I'LL NEVER CRY AGAIN

A MILLION MIRACLES BOOK ONE

USA TODAY BEST SELLING AUTHOR

ROBERTA KAGAN

ISBN (ebook): 978-1-957207-79-7
ISBN (Paperback): 978-1-957207-80-3
ISBN (Hardcover): 978-1-957207-81-0

Title Production by The BookWhisperer

PROLOGUE

They referred to it as the most beautiful place on earth, but when he stood on the mountain and looked out over Salzburg, he felt a sense of danger. It was surely lurking, waiting for him. His heart raced, and sweat beaded on his brow. His knees felt weak and heavy as he made his way through the narrow tunnel. He hated this place, hated how high above the ground it stood. He had to own it because everyone he knew admired its magnificence. But he knew that this mountain was not his. This mountain belonged to God. He couldn't explain exactly why he was so afraid of the mountain. Perhaps it was that, even when he stood outside surveying the beautiful landscape, all he could see— or feel—was the deepest, darkest danger. Or perhaps he felt the power of God when he looked out over the land beneath him. And although he told his followers that there was no God, he knew that there was, and he was both afraid and in awe.

His boot heels hit the cobblestone floor, and in the absence of any other sound, the clicking echoed loud and ominous. The noise pierced through the silence of the damp, dark passageway. Though the elevator wasn't far, it always seemed to him that he walked for an eternity before reaching the small mechanical room that would carry him to the top of the mountain. He shivered as the frigid wind swirled and danced around him. It was June, and it was sunny outside, yet an eerie chill filled the tunnel. When he finally reached the elevator, fear struck him. For a moment, he thought of turning back. But he dared not. He had an important announcement to make tonight. Eva, his longtime girlfriend, had ensured everyone of significance would be there.

He stepped into the oddly shaped dome room while he waited for the elevator to arrive. He was terrified of the elevator. *I can't take this elevator. What if we're hit by lightning while I'm inside? Or bombed?* But he clenched his jaw to hide his fear.

It had taken thirteen months to build this place—elevator and all. A project like this should have taken years, but his staff had driven the workforce to work relentlessly. In just thirteen months, they'd carved the elevator into the mountain and constructed the lovely banquet hall and sunroom upstairs. They had built it as a surprise for him. A surprise designed to offer him protection from his enemies. He'd only been up here a dozen times, maybe thirteen at most, since its construction, but each time he remembered. And each time, he'd been paralyzed by fear, though he knew he must hide it. If his devoted followers ever saw his cowardice, he was sure that they would abandon him.

The elevator door rattled slightly as it slowly opened. Inside, it was beautifully decorated in all gold—a state-of-the-art project, complete with a black rotary phone he could use in an emergency and a clock to mark the time. The sound of the door opening unsettled him, but reluctantly, he stepped inside. A white-hot light bulb hung from the center of the elevator, and when he glanced up at it, the brightness stung his eyes. He stood there for several moments, trembling as the elevator door shut. He closed his eyes and swallowed hard. So many things could happen to him on this ride to the top of the mountain. The elevator could plunge down the shaft, trapping or killing him. But when the doors finally opened at the top of the mountain, the beauty of the place, known as the Eagle's Nest, stole his breath away.

He looked out over the lush green earth and eyed the lovely little town in the distance. It was Salzburg, Austria, his homeland. He sucked in the crisp, thin air. It was certainly breathtaking, but he was careful to stay far away from the edge. *Just in case God was watching.*

Then, a pretty, vivacious young woman wearing a white dress with yellow flowers, a cigarette in hand, and a welcoming smile rushed up to him. "Adolf," she said, "I'm so glad you're here. Everyone has been waiting for you to start the party."

He managed to give her a trembling smile.

"And wait until you see the lovely gift Mussolini sent you," she continued.

"Oh?" he said, trying to show interest, but he was not interested in anything right now but his safety. He knew he must not allow himself to be distracted. He had to be very careful on this mountain— very careful. God was watching and waiting.

The attractive young woman smiled at him and took his hand. "In case you want to know, Mussolini sent you a gift. It's a red marble fireplace. And, I must say, it's magnificent. I had them put it in the banquet room so everyone could see how much Mussolini adores and respects you. It's good that everyone knows just how strong your rela- tionship with Italy is. Anyway, it will be a glorious addition to the Eagle's Nest. I hope it's all right that I had them place it in the banquet room."

"Yes, of course, it's fine," he said, not caring much about Mussoli- ni's gift. Then he asked, "Have the children arrived yet?"

"Not yet. I expect them any minute. They left Steinhoring over an hour ago."

"Good. Let me know when they arrive, will you?"

"Of course I will." She smiled.

"All right. You go back to the party and keep them all entertained. I just need a few minutes alone to enjoy this beautiful view. Then I'll come into the great room and greet everyone."

"Perhaps I should stay here with you?"

"It's not necessary. I prefer that you go back and make the guests comfortable. Like I said, I just need a moment alone, and then I'll come in."

She shook her head and frowned at him for a moment. He knew why. He knew she wanted to enter the room with her arm locked in his. The only way to get rid of her was to bring up her least favorite subject, which was her cigarette addiction. He softened his gaze, then, in a serious tone, said, "You really should quit smoking, Eva. It's bad for your health."

"I know, dear. You've told me a thousand times. And I will, I promise. But not tonight. Tonight, we're having a party, yes? Tonight, we will have fun."

He nodded and smiled, but an icy imaginary finger traced down his spine, and he shivered. Glancing around quickly, he thought, *I can feel someone watching. I feel eyes on me. The eyes of an enemy who wishes me harm. Maybe they are the eyes of an angry God.*

"Come, Adolf. Let's go into the dining room together."

He was irritated with her. It was difficult for him to breathe. His heart was racing, and he felt sweat trickling down his face. "I told you, I'll be there in a few minutes. I'm losing patience with you. Now, go on without me." His tone was firm, and she knew he would get angry if she didn't do as he said. And if he got angry, it would spoil the entire night. So, she did not continue to try to convince him to go with her. She smiled, turned, and walked back to the room where the party was already in full swing.

Without looking at her, he turned and walked in the opposite direction toward the sunroom. He loved the sunroom because it was all encased in glass, and the view was stunning. He suddenly felt that he would be safe once he entered the room. He doubted that anyone from the party would wander in. So this would give him an opportunity to be alone and gather his thoughts before going into the dining room to speak to the crowd.

Slipping into the sunroom, he looked around. The stone tiles were spotless, polished to a shine that reflected the sunlight filtering through the windows. He was very nervous tonight, and his breathing was shallow. Was it because the air was so thin, or was it the weight of what he needed to say to the waiting SS officers? Gasping, he leaned against the wall. Then he saw them—two dark-haired young girls, both smiling. They couldn't see him. One of them bent down and lifted a child lying on a blanket on the floor. He realized that there were five of them. Five little blond boys and girls, ranging from infant to around six years old.

The infant let out a small cry. One of the girls rushed to him, picking him up and whispering softly, though Adolf could not hear what she said. She cradled the baby, and the look of love in her eyes reminded Adolf of his own mother. She had loved him. He smiled because he knew this to be true. He had never doubted his mother's love. And though many had professed their love for him in the years since her death, he was never certain who to believe, never sure who to trust.

Adolf knew his guests were waiting for him and remembered why he had invited all of these SS officers to his mountain. *There are not enough pure German children to secure the future of our nation. I know that Reichsführer Himmler will be here tonight, and he is very proud of his creation of the Lebensborn program. And I must admit that the beautiful children I saw earlier with the little brown sisters in the sunroom are evidence of the wonderful success we are having with Himmler's program. However, it has been impossible to produce children at the necessary rate. Therefore, my officers must go into Poland and kidnap blond-haired, blue-eyed children. Then, I will send them to the Lebensborn homes to be Germanized.*

As he walked into the room, a large, muscular, blond man watched him. Himmler had hired this handsome blond Aryan man to be Adolf's new bodyguard. He hadn't met the man yet, but from the way he looked, Adolf decided Himmler had made a good choice. This man, who was his bodyguard, was strong and intimidating. There was something about the presence of his new bodyguard that made Adolf feel safe. Someone in the crowd noticed Adolf had entered the room and immediately told everyone else. They all looked up at Adolf. Adolf saw the admiration in their eyes, and he was glad they could not see his lips trembling as he smiled under his tiny mustache.

Adolf made his way toward the podium that had been set up for his speech, smiling at the crowd, who stared at him with admiration. They applauded as he climbed the stairs. Once he was standing behind the podium, he raised his hand in a salute. Everyone in the room stood up. They raised their right hand and saluted him. "Heil Hitler," they said in unison.

Adolf smiled and raised his hands to show his approval. Then he said, "I have a couple of things that I would like to discuss with all of you this evening. First, as all of you know, the Jewish question has always been a burden. So, I have decided to liquidate the Warsaw Ghetto in Poland. It is a filthy, overcrowded place. Beginning on July 22, the Judenrat will post notices inside the Warsaw Ghetto informing their fellow Jews that they will be deported to work camps in the east. However, arrangements have been made for them to arrive at Treblinka."

A hush fell over the room. Everyone who was there knew that Treblinka was a death camp. "And, unfortunately, we Germans are not reproducing fast enough. Therefore, I am requesting that you find children in Poland who are Aryan—blond and blue-eyed. Take these children to the Lebensborn homes, where they will be Germanized. Try to get them as young as possible. When they are very young, it is much easier to teach them. But for those who are unable to forget their families or their countries of origin, we will have to eliminate them."

The room erupted into applause. Adolf smiled and said, "Enough talking for now. Enjoy the party and enjoy your dinner." They all loved him. But as he walked over to his seat beside Eva, he felt the weight of God's hand pressing down on his back. Fear shot through him like a bullet.

Then Adolf connected eyes and smiled at the new bodyguard. It was rare that anyone he did not know very well could attend a party on this mountain. His mountain. But he knew that this new bodyguard would attend tonight. He'd been told all about him. His name was Konrad Hoffmann, and he looked so sincere and dedicated as he returned Adolf's smile. Adolf liked him instantly. The bodyguard's appearance was perfectly Aryan. He was blond, with high cheekbones, a strong jawline, and perfect white teeth. For reasons he couldn't explain, Adolf trusted this new man instantly. Adolf had never met or spoken to him, but he believed Hoffmann's appearance made him trustworthy. In fact, he was exactly the kind of man Adolf wished he could be—a perfect Aryan. But Adolf didn't know this handsome bodyguard was hiding a dark secret.

CHAPTER ONE

WARSAW, POLAND
SUMMER OF 1931

Pitor Barr sat on the edge of his mother's bed, holding her hand. He glanced out the window at a group of children playing with a ball. His family had moved to this run-down, cold-water flat in Poland from their small house in Frankfurt, Germany, a year ago. Though the living conditions were not as comfortable, he loved the big city. He didn't mind the crowds or the dirt, but he hated that his mother had taken a job as a maid working for a wealthy family. Two nights ago, she had come home from work sick, and now she was getting worse.

"You caught this from one of those lousy rich jerks you work for," Pitor said angrily.

"Pitor, don't say such things. The Wolinski family is very kind to me. They are generous, too," his mother, Rivka, replied softly. "It's not their fault that Pan Wolinski got sick. No one meant for this to happen."

"But he did get sick, and now you're sick. When you get better, you should quit that job. I'll find a way to support us."

"I'm dying," Rivka told her son in a gentle voice.

He shook his head, his voice cracking. "No, *mutti*, you can't die. Please, *mutti*. You are the only person in the world who believes in me,"

"It's my time, Pitor."

"Then I want to die too."

"You are only fifteen years old. You have your whole life ahead of you. Someday soon, you will marry and have children of your own. But first, you must try to stay out of trouble. I have protected you so far, but now you will be on your own. You know as well as I do that your friends are not good people. They are constantly in trouble with the law. You must promise me that you will stop getting into mischief. You are smart. Perhaps too smart for your own good. And these people, who you call friends, are going to end up in prison. You must promise me that you will try your best to be a good boy from now on. Your father is weak-minded, and he is going to need your help. Without you to guide him, he will not survive."

"Why do you care so much about him? He is lazy and has not been a good father or husband since he started drinking. I don't know why he became so driven by alcohol. When I was younger, he was better. He taught me to hunt and fish. He seemed to care about us then, but something happened to him, and he changed. He stopped loving us for some reason, but you still love him. I know you do. Why?"

"I care about him because he is my *bashert*. That means that even before we met, your father and I were destined to go through life together."

"But how can you know that?"

She smiled and patted his hand. "My son," she said as she looked into his eyes, "when you meet your *bashert*, you just know."

"I don't think I have a *bashert*."

"Oh, but you do, and when you see her, you'll know that she is the one. That's why I'm telling you that you must stop getting into trouble and start thinking about the future. Once you meet her, you will want to be able to earn enough money to support her. You are smart enough to stay in school, but there's not enough money. So, you should try to learn a trade. As I said, soon enough, you will find her and get married. Then you will be a father with children of your own."

"So, you have to get well. You have to! If you die, you won't be there to see my children. So, you have to live. You have to live for me," Pitor pleaded with the selfishness of a fifteen-year-old. "Life will never be the same without you."

"No, it won't. But if you do as I say and try to find an apprenticeship where you can learn a good trade, you will have a new life. You'll see."

"How will I know who to marry if you aren't there to direct me? You know *vater* isn't capable of doing anything, right? Don't leave me, *mutti*. Please don't leave me."

"You'll know your betrothed when you see her. Something inside of you will tell you that she's the one for you," Rivka smiled at her son. Then she squeezed his hand. "Now, promise me that you will stop getting into trouble. Promise me that you will be a good boy and learn a trade. I have a brother who lives in a village outside Warsaw, and he owns a butcher shop. Write to him. Maybe he will give you an apprenticeship," she said.

He nodded. "If that's what you want."

"It's what I want. Promise me, Pitor. Promise me so I can die in peace."

"I promise," he said. Rivka smiled, satisfied. And the light in her eyes grew brighter. Pitor looked at his mother, and for a moment, he believed she was growing stronger, but then she closed her eyes, and her hand dropped from his.

He knew she was gone.

PITOR WEPT FOR A WEEK. He spent every day lying on his bed, refusing to go to school or to work. But he finally got up and walked into the living room when he heard his father arguing with the landlord about the rent. His father had never been a good provider, and he did not have a job. If it had not been for his mother, the family would have been out on the street long ago.

"How much do we owe?" Pitor asked the landlord

"Two months."

"Have a heart. The boy is still mourning the loss of his mother. And I have lost my wife. Give us a little time," Pitor's father said.

"You have one week. After that, either you pay or you leave." The landlord walked out of the apartment, leaving the door open.

"What are we going to do?" Pitor's father asked, his voice heavy with despair.

"I don't know," Pitor said. "I suppose we're both going to have to get jobs."

"I'm an artist. I have no practical trade. Who will hire me?" his father said bitterly.

"You're going to have to get a real job. I'll drop out of school and find work, but you must help, too."

"My heart is broken from losing your mother. She was the love of my life, my bashert. I don't think I can go on without her."

"You should have been better to her when she was alive," Pitor said. "You let her work herself to death because you were too lazy to help her."

"Shut your mouth! What about you? You could have gotten a job! Oh yes, I forgot. Your mother insisted that you stay in school like some kind of Little Prince. You were always her main concern. She wanted you to go to the university, but I told her you were too much of a rabble-rouser that you'd never get in. But she wouldn't listen. She loved you no matter what you did." His father burst into tears. "And now she's gone. Who will take care of me in my old age? You can't understand what I'm feeling or what I'm going through. Don't worry yourself about me, not that I ever thought you would. You're a selfish boy. I will have to find a way to fend for myself. I don't know what I will do, but that's none of your concern. You just need to decide what you're going to do and then go and do it."

"I'll tell you what I won't do," Pitor said coldly. "I won't sit around this apartment and cry. Weeping like a child won't bring my mother back, so it's pointless. In fact, from this day forward, I swear I'll never cry again. It doesn't solve anything."

"No, I suppose you're right. It doesn't," his father said, but tears still streamed down his cheeks.

Pitor went into the other room and grabbed a pen and some paper. Then, he sat down on a wooden chair in front of the kitchen table.

"What are you doing?" his father asked.

"I'm writing a letter to *mutti's* brother, the one who owns a butcher shop in the little village just outside of Warsaw. I'm going to tell him that *mutti* passed away, and then I'll ask him if he can help us. If I remember correctly, he has no children. Maybe he will take me on as an apprentice."

"We can only hope," Pitor's father replied, wiping his eyes. "You know he is married to a *shiksa*. But he lives in an Orthodox Jewish village. From the letters he wrote to your mother, I know that he's shunned by the Jewish people there. They don't buy from him, so he might not earn enough money to hire you."

"Well, I am going to write to him, and we'll see what he says."

CHAPTER TWO

A SMALL SHTETEL, OUTSIDE OF WARSAW

SEPTEMBER 1931

Pitor's uncle, Sam, and his wife, Maria, lived in a modest house near the butcher shop they owned. Though the house was not really large enough for Pitor and his father to live there as well, they had no money and nowhere else to go. So, they moved in. It was cramped, but Maria made the best of it. She converted part of the living room into a bedroom for Pitor and his father.

A week later, Pitor began his apprenticeship at the butcher shop. He remembered the promise he made to his mother. *I will stop getting into trouble and learn a trade.*

Pitor and his uncle rose at 4:00 a.m. every morning to start their day at the butcher shop. At first, the early mornings were difficult for Pitor, but as they walked from the house to the butcher shop, Pitor pointed out how peaceful and beautiful the earth was while everyone slept. As they prepared the meat they planned to sell that day, Uncle Sam would hand Pitor a cup of coffee and tell him to take a minute and stop working so they could watch the sunrise. Sam was a kind and patient teacher, and Pitor was a quick learner. Pitor liked his uncle and aunt; his uncle reminded him of his mother in many ways. But despite the quiet comfort of village life, Pitor was bored. A small shtetl didn't offer the same excitement as a big city.

He missed Warsaw and the wild crowd he used to run with. Pitor had always been a handsome boy, and the girls he ran around with liked him. They were girls with loose morals, and he found them intriguing. Many mornings, he woke up in bed beside a girl whose name he did not know. He had been so drunk the night before that he couldn't remember whether she had ever told him her name. Sometimes, the girls would think they were in love with him. They would pursue him relentlessly, but he had no interest in settling down with any of them. Pitor loved his freedom, and he couldn't imagine that there really was a woman out there somewhere who would change his mind about settling down. He was an excellent pickpocket. He could tell if a man was wealthy just by looking at him, and he could lift his wallet without being detected. Not only did he steal from the wealthy shoppers in the marketplace, but he sometimes swiped food from the vendors.

Religion was never important to Pitor. His family was not religious. They lived in a mixed area of Jewish and non-Jewish people. Some of the Jews he met were religious, but most were secular. Both of his parents were Jewish, though not practicing. However, his mother had kept some of the old traditions alive, like telling him that one day he would find his bashert—the woman who would change everything for him. His twin soul, as his mother called her. Pitor would smile and listen, but he never truly believed in the idea of finding his one true love. Still, he enjoyed hearing her tell him about how somewhere in the world, there was a woman whose soul was the other half of his soul. He enjoyed it, not because he was eager to find his bashert, but because he relished how her eyes lit up when she spoke of how she had fallen in love with his father.

Pitor had little respect for his father. He could not respect a man who would allow his wife to work and slave as a maid while he pursued an unsuccessful career as an artist. But his mother never seemed to mind. "I knew what he was when I married him. I loved him then, and I still love him today," she would always say. And because Pitor loved and respected her, he never confronted his father.

Pitor missed his mother terribly. No matter how much trouble he got into, she always stood behind him, and now he felt alone. He considered running away, leaving his father in this little village with his aunt and uncle, and disappearing back into the hustle and bustle of Warsaw.

"Daydreaming again?" his uncle asked kindly. "Maybe you're hungry?"

"I am," Pitor replied, then added, "I was missing my mother."

"I understand. This move has been hard for you. Everyone you know is in Warsaw, and it's hard for a young man to start over in a new place."

"Yes, I miss my friends," Pitor confided. "But I do want you to know that I appreciate everything you have done for my father and me."

"You're not planning on leaving us, are you?" His uncle's voice was gentle, but there was concern in his eyes. "I hope not, because you're doing very well learning the business. You're actually a very good butcher."

Pitor nodded but didn't speak.

"Let me get you one of the sandwiches your aunt packed for us. It will do you good to eat something."

Pitor felt bad as he watched his uncle disappear inside the building. The man and his wife had been so kind to him, yet all he could think about was running away.

Just then, Pitor looked up and saw two young girls walking towards the Jewish sector of the marketplace. His eyes landed on one of them, and when they did, his breath caught in his throat. With long black curls blowing in the wind, she was the most beautiful girl he had ever seen. She caught him looking at her and blushed. When their eyes met, he saw her eyes were the deep, inky color of a raven's wing. He couldn't control the smile that spread across his face, and to his surprise, she smiled back at him. His heart melted. Then he heard his mother's voice in the back of his mind. *I told you, Pitor, you would know her when you saw her.*

"My *bashert*. She is my *bashert*. The dark beauty with those deep black eyes. It's her. I know it's her. Even though she is still just a child, she will be my wife someday when she grows up."

Yes. Can you feel it? Is it not as I said it would be? Do you not know for certain that it is her?

"Yes, *mutti*, I am certain, and it is just as you said it would be."

Don't let her get away, Pitor. Go and speak to her.

"But what should I say? How can I approach her?"

Just go to her. You will know what to say. You will know what to do.

"I must learn her name before she walks away. If I don't speak to her now, I may never see her again."

Then stop wasting time and go before the opportunity is gone. His mother's voice urged him.

Pitor jumped up and ran over to the raven-haired girl, unsure of what he was going to say.

"Hello," he greeted her breathlessly.

Neither the girl nor her companion replied at first, both at a loss for words. From the modest way they were dressed, he realized they were likely religious and perhaps not permitted to speak to boys. But he wasn't ready to give up. This girl, whose name he did not even know, was his *bashert*. She was his twin soul, and as he looked at her, his soul yearned to join with hers.

"Hello," she said softly, then giggled and looked away. Pitor knew she was not laughing at him. She was only giggling because she was shy.

"I'm Pitor Barr," he said. "May I ask your name?" He looked down at his butcher's apron and was suddenly ashamed of how he looked. He wished he had had time to put on his only suit before speaking to her. But she didn't seem to notice.

"No, we had better go," the other girl said. "Come on, Mila. Mama and Sarah are waiting for us. We need to bring the potatoes for tonight's soup."

"Mila," he whispered. "Your name is Mila?"

The girl nodded.

"Don't go. Let me give you some meat to take home to your mother," he offered, not caring whether his uncle would approve.

"No, we can't take gifts from strangers," the other girl said quickly. "Besides, your shop isn't kosher. We can't eat the meat anyway."

Pitor felt a pang of disappointment but pressed on. "Can I see you again? Can I take you out to dinner? Or maybe for ice cream? Or whatever you want?" He knew he sounded foolish but couldn't just let her leave.

Mila's eyes flickered with interest. "I'm sorry. I must go," she said, though her voice hinted that she didn't want to.

"Come on, Mila," the other girl pulled Mila's arm, and the two girls began to walk away. Pitor stood watching them, helpless but determined to see Mila again.

That night, as Pitor lay in his bed trying to sleep, he couldn't stop thinking about Mila. *How am I going to win her? What am I going to do?*

Once again, he heard his mother's voice. *Pitor, become a good butcher. Learn the trade from my brother and learn it well. Now that you have found your bashert, you will want to provide for her.*

"But she is from another world. She comes from a religious family, Mother. Her parents will never allow me to marry her."

You'll find a way, my son. You'll see. She is your bashert, and you must fight for her. Start preparing for your future.

OVER THE NEXT FEW YEARS, Pitor worked hard and learned the business. He searched everywhere for her face. In the market-place, at the river, in the park, and each time he laid eyes on the girl called Mila, he was more confident that someday they would be together.

CHAPTER THREE

1933

One day, Uncle Sam left early, and as Pitor was wiping down the counter, one of his favorite customers entered the shop. "How are you, Pitor?"

"I'm doing well, Professor Borkowski. And how are you and your family?"

"We're all well. Thank you for asking."

"What can I do for you today?"

"I need a chicken. Cut-up in quarters, please."

"Of course. I'll get that for you right away," Pitor said. He always looked forward to the professor's visits, as the professor brought fascinating news about the world outside this little village.

"Today, I bring news that I am not so happy to share," the professor said, "but I think you should know it."

"What is it?" Pitor asked, looking up from the counter where he was wrapping the chicken in white paper. "Is something wrong?"

"I'm not sure yet. But I don't have a good feeling about this."

Pitor finished wrapping the package, then wiped his hands on his apron and looked at his friend. "What is it? What are you talking about?" Pitor asked.

"Well, I don't know if you've heard, but Hindenburg has died."

"Who is Hindenburg?"

"The president of Germany."

"And how does this affect us? We're in Poland."

"I know, but before he passed away, he appointed a man named Adolf Hitler as chancellor."

"And so?"

"Well, this Hitler fellow is not of good character. I've heard of him before. He was the head of the National Socialist German Workers' Party."

"But what has this got to do with us?"

"Hitler wrote a book that I read a few years ago. It's called *Mein Kampf*. That means *My Struggle*."

"Yes, I know. I speak fluent German."

"So, how did you come to learn German? Did you learn it in school?"

"I actually grew up in Frankfurt, before moving to Poland. When I was in Germany, I ran with a wild crowd. We got into a lot of trouble, and I gained quite a reputation. They taught me a lot of things I would have been better off not knowing. That's a part of my life I'd like to forget," Pitor said, shaking his head at the memory. "Anyway, most of those boys were really into German politics, and I kept up with them, but once we moved to Poland, my whole life changed. I left all those friends behind, and I eventually started working for my uncle, and I met my wife, and I stopped paying attention to anything that happened in Germany. So, may I ask how does Hitler's book affect us here in Poland?"

"In his book, Hitler talks about his hatred for Jews. I am worried about his influence. Hatred like this is not good for the Jewish people. I am not a Jew, but so many of my good friends, like you, are. And, well, it worries me."

"You think there could be a pogrom? Here in Poland? Why would Germany want to bother with us?"

"This Hitler fellow seems rather insane. If he hadn't managed to get himself appointed chancellor, I wouldn't worry about him at all. I'd think he was just another madman. But I am concerned. I am afraid that he's different. He has somehow weaseled himself into a place of real power. And from what I can gather, he has plans to somehow create a Jew-free Europe. If I were you, I would consider getting out of here."

"Where would we go?"

"Take your family to America."

"America? What would I do there?"

"You'd be a butcher, the same as you are here. I might be over-stepping my boundaries by suggesting this, but I've always liked you. And I don't know why, but I am worried."

"Well, thank you for your concern, but I am not running away. I won't leave my home and business. I've helped build this place, and I have a nice clientele. I can't see leaving everything behind on a whim."

"I understand. I just wanted to share my thoughts with you. I could be wrong. Now that Hitler is chancellor, he might just abandon all of his crazy ideas. We can only hope so."

"At least he's not here in Poland. He's the chancellor of Germany. So, as far as Hitler is concerned, we here in Poland don't really have much to worry about." Pitor handed the chicken to the professor.

CHAPTER FOUR

January 26TH, 1934

On January 26, 1934, Hitler signed a non-aggression pact with Poland. In that document, both countries promised not to engage in armed conflict with each other for the next ten years.

A few days after the pact was signed, Pitor read about it in the newspaper. As he read, he recalled the conversation he had with Professor Borkowski about Hitler, and a slight chill ran through him. He remembered Borkowski's warning about Hitler's hatred for the Jewish people. *At least Hitler has signed this pact and agreed not to invade us here in Poland,* Pitor reassured himself. *This is good news. As long as the Germans leave us alone, I know that my family will be safe here in Poland.*

CHAPTER FIVE

1936

In the heat of summer in 1936, tragedy struck. A deadly flu epidemic swept through the village. First, it claimed Pitor's father, and within a few weeks, both his aunt and uncle had also fallen ill and passed away. Pitor was devastated. He had come to love his aunt and uncle as if they were his own parents. His uncle had taught him everything he knew about running the butcher shop, but now, faced with the overwhelming task of managing it alone, Pitor didn't think he could handle it.

At first, Pitor thought about selling the shop and moving back to Warsaw. He figured he could probably get a job working for another butcher. It would be easier than trying to run his own business. But then he remembered the raven-haired girl, Mila, and he decided that no matter what it took, he was going to stay in the little village until she was old enough to be his bride.

CHAPTER SIX

A LITTLE VILLAGE ON THE OUTSKIRTS OF WARSAW, POLAND

1937

Mila Zielinsky combed her long black hair and thought about her upcoming marriage to Anshel Minsky. She felt a sting of loss shoot through her as she caressed her hair, knowing that the day after the wedding, her mother would arrive at Mila's new home and shave her head. Once she was a married woman, it was no longer acceptable for her to walk the streets with her hair exposed. From that day forward, whenever she was outside, her head would be covered, and the only man who would see her hair would be her husband.

Mila closed the door to the room that she shared with her sisters. Once she was sure that she was alone, she opened one of the drawers in her dresser and took out a looking glass that she kept hidden so her Orthodox Jewish parents wouldn't think she was vain. She stared at her reflection. *I am not ready to marry. And I am certainly not ready to marry Anshel. He's short and fat and terribly boring. My father may be impressed with him because he is an intellectual, and the rabbis like him, but I don't want to be his wife. He expects me to bow down to his every wish. I am expected to go out and work so I can earn money while he prays and studies all day. Then I must prepare his meals and keep the house. And worst of all, I must lie beside him every night and allow him access to the most sacred parts of my body. I know that our women have done this for centuries for their husbands, and it is what is expected, but I find it unbearable. Especially because I don't like him at all. My father pretends he is so religious, but he's a hypocrite. If he really followed Jewish law, he would allow me to accept or reject his choice for my husband. But he only follows the laws when they suit him.*

"Mila." Her mother walked into the room. She was carrying a bolt of beautiful white lace. "The lace for your veil just arrived. Take a look. It's gorgeous. However, time is ticking, and we must hurry and finish the dress and veil. There are only two months left before the wedding."

"It's lovely, Mama. You did a wonderful job of choosing the lace."

"Oy vey. I have so much to do. I hope I can finish everything in time," she said as she laid the fabric down on Mila's bed. Then she ran her fingers over the lace.

"Would you just look at his lace? Your father complained about how expensive it was, but I can't wait until he sees it. He will be proud to walk down the aisle at your side. All the young women will be so envious of you. That's for sure. Don't you think so?"

Mila nodded, then shrugged her shoulders.

"What is it, my *shayna maidel*, my beautiful girl?" her mother asked, sitting down on the bed and patting the area beside her. "Sit, *mayn kind*, my child. Tell your mother what's bothering you."

Mila sat beside her mother.

The skin on her mother's hand was rough when she reached up and gently caressed Mila's chin. "You look so sad. I know you are scared. Every girl is scared when she is getting married. I was scared, too, when I married your papa, but things have a way of falling into place. You'll see, it will be alright. It will all work itself out."

"I'm not afraid of getting married, Mama. I just don't want to marry Anshel. I know he is a good man from a good family, but he is wrong for me. When I look into his eyes, I can feel it. He is not my *bashert.*"

"You hardly know him. You only met him once, and you haven't spent a single moment alone with him. Everyone was sitting at the dinner table, so the two of you didn't really have a chance to talk to each other. After you're married, you will get to know him better. Every man has good and bad qualities. As the years pass, you will come to understand him, and you will learn to be happy."

"I know for sure that Anshel is a nice man, but I also know he is not for me. He's Papa's choice. Not mine. I don't want him for my husband. And according to our laws, Papa should not force me to marry him. He is supposed to bring the man he chose to me. And then he should allow me to say yes or no."

"Yes, I realize this. But we both are aware that your father would never do that. He expects you to do as he says. He will not go back on his word, and since he has already agreed to the match with Anshel's parents, he will insist that you marry him. Besides, your father and I have made all of the arrangements for the wedding. If you try to change things, your papa will lose money. And if he does, he will be livid."

Mila sighed, feeling tears welling up in her eyes. "Oh, Mama, my whole life, my entire future happiness is at stake here, and yet you expect me to worry about Papa's pride."

"I'm sorry, *Milaleh,* but you have no choice but to become Anshel's wife. Your father won't listen to you if you try to tell him otherwise. You and I have no say in the matter—we must go through with the wedding. I wish I could help you, but your father is the man of the house, and as always, what he says, goes."

Mila looked away. Tears burned behind her eyelids before spilling down her cheeks. She wanted to cry out loud and scream and kick her feet, but she knew that her mother was right. No matter how hard she protested, she knew that in the end, she would be forced to do as her father demanded.

Her mother took Mila in her arms, hugging her tightly. That was when Mila broke down, crying in long, heart-wrenching sobs. "Shh, shh. It will be alright. You'll see. I promise you." Her mother soothed. "I know it's hard for you to believe because I am so much older than you. But I understand how you feel. I felt the same way when I first met your papa. I must say that I didn't like him very much. He was outspoken and terribly arrogant. But my parents made the match, and when I tried to protest, my father told me this was the man I was going to marry. I had no other choice. So, I did what he told me to do." Her mother paused for a moment before continuing, her voice softer. "I've never told anyone this before, but as I stood under the *chuppah* beside your papa, I was crying under my veil. It didn't matter. Nothing I did or said mattered. We got married. He wasn't perfect, but I learned to live with him. And to tell you the truth, I wasn't perfect either. Over the years, I guess you could say I learned to love him. And if not, well... at least I got used to him."

That's not what I want for the rest of my life, Mila thought. *I don't want to live with a man who I've simply gotten used to. I know we are Jews, and we aren't supposed to marry for love, but I want that. I want love in my life. Is that so terrible?*

"Come on, Mila. Go and wash your pretty face. I need you to go to the market for me. I want a few potatoes and cabbage for the soup I am preparing for dinner tonight."

"Yes, Mama," Mila said, resigned. She went to the bathroom to wash her face and brush her hair. It was useless to ask her mother for help. Her mother was weak and would never stand up to her father. Mila wanted to shake her, to tell her she didn't want to make the same mistakes, but she knew it wouldn't make any difference. The truth was she was relieved to be going to the marketplace. She couldn't wait to leave the room where her mother sat, still staring at the bolt of lace.

CHAPTER SEVEN

When she arrived at the market, Mila made her way to the fruit and vegetable stand, where she knew the owner always had the freshest produce. On the way, she spotted one of her close friends, Fanny Goldstein, who called out to her.

"Mila!"

"Hello, Fanny," Mila said as Fanny walked over. The two had been best friends since they were very young.

"What's wrong with you? You look like you're about to cry."

Mila shrugged.

"Tell me. What is it?"

"You have to promise not to tell anyone."

"What is it?"

"Promise first, and then I will tell you."

"All right, I promise. I promise never to tell anyone."

"I'm betrothed to Anshel Minsky."

"Everyone knows that. The wedding is right around the corner. So, what's the secret? Why are you crying? I don't understand."

Two older women, sitting on a nearby bench, were watching Mila and Fanny and listening intently. "Come, follow me. We need to go somewhere we can talk privately," Mila said.

Fanny followed her, and they walked in silence for a few minutes. Once they were out of earshot from the crowds in the marketplace, Mila turned to Fanny and whispered, "I'm scared. I don't really know Anshel at all, and I don't want to get married."

"Every girl wants to get married," Fanny said. "I'm eagerly waiting for my father to bring home some prospective grooms."

"I don't know. I don't feel like I am ready. And... if I tell you something, you promise not to say anything, right?"

"Yes, of course. I promise."

"I don't think Anshel is my *bashert*. I really don't believe that he is the right person for me."

"You should tell your father how you feel. According to Jewish law, he can't make you marry him."

"Yes, I know this. But my father only follows the Jewish law when it benefits him. He won't even listen if I tell him I don't want to marry Anshel. He will just get angry and insist. You don't know my papa. He's very strict, and once he promised me to Anshel, he won't break his promise. His promise is more important to him than my feelings. He's always been worried about what other people think."

"Oy, that is terrible," Fanny admitted. "What are you going to do?"

"Marry him, I guess. I don't have any choice."

"Oh, Mila. That's awful."

"I know. I know it is. And that's why I can't help but cry when I think about it."

Fanny cleared her throat, then said gently, "You know, my mother says that sometimes you don't realize that the man your father chose is your *bashert* until after you've been married for a while. Hopefully, you will feel differently about Anshel after you have children."

"Yes, perhaps you're right," Mila said. "Anyway, I'd better go and buy some potatoes and cabbage. I have to hurry and get home. My mother is waiting for me to bring the vegetables so she can make soup."

"Good luck to you, my friend."

The two girls hugged. "Good luck to you, too," Mila said, closing her eyes and holding her friend for a moment. Then, the girls parted ways, and Mila headed back to the vegetable vendor's stand.

After buying the potatoes, Mila began her walk home. On her way, she passed the butcher shop. It was the shop that most of the Jewish residents avoided because they did not consider it to be kosher enough. It had been a while since her family had any meat or chicken, and she wished she had extra money to buy some. For a moment, she stood gazing into the window of the butcher shop. Everyone knew it was cheaper than the kosher butcher a few streets away. Mila sighed. *I can't afford to buy meat anyway, so it doesn't matter if the store is kosher or not.* She turned to walk away when a tall, handsome, muscular young man, only a few years older than her, stepped out of the shop. His golden-blond hair and neatly groomed beard matched, and he wore a white apron that was stained with dark patches, which Mila assumed were animal blood. "I saw you looking in my shop. Can I help you?" he asked.

"Oh, no, thank you," Mila replied.

"We have fresh chicken today," he said. His eyes were a striking aqua blue, and his face was chiseled, with high cheekbones and a strong jaw. He was so handsome that Mila's breath caught in her throat, and her heart skipped a beat.

"I would love to make chicken soup, but I don't have enough money to buy a chicken, I'm afraid," she admitted.

His eyes twinkled. "Come with me," he said.

She looked at him skeptically, feeling a bit nervous. She didn't move.

"It's all right. We're only going into the butcher shop. I'm not leading you anywhere dangerous. Come on in," he said with a reassuring smile.

Mila hesitated but followed him through the front door. He

walked behind the counter. "There is no reason for me to be here. Like I said before, I am sorry, I just can't afford to buy chicken today," she protested.

"I heard you. But this is my gift to you." He smiled as he cut up a chicken, wrapped it in white paper, and placed it on the counter. "By the way, my name is Pitor. Pitor Barr."

Pitor, she repeated silently to herself. "Barr?" she asked aloud. "Are you German by any chance? Your name is Polish, but you have a German accent."

"Yes, I was born in Germany, so I suppose you could say I am a German Jew."

He was certainly handsome, with curly, golden-blond hair—a rarity in her village, where most men had dark hair, beards, and payot, the long curly sideburns of observant Jews.

"I'm Mila," she said, unable to suppress a smile.

"I know," he said. "I know who you are. You're Mila Zielinsky, the prettiest girl in town."

She giggled, and Pitor took the package and walked out from behind the counter. Then he tried to hand it to her, but she wouldn't take it. "Please take it. It's for you," he insisted.

"This is very generous of you," she said, "but what will I tell my mother? She'll want to know why you gave me a chicken."

"Just tell her that I gave it to you because you won it as a prize for being the prettiest girl I have ever seen."

Mila blushed, her olive skin glowing with just a hint of pink on her cheeks. She self-consciously reached up and touched her long, dark hair, and then she cast her eyes down, feeling shy and intimidated by this handsome man.

"And though I thought you were quite lovely before, now that you're blushing, you're even more beautiful," he said, his eyes glued to her.

"I'd better go," Mila murmured without looking at him. She turned to leave.

"Please, take the chicken. What harm can there be in it?"

"My mother would be angry."

"But why? I only want to do a nice thing for you and your family. Tell your papa I'd like to speak with him and ask his permission to get to know you better. I only have the best of intentions," he said, beaming.

"You are very bold," she said, shaking her head. "And I really had better be on my way."

"A person must be bold if they are to get what they want in life."

"I'm sorry. I—"

"You can ask your father, can't you? At least just ask him, no?"

"No," she said firmly. "I can't. I'm sorry, but I'm betrothed to someone else. I am getting married soon."

"Oh," he said, the disappointment clear in his voice. Mila's heart sank. He was so good-looking and even more handsome as he looked at her with longing in his eyes.

"I'm serious. I had really better go," she repeated.

"Who is it?"

"I'm sorry? Who is what?"

"Your betrothed? Do you feel certain that he is your *bashert*?"

At hearing the word *bashert*, tears welled up in her eyes. "I didn't say he was my *bashert*. I said he was my betrothed."

"You don't like him?"

She couldn't answer him. "I'd better go. What if a customer walks in here and hears us? If someone hears our conversation and tells my parents, I'll be in trouble. The entire community would look at me as if I were a fallen woman. I'm sorry, Mr. Barr, but I must leave right now. People are watching. In our little village, the people are very nosey, and they are always watching and paying attention to others."

"I understand. And, of course, you must go. But, please, meet me somewhere later so we can talk privately. I won't try to stop you from marrying the fellow you are betrothed to, but at least take the time to think it all through. I just want to help you make sure you are making the right decision."

She shook her head. "It's not as if I have any choice. What you don't understand is that this is not my decision to make. I must do as my father commands. He would be furious if he even knew that I was speaking to you. And he would be even more livid if he knew that I was talking about my betrothed with you."

"Then he won't ever know. But Mila, this is *your* life. If you marry this man and you are not happy, you will spend the rest of your days without joy. I can't let that happen to you. You are too young and beautiful to live a life sentence with a man you don't love."

Suddenly, she had the urge to laugh. She let out a small giggle.

"What's funny?" he asked.

"You can't *let* it happen?" She laughed again. "You're a nice fellow, but you really have no say in my future. My father wouldn't even speak to you, even if I begged him. He knows everything about everyone, and I am sure he knows that your uncle owned this butcher shop and that you cater to a non-Jewish crowd."

"Please, just meet with me so we can talk. Just give me a chance."

Mila was silent for a moment, knowing he was right. If she married Anshel, she would be stuck with him for the rest of her life. She would cook his food, wash his clothes, keep his house, and bear his children in silent misery. *I've never been bold. I've always been afraid of my father. But this man makes me feel strong, even reckless. I want to meet him. I want to talk this out with someone who understands how I feel.*

"All right," she said.

"All right?" He was shocked but thrilled. His face broke into a wide smile, and she noticed a dimple on his right cheek.

"I'll meet you. Do you know where the weeping willow tree is at the edge of town?"

"Yes, of course. The big tree with the bench nearby, right?"

"Yes, that's the one," she said. "Can you be there tomorrow?"

"I will be there anytime you want me to be there, even if I have to close the shop."

"Tomorrow, after my parents go to sleep, I will sneak out of the house and meet you." She was surprised at her own *chutzpah*.

"What time?"

"Nine p.m.?"

"I'll be waiting," he said, then added, "Take the chicken, please. It would make me happy."

"I can't. If I come home with a chicken, my parents will be suspicious. They know I don't have enough money to buy that, and they'll start asking questions. Please understand, I appreciate your generosity, but I just can't accept it."

He nodded. "I understand."

Mila turned and left.

CHAPTER EIGHT

All the way home, Mila thought about her promise to meet Pitor. *I shouldn't go. It is very wrong for a nice Jewish girl to meet with a man alone. And even worse, I am betrothed to another man. If anyone in town learns of this meeting, my whole family will be ostracized. It will ruin my younger sister's chances for a good match in the future. And that is so selfish of me. This is unforgivable behavior. If Papa finds out, he will never forgive me. He will punish me. He might even beat me. I shouldn't have promised Pitor. It was a bad idea, terrible.* But even as she told herself that she shouldn't even entertain the thought of meeting Pitor secretly, she knew she was going to meet him.

"What took you so long?" Mila's mother asked when she entered the house. "I told you I needed the potatoes and cabbage for the soup I'm making tonight. Oy, what am I going to do with you? Soon, you'll be a wife and then a mother, and you're still like a child—so irresponsible. I'm sure you were wasting time kibitzing with one of your friends. Sophie? Maybe Esther? Fanny? You don't have to tell me who it was. It doesn't matter anyway. I know I am right. You get started talking with your friends, and you lose all track of the time. Well, Mila," she sighed, "now, the soup won't be ready when your father gets home from work, and you know how he hates waiting for dinner." She shook her head. "You'd better grow up fast, my girl. You're about to be married."

She began peeling the potatoes quickly with an experienced hand. "Soon, you will have to act like an adult, with a home and husband of your own. Grown women do not have time to waste talking to their girlfriends at the market. Certain things will be expected of you. You will have responsibilities."

"Yes, Mama," Mila said, not wanting to argue. *She thinks I was talking to Sophie or Esther. At least she doesn't suspect the truth. I wish I could have brought that chicken home. My sisters would have enjoyed a little chicken for a change. But I suppose it doesn't matter. My mother would have given most of it to my father, anyway. She gives him the best of everything because he is the man of the house. And a good wife takes care of her husband because he is the provider.* She snorted, and her mother turned to look at her, but Mila quickly looked away. *I resent my father. I resent the way he wields his power over all of us. I wish I had the courage to defy him and run away.*

"Why are you just standing around daydreaming?" her mother asked sharply. "You're looking out into the empty space? Nu, Mila, what is wrong with you? Come on, help me. I'm peeling the potatoes; you can cut the cabbage." She handed Mila a large chopping knife.

Mila began to chop the cabbage, but her mother's eyes stayed on her. "Ehhh, maybe you're just nervous about the wedding. Yes, that must be it. I am sure it's weighing heavily on your mind. But you need to wake up Mila and pull yourself together. Anshel expects you to behave like a good wife. You must do your duty and take care of his home. You must provide him with a hot meal each night. You can't spend your time laughing and talking to your friends anymore. Do you understand me?"

"Yes, Mama," Mila said, but frustration boiled inside her. *I am tired of learning how to please Anshel. Since I became engaged, everyday has been about how and what I must do to keep him happy. But what about me? What if I am not happy?*

Her mother's voice was harsh as it broke through her thoughts. "Mila, what is the matter with you. Pay attention to what you are doing! I need this cabbage chopped up now. The water is already boiling."

"I'm sorry, Mama," Mila said, snapping back to the task. She focused on chopping the head of cabbage.

Mila's mother nodded. "That's better. I'll be right back." She walked into the living room, and Mila could hear her speaking to her sisters. "Sarah, Ruth, come on, put your schoolwork away for now and go and wash up. I never could see the purpose of girls going to school. It's a terrible waste of time."

Sarah and Ruth began walking towards the bathroom. "After you wash your face and hands, come back in here and set the table for dinner. Look at the time. Oy, we must hurry—your papa is probably on his way home."

My mother is like a slave to my father. She jumps at the sound of his name, even after so many years of marriage. Everything she does is to please him. In fact, I am so disgusted by the fact that she once told one of her lady friends she felt guilty about not being able to give my father a son. She gave him three girls. That should have been enough. But to her, having a boy is the ultimate gift a woman can give her husband. And because my mother didn't have a son, she feels like a failure.

Mila thought about the way her mother and father interacted with each other. *And he never makes her feel better. He never thanks her for the things she does for him. He just expects it. In fact, he doesn't even listen to her or take her seriously when she speaks to him. Which she hardly ever dares to do. He walks in and goes to wash up. It's a given that the bathroom must not be occupied when he is going to use it. Then he walks into the living room and plops down on his special chair like a tyrant. He doesn't even acknowledge any of us. My father behaves like we are not important to him at all. He just starts reading his holy books. The room must be completely silent. No one dares to speak or disturb him. It's as if he sees himself as some great Talmudic scholar. He's not; he's a working man. But in his own house, my papa is king. And my mama makes sure of it.*

"Mila? Is the cabbage in the soup pot yet?" her mother called.

Within fifteen minutes of arriving home, Mila had finished chopping cabbage, and it was already in the pot. Her mother glanced over and saw that the soup was boiling. "Good girl," she said approvingly.

She then placed the challah dough, which she had braided a little while ago, into the oven. Within half an hour, the sweet fragrance of fresh bread began to fill the small kitchen.

"I was hoping you would at least try to make the challah tonight. You must be prepared to make challah on Shabbat. Anshel will be expecting it."

"I've made challah before, Mama," Mila said, trying to hide the annoyance in her voice.

"I know you have, but you're very slow when you knead the dough. It takes you forever. And besides that, I also want you to get used to braiding it properly."

"Yes, Mama. I'll make the bread this Shabbat. I will try to be faster and make the braids neater, the way you like them." It was easier to comply than to argue. But inside, Mila felt a deep sadness. *I don't want to spend my life making bread for a man I have little to no feelings for.*

Suddenly, without warning, her mother wrapped her arms around Mila and hugged her. "Oh, my sweet girl. I know you are trying to do what is right. I remember when I was young and about to get married. I was afraid, too. But, you'll see, as time goes by, you and Anshel will build a life together. He is a good boy—a smart boy, a scholarly student. The rabbi likes him. The other women in town will envy you because you have made such a good match."

"Yes, Mama," Mila sighed, but hot tears stung her eyes. "Oh, Mama, all I want is to be happy."

"I know. And right now, you think that your husband will be the reason for your joy in life," her mother continued. "But it's not that way. Once you have children, they will be your true joy in your life.

Your children will mean everything to you. Marriage isn't wonderful for the woman, but the children that come from the marriage are what bring the woman happiness. Even if you only have daughters. God forbid."

"Mama? Do you love us? I know you wish you had a son, but do you love us?"

"That's a crazy question. Of course, I do."

"Can I ask you something very personal?"

"Of course, Mila. You can ask me anything. I know you have many questions right now, especially with your wedding so close at hand."

"I want to know... are you actually in love with Papa?"

"Love?" Her mother laughed. "That kind of romantic love isn't for us, my girl. That kind of love is only in forbidden storybooks, and it's something the goyim chase after. They marry for love and have lots and lots of problems because of it. Not us Jews. We do what we can to make the best possible match. Your father is not perfect, but he is a good provider. We have a place to live and food on the table. So far, he has never hit me. So, I can't complain."

"Did you ever want to be in love? I mean, it seems so magical."

"Oy, Mila," she sucked in her breath. "You've been reading those forbidden books again, haven't you? I don't know why you do this to yourself. You know that your papa forbids you to read them. He does that for your own good. You don't want to chase after something that isn't real. Love isn't real, not like that. That's why you are only permitted to read religious text."

"I haven't been reading them lately... but I did read them in the past before Papa decided to forbid it. And I found the idea of being in love to be, well, to be, sort of wonderful. Do you know what I mean?"

"It's not real. A real marriage is built on solid things, like mutual respect. This comes from both parties understanding what is expected of them. Each of them carries out their duties so that they can build their home together. That's why I insist that you learn to cook and to sew. These are things your future husband has been told are your responsibility. You don't want to disappoint him."

"I realize that, but..." Mila felt a surge of anger in her soul, and for a moment, she was bold. "If I am working as a teacher, and I am cooking, cleaning, sewing, and caring for the children, shouldn't he be doing something more than just studying the Torah and Talmud all day? He won't be supporting us financially. Papa will be paying for everything except for what I can afford on my teachers' salary. It seems to me that very little is expected of Anshel."

"Yes, that's true. But your father likes the match very much. He doesn't mind giving money to Anshel so you two can have a decent life. I know for a fact that he feels proud and lucky that you are betrothed to a scholar."

"But it seems like we have to bow down to Anshel. I can't understand why."

"Mila, do you have any idea how many girls wish they had the opportunity to serve a husband like Anshel?"

Mila shrugged and looked at the floor. "I know that, but it just seems like our family is making such a fuss over him."

"That's because it is an honor to serve a scholarly husband. A boy who is as studious and respected by the rabbi as Anshel could have made a match with many other girls in this village. I'm sure his papa had a list of potential wives for him. But he chose you. You should be grateful, Mila. You shouldn't be questioning whether you are going to be happy with him. You should just be glad he picked you."

"I suppose you're right, Mama."

"I know I am."

In the dining room, Sarah and Ruth were talking and laughing as they set the table for dinner. Mila watched as her sisters worked side by side, occasionally teasing each other. Sometimes, Mila envied them. Sarah was born when Ruth was one year old, making them only one year apart in age, and they were best friends. She often wished she had someone who she could confide in and trust the way Sarah and Ruth trusted each other.

When her father walked in from work, the house instantly grew quiet. He didn't say hello or announce himself. Instead, he went straight to the bathroom to wash up, then into his bedroom, where he changed into something less formal for dinner. Once he was done, he walked into the dining room, sat down at the table, and waited for his wife and daughters to serve him his evening meal.

Mila and her sisters were quiet during dinner. Their father didn't like it when they talked at the table, so no one spoke. Most nights, Mila found it frustrating to wait until her father had finished his meal before she could speak. Sometimes, she had important questions to ask but was forced to remain silent until he had eaten and was satisfied. Tonight, however, she was lost in thought, rethinking the conversation she'd had with her mother. Instead of feeling grateful to be engaged to Anshel, she felt even more determined to meet Pitor.

When her father finished eating, he placed his napkin on his plate and stood up, leaving the table. Like robots, Mila and her sisters began to clear the dishes while their mother washed them at the sink.

Once the kitchen was spotless, Mila escaped to the room she shared with her sisters. Since Ruth and Sarah were still in the living room, she felt safe enough to take out her forbidden book from under the bed. It was a love story about a knight who would do anything for the woman he loved. He brought her candy and flowers and fought battles to protect her. Mila had read the book many times before, but each time she read it, she was swept away into the beautiful dream it offered. She placed her hand on her heart as she read, longing to be the woman in the story instead of Anshel's wife.

CHAPTER NINE

The following day, Mila still had mixed feelings about going to meet with Pitor. She wanted to see him, to speak with him, but as the time drew nearer, the very idea of breaking so many rules terrified her. *The stakes are high. If I get caught meeting this man all alone at night, Anshel will break our engagement. The whole town will call me a curva, a whore. My parents will be ashamed to face any of our neighbors. I will undoubtedly be shunned, and I'll never have another chance to get married. And...my father will probably be so angry he'll beat me.*

Mila was no stranger to her father's terrifying disciplinary tactics. He had used the threat of physical violence to keep his family in line for as long as she could remember. He hit her and her sisters when they defied him. On the rare occasions when her mother voiced an opinion that he did not agree with or stood up to protect one of her daughters from his beatings, he would yell at her. Mila feared him, and sometimes, she thought she hated him. But she knew that no matter what he did, he was still her father, and there was a part of her that loved him, regardless of how despicable she found his behavior to be.

Despite her fear and trepidation, Mila decided she had to meet with Pitor. If she didn't go, she felt it meant that she was ready to seal her fate and marry Anshel. And though she had always been the obedient daughter, she just couldn't sign her life away so easily. She had to at least hear what Pitor had to say.

That evening, she waited patiently, listening closely for her father to start snoring. She'd listened to him snore her entire life. It was usually so loud that she would lie awake, disturbed by the noise. But this time, she welcomed the snoring. It let her know he was fast asleep. Once she heard the loud snoring coming from her parent's room, she got out of bed and checked on her sisters. They lay in their beds, and they, too, seemed to be asleep. Her heart pounded so hard that she felt dizzy. *I've never done anything like this before. This is so deliberately defiant. And yet, I must find the courage to go. Once I hear what Pitor has to say, I will know what I must do.*

First, Mila fixed her pillow under her blanket so that if one of her sisters awakened and looked over, they would think she was asleep in her bed. Then, quietly—so quietly—she climbed out the window of her room and lowered herself to the ground. As soon as she felt her feet hit solid earth, she began to run. If she didn't keep moving forward, she was afraid she might turn back. But before long, she saw Pitor standing where they had agreed to meet.

"Mila," he said, his voice warm, "I'm glad you came."

She smiled shyly, breathless from running and also from being very nervous.

"Sit down, please," he said, motioning to the ground. As Mila began to sit, he touched her shoulder and stopped her. "Wait, just one moment. The ground is still a little damp from the rain earlier this afternoon."

She nodded. "Yes... it did rain," she managed to say.

Before she could sit, Pitor took off his jacket and spread it on the ground. "Here, sit on this," he said, offering a kind smile. "I wouldn't want you to get dirty."

She sat down on his jacket, the air between them thick with

nervous energy. After a moment of silence, she spoke. "I don't know why I came. I've never done anything like this before."

"But you did come, and that means a lot to me. I... I've been watching you at the market since we were both children. I still remember the first time I saw you."

"I don't remember you," she said honestly.

"I know," Pitor said with a soft chuckle. "Back then, I was a shy, skinny boy hiding in the back of my uncle's butcher shop. I was learning the trade."

"How old were you?"

"You mean the first time I saw you?"

"Yes."

"Fifteen. I had just moved here to apprentice at my uncle's shop after my mother passed away." He looked down, pausing for a moment before continuing. "The first time I really saw you, I was so taken with you that I couldn't forget you. I heard my mother's voice in my head. She always spoke about finding my *bashert*."

She shook her head and muttered, "What do you know about *bashert*?"

"I know enough." He smiled at her. "And I said to myself that day that you were the girl I was going to marry."

When he said those words, Mila was stunned. "That's insane," she blurted, suddenly feeling nervous. She began questioning her motives for coming. *What am I doing here? What did I expect to accomplish by meeting with Pitor all alone without a chaperone? This was a mistake—a mistake that can only be trouble for me and for him.*

"I should go," she said, her voice shaky. "I don't know what I was thinking, coming here alone at night to meet with you. I don't know what I was expecting would happen. But before anything happens, I really must go home."

"No, please," he said gently. "You came, Mila. That means that something in your soul is unsettled with your upcoming marriage. Are you sure that the man you're about to marry is the one you want to spend the rest of your life with? Because I don't think you are. I believe that you aren't sure about this upcoming marriage."

"Don't say that. Please," Mila whispered, turning away from Pitor, about to leave. But when he gently reached out and touched her arm, it sent shivers through her entire body. The warmth of his hand on her arm set off an incredible rush of life through her. When she thought of Anshel, she often felt as if something inside her had died. Mila's heart raced. It was very forbidden for a man to touch her like this. And this boy's hand was still resting on her arm. It took all of her inner strength to shake it away. But when he let go, she felt an emptiness where his hand had been.

"It's true. You know I am speaking the truth, Mila. Why else would you have come here tonight? You have feelings for me, too. You must, or you wouldn't be here."

Tears flowed down her cheeks. She saw the look in his eyes. He was gazing at her with such deep warmth, caring, and compassion like she had never known before, especially from a man. Before she knew it, the words flowed out of her mouth like the tears streaming down her face. "I don't want to marry Anshel. My father is forcing me. I don't know what to do. I can't fight him. My papa is too strong... he *will* beat me."

"I will fight him. I'm not afraid of him. I'm not afraid of any man."

Mila shook her head. "It's no use. He is my father. And as I am sure you know, the Ten Commandments tell us that we must honor our parents."

"Yes, yes, I know all of that. But I also know that no father should beat his daughter. And also, I know that you should have some say in who you choose to marry."

"Anshel, my betrothed, is a scholar," she said, her voice trembling. "I know I should be grateful and honored that he chose me as his potential bride. My father is proud and happy that Anshel could have married any one of the other eligible girls in our village, but he chose me. If I even tried to defy my father's will, he would be so angry..."

"You need not be afraid of your father. I will go with you when you speak to him. I will be there at your side."

"I don't even know you," she said, looking away from him. Her hands were trembling, and as she stood, her knees threatened to buckle. "I should really get going. This is wrong. Being here with you is wrong." Tears ran down her cheeks, and she sat back down.

"It's not wrong. We haven't done anything wrong. We're just talking."

"Talking to a man and being alone with him is forbidden."

"*Forbidden.* So much is forbidden in your little community," he said, shaking his head. "That's because they don't want women to learn to think for themselves. You are expected to do whatever your father or husband tells you to. But believe me, Mila, you have a mind of your own. All you have to do is use it."

She looked away, feeling a warmth inside her at his words. He was the first man who had ever acknowledged the fact that she could think for herself. And even though she knew it was wrong, she really liked Pitor. Not only was he devastatingly attractive, but he respected her in ways no other person had ever done. Pitor cleared his throat and continued, his tone calm and logical, "Now, you say you don't know me. But the fact is, you don't know Anshel either, do you?"

"No," she admitted softy. "I don't know him at all. I know only that my father chose him," she admitted.

"Well then, if your father likes him so much, let *him* marry Anshel," Pitor said with a small laugh, trying to lighten the mood. "This is your life, Mila. No one, not even your papa, should ask you to sacrifice your happiness for him."

She couldn't help but let out a short laugh. Then she wiped the tears off her cheeks with the back of her hand.

"You're even prettier when you laugh," Pitor said earnestly. Then he added, "Don't let your father ruin your life, Mila. Look inside yourself and trust your own feelings. I know you feel something for me that you don't feel for your current fiancé. I know because if you were certain that you wanted to marry Anshel, you would never have come here tonight."

She shook her head. "You scare me," she admitted.

"Please don't be afraid of me. I would never hurt you, and I would never do anything you didn't want me to do."

"I'm afraid… because what you are saying might be true."

"You know it's true. And that's what is scaring you. I know it goes against everything you have been taught but listen to your heart, Mila. Do what your heart tells you to do. I am here to help you."

"I'm feeling so many different things," she said, her voice wavering.

"I understand," he replied gently. "And if you want me to, even if I am not your choice for a husband, I'll talk to your father. I'll tell him that he must call off the wedding."

She laughed. "You certainly are confident, aren't you?"

He shrugged. "I suppose so. I've never backed down from anything that I've had to face in my life. And I've had to face plenty. I grew up Jewish in Germany, and there were a lot of people who hated Jews, and a lot of people I went to school with hated them, too. When I was really young, they beat me up. But then I grew up, and I wasn't such an easy target."

"But you're not religious, are you?"

"That didn't matter to them. Religious or not, I was a Jew, and that was the reason they needed to hate me. I've fought my whole life. So, I am not afraid of your papa. The only thing I am afraid of… is losing you. I want to get to know you better. I feel things for you that I have never felt for anyone before."

Mila was afraid of what her father would do if she brought Pitor home to speak with him. Pitor wasn't part of her very strict Orthodox community. His butcher shop wasn't even considered kosher, and she wondered if he even belonged to a synagogue. She knew he was not a member of the one she attended. And through the years, when she'd heard her parents talking about Pitor's uncle and his *treif*, non-kosher butcher shop, they also said that his nephew Pitor was a rebel. He was not considered a good match for any decent *frum* girl. In fact, there were whispers he had been involved in unsavory relationships with secular women, and she'd heard that he had even dated a *shiksa* once. She remembered overhearing her parents talk about Pitor and his unacceptable behavior, but she had never dared to ask them anything.

As she sat with him now, having broken the rules by meeting a man her community shunned, she found herself wanting to know everything about him. "I've heard things about you," she said softly.

"Oh?" he replied as if he was surprised, but she was sure he wasn't.

"Yes," she sighed. "You know how people talk."

He laughed a little. "I sure do. So, tell me, what do they say?"

"Well, I've heard you've had girlfriends... who were, well, kind of loose. If you know what I mean."

"Of course, I know what you mean," he said.

"But you never married any of them. Why?" She hesitated, took a deep breath, and continued, "Am I getting too personal?"

"Not at all. I want you to know everything there is to know about me," Pitor said with a smile.

"I heard that the girls you were seeing were secular... and that one was not Jewish at all."

It was getting too dark to see his facial expression, and for a moment, Mila worried that he might be angry. "I am sorry. I had no right to pry. I should go," she said, though she didn't move to stand.

"No, it's all right," he reassured her. "Like I said, I'll tell you whatever you want to know. First of all, I didn't marry any of them because I had no intention of marrying them. I have been waiting my whole life for you."

"You were waiting for *me*?" she asked, unable to keep the shock out of her voice. "Now you're being silly."

"No, I am not. I knew."

"Did your parents tell you that they were planning to arrange a match between us?"

He laughed. "My father would have loved to arrange a match between us. But, I suppose you might say he knew I was considered a bad boy. I was always getting into trouble. So, between my behavior and the fact that I was never religious, he would have known, even before asking, that your father would never accept me."

"So, if you already know my father won't accept you, how can you expect to go and speak to him? How can you think he will allow you to marry me? What are you thinking?"

"Back then, I was a child. Now, I'm going to tell your father the truth. I'll tell him that I have a good business. The secular Jews are my best customers, but I have plenty of non-Jewish customers, too. I earn a nice living so I can afford to take good care of you, and if that's not enough, I will tell him that you are my *bashert*."

"*Bashert?*" she repeated.

"Yes, you are the one for me, Mila. You are my twin soul, the other half of me. I will never be complete without you."

"Oh, I see," she said, her voice laced with sarcasm. "And you think that telling him all of this will convince him?"

"I do. It should. He is your father—he should want you to be happy. And even if he doesn't agree, we can marry anyway."

Mila sighed. "I can see why you don't fit into our way of life."

"The Orthodox life?" he echoed. "I could never fit in there because it's too rigid for me."

"How old are you, Pitor?"

"How old do you think I am?"

"I don't know. But I am a grown woman now, and so far, I've spent every day of my life living under the rules of my community. There are so many rules—for everything we do. I have followed them for so long. How can you expect me to change and behave in a way that is so foreign to me?"

"I am twenty-one years old," he said. "And it's not that I expect you to act in ways that are foreign to you. I am trying to help you. Once again, Mila, if you were happy with the way things were going, if you were ready to marry Anshel and live your life with him, you would never have come here tonight. You don't have to say a word, but I know you realize that I am right."

He paused for a moment, then continued with a sigh, "As far as we know, we only have one life. Why should you spend your entire life being miserable?"

She shook her head, her small, delicate hands trembling. Even in the darkness, Pitor could see them shaking. He looked at her and wished he could hold her hands and somehow make her feel safe.

"I am lost," she whispered, and there was a slight cry in her voice. "I don't know what to do. I wish I knew. My father is not the kind of man who would care if I was happy or not. All he cares about is what people will say about our family. And you know that what they will say if they ever find out about me meeting you here tonight will not be good. I will never be able to live it down. I will be labeled a *kurveh* —a whore. I'm sorry, Pitor, but I really have to go. I have so much to think about."

She stood up and turned to walk away, but Pitor grabbed her arm gently but firmly and swung her around to face him. In one swift motion, he put his arms around her and pulled her to him. At first, she struggled to get away, but when his lips met hers, her body surrendered completely. Mila's knees were so weak that Pitor was practically holding her up. The kiss was long and slow, and she could feel his passion as he pressed against her.

When he finally let her go, Mila stood there, stunned, gazing at him. "Think about that," he said softly before turning and walking away without looking back.

Mila stood frozen for several minutes as she watched him go. Her lips still burned from his kiss, and her mind swirled in confusion. A shooting star cast a fiery glow across the dark sky, breaking the spell. She looked up and watched it for a moment, then she turned and ran home. But even as she hurried away, the memory of Pitor's kiss still lingered, refusing to fade.

CHAPTER TEN

"Where were you? Where did you go? You went out alone at night? Papa would be furious if he knew," Ruth whispered. She was awake, watching as Mila climbed back through the window into her bedroom. "I was worried sick about you."

"I..." Mila tried to think of an acceptable lie, but she knew Ruth would see through her. "I had to meet someone."

"Anshel?" Ruth asked.

"No."

Sarah, who was still asleep, stirred in her bed.

"Who then?" Ruth pressed. "You know I won't tell on you, but you shouldn't be going out at night alone. It's very dangerous. Besides, what about your reputation? What would happen if Anshel's parents found out that you were wandering around at night. It would not be good. You know how strict his family is. And what about papa? He would be so angry."

Sarah sat up. "What's going on in here?"

"Nothing, go back to sleep," Mila said quickly.

"Ruth, is something wrong?" Sarah asked, her voice groggy.

"No, everything is fine. Just go back to sleep. Really. I promise you everything is all right."

Sarah lay back down, but even in the darkness, Mila could see that Sarah's eyes were wide open. Mila adored her sisters, and she knew they loved her too. Because they were only a year apart, the two babies were small at the same time. Her mother had needed Mila's help to raise them. Mila had been like a second mother to the girls. She'd changed their diapers and rocked them when they cried. She had watched them as they slept. And she knew that because they were so close in age, they were very close. They could almost communicate without speaking. Mila had watched them interact with each other from the time they were very young. But even though they were as close as two people could be, they never made Mila feel left out. They embraced her and included her in their private world.

Mila felt strongly that she could trust her sisters, but she was conflicted. She had strong feelings for Pitor, and she couldn't deny that she didn't want to marry Anshel. No one in her family knew her true feelings about the upcoming wedding. But her wish to break things off with Anshel was driving her crazy, and she felt she had to share her secret with someone. She needed to decide about her future, and she could not do it alone.

So, she whispered. "I was out meeting with another boy."

Sarah, who was supposed to be asleep, gasped and sat up again. "Are you crazy? You went out the window at night, alone, to meet with a boy? If anyone in town saw you, your reputation would be destroyed. What are you thinking, Mila? Why would you do this? You do realize that if you get a bad reputation, it will ruin our chances, too, right? It will have a terrible effect on the boys who are eligible when Ruth and I are ready to get married?"

"I am sorry, but I just can't marry Anshel."

"Did he do something bad to you? Did he ruin you?" Ruth asked, her voice tense.

"No, he's never touched me. In fact, it's nothing like that," Mila admitted. "It's just that I can't see myself spending the rest of my life with Anshel. I know a lot of girls would think he's a catch, but for me, well, he is just not the right fellow. He is not my *bashert*."

"If he wasn't your *bashert*, you wouldn't be betrothed to him," Ruth said firmly.

"Papa made a mistake," Mila snapped.

"Can that happen?" Ruth asked honestly.

"I think it can," Mila said. "in fact, I know it can." She hesitated, then she asked both of her sisters, "Can the two of you keep a secret?"

"Of course. For you? We will do anything," Sarah said quickly.

"I think I know who my *bashert* is. In fact, I think I am in love."

"In love?" Ruth said, skeptical. "Really?" She took a deep breath. "Did you let him... do anything to you? You know what I mean..."

"Of course not. I am not that kind of girl," Mila said, her cheeks flushing.

"I know you're not, of course. But...well... what did you do when you were out tonight?"

"I didn't do anything. We just talked. And..."

"Nu? And?" Ruth said.

"He kissed me."

"Oy vey," Ruth shook her head. "Who is he?"

"If I tell you, you have to promise to keep it a secret?"

"I would never tell on you. I already told you that. Who is the boy?"

"Pitor Barr, the butcher."

"Oy! Pitor from the *goyish* butcher shop? Papa wouldn't even consider that boy to be a Jew. His shop is not kosher, and... oy... from what I have heard, his reputation is not so good. And now yours is going to be the same if anyone ever finds out you've been meeting him alone at night," Ruth grabbed her older sister's arm. "Listen to me—you must never see him again. You shouldn't be going to his butcher shop in the first place. It's not *Glatt* kosher. Go to Weinstein's around the corner from now on. Just avoid him at all costs, and eventually, your feelings for him will go away."

"I understand what you are saying, but I know I can't marry Anshel," Mila said, her voice resolute.

"Because you met with Pitor?" Ruth asked.

"Because I have feelings for Pitor, and it would be wrong to marry Anshel while feeling the way I do."

"Papa will hit you," Sarah said, biting her lip. "I hate it when Papa hits one of us. He will be so angry if you try to break up with Anshel."

"Then I'll run away."

"No, no, please don't," Ruth pleaded. "We'll be forbidden to see you again if you do that. Papa will never let us speak to you."

"What else can I do? You two will have to find a way to come and see me in secret during the day. I don't know what else to do."

Ruth shook her head. "This is terrible. Just terrible. You have been more than an older sister to us. You've been like a mother, and I can't bear to lose you. I know Sarah feels the same."

"I do," Sarah said softly.

Mila sighed, her heart heavy. "I realize this. And I love you both very much. But you're going to have to understand that I have no other choice."

CHAPTER ELEVEN

The following day, Mila got up early and did her chores. She swept and washed the floor, dusted all the furniture in the house, and scrubbed the laundry. Then she took the wet clothes outside to hang them on a line. It was mid-July, and though it was still early morning, it was already getting hot outside. Mila felt flushed and nervous. She'd been unable to sleep at all the previous night. All night long, she agonized over the consequences of what she was about to do. But no matter how much she wrestled with it, she could not see any other way.

She had to tell Pitor how she felt about him. If he still wanted to marry her, she had to let him know she was willing to run away from home and marry him. But first, she knew she would have to tell Anshel that their wedding was off. *This will be very difficult for me because he is a nice person, and I don't want to hurt him. I can't say anything bad about Anshel. He is so smart, and so many girls would love to be his betrothed. So, I know he will find another match quickly.*

But then... she wasn't sure how she was going to tell her father. If she ran away and got married before her father could stop her, she was certain that he would never allow her to see her mother or her sisters again. But even if she didn't run, even if she faced him and told him everything, he might still forbid her to see her family. The weight of it all made her chest tighten.

Mila walked through town until she got to the window of Pitor's butcher shop. She saw two women inside; they were buying meat. Pitor was busy wrapping up their purchases, so he didn't notice Mila at first. But when he looked up to hand the women their packages, his eyes met hers. His handsome face lit up, and he smiled. Mila felt her heart melt, her hand instinctively moving to her chest. She looked away, but she couldn't help but smile back. Pitor rushed out the door and went straight to where she stood.

"You came."

"It seems like those two words are the only two words you know," she said teasingly, her eyes sparkling with mischief as she leaned against the doorframe.

"I know plenty more. Just give me a chance," he laughed. "But right now, those two words are the most important words in the entire world to me. I am so glad you came to see me."

"Who says I came to see you?" she asked, raising an eyebrow and crossing her arms playfully. "Maybe I was just walking through town and happened to pass your window."

"Is that so?" He folded his arms, his lips curving into a knowing smile.

"No, it's not." She looked away, a blush creeping onto her cheeks. "Actually, I did come to see you."

He smiled at her. "Come into the store. Please."

She looked around before she followed him inside.

"Do you want to sit down? There's a chair in the back."

"What if someone from town looks through the window and sees me go back there?" she asked, her eyes darting nervously to the street outside.

"So? What if they do? What if they see you in my store and think you are shopping here? Everyone knows I don't follow all of their strict kosher laws. That would be enough for them to start gossiping," he sighed. "If you spend all of your time worrying about what the community will think of the things you do, you'll never be happy."

"You're right," she said, her shoulders relaxing slightly. She glanced at him, a flicker of warmth in her eyes. "And…" She cleared her throat. "That's why I'm here. I came to tell you something."

"Sure… yes, go on. Tell me anything," Pitor said, searching her eyes.

Just then, the bell above the door jingled, and a woman who Mila did not recognize as a part of the Jewish community walked into the butcher shop. "Hello, Pitor," she said, "I need a chicken. Do you have one? And can you cut it up for me, please?"

He nodded, giving Mila an apologetic look. "Of course, Frau Hermann. I will get that for you right away."

Quickly, Pitor expertly cut the chicken into pieces. Then he carefully wrapped it and handed the package to Frau Hermann, who paid him.

"Enjoy your dinner," he said.

"Thank you," Frau Hermann replied, then she left the store.

Once she was gone, Pitor turned to Mila and said, "I'm sorry for the interruption. You were saying?"

Mila hesitated, then asked, "I suppose a lot of *goyim* shop here. Yes?"

"Yes, they do. I have good quality meat at a better price than the kosher butcher down the street, and they realize it. My store is just not good enough for the ultra-Orthodox community, I suppose. They don't like me."

She nodded. It was true; they didn't like or accept him as one of their own. But she felt bad for him, and so she tried to make him feel better. "You don't follow the rules of Glatt kosher. That's all it is. It is nothing against you."

"It doesn't matter." He smiled. Then, in a softer voice, he asked, "Mila, what were you about to say when Frau Hermann came in?" He was still standing behind the counter.

She took a deep breath. "This is very hard for me. I don't know how to tell you this."

"Just tell me," he said gently. "Believe me, you can tell me anything."

Mila looked down, her heart pounding. "I have decided that you are right. I can't marry Anshel. I must break off the engagement."

Pitor nodded and swallowed hard enough for her to see his Adam's apple bob up and down. Mila watched his face carefully. Then she saw the hint of a smile behind his eyes. His lips were quivering, and she knew he was as nervous as she was.

"I don't know how to ask you this," she said, her hands trembling.

"What is it you want?" he asked. "Whatever it is, I'll do my best to see to it that you get it. I love you, Mila. More than anything in this world, I want you to be happy."

"I want to be happy, and I really believe I could be happy with you." Her face felt hot, and she was sure it was probably as red as a ripe strawberry. "I just... I don't know how to ask you this. Girls don't ask boys... This is not the way it's done."

Pitor stepped out from behind the counter. "It's all right. I'll ask you. I'm not afraid to go after what I want. And I want you." He took a deep breath, his voice softening. "I want to marry you, Mila. I promise that I will spend every day for the rest of my life trying to be a good husband to you. You couldn't ask for more from any other fellow."

She giggled, looking away from him.

"Why are you laughing?" He was offended. She could hear it in his tone of voice.

"I'm only laughing because you knew what I wanted to ask, but I could never have found the words to ask you to marry me."

"I didn't know that was what you wanted. I only hoped it was."

"It was," she said softly, shyly.

"So... you will? Are you actually saying that you will marry me? Are you really saying yes?" He practically jumped over the counter to stand beside her.

She giggled again. "I'm sorry for laughing, but you are terribly cute when you are passionate about something."

"You didn't answer my question... Are you saying yes?"

She nodded, then cleared her throat and said firmly, "Yes. I am saying yes. I will marry you, Pitor Barr."

Pitor's face lit up, and he put his hands on her waist, lifting her in the air. Then he spun her around. Mila glanced outside through the large plate-glass window and froze. Frau Nachman, her neighbor and the town gossip—who was also her mother's friend—was staring at them in horror. Her eyes were wide, and her mouth was hanging open. Suddenly, Mila was terrified at her own brazen behavior.

"Please put me down," she whispered.

"What is it? I was just so happy that I couldn't help but spin you around. I didn't hurt you, did I?"

"No, not at all." Mila was staring out the window, her eyes fixed on Frau Nachman, who shook her head and wagged her finger disapprovingly. Mila felt a chill run through her.

"What is it? You look like you've seen a ghost," Pitor said.

"Do you see that woman over there? That's Frau Nachman. She's my neighbor and like a neighborhood watchdog. And to make matters worse, she is friends with my mother." Mila said. "She's a widow with nothing to do but gossip and cause trouble. Look at her face. She's going right to my house to tell my parents what she just saw. Once my father hears that I was in your store and that you put your hands on my waist, he will lock me up. He'll be so afraid of what Anshel's family will say that he will beg Frau Nachman to keep silent. And if I go home now, we won't have a chance to get married. My father won't let me out of his sight again until after my wedding to Anshel."

"That's all right," Pitor said, his eyes determined. "I don't care if we have a wedding or not. Let's just get married right now. I'll close the store, and we'll go."

"Who will marry us? Not the rabbi from the synagogue I attend. He would never do it without my papa's approval."

"Don't worry. I just happen to know a rabbi who will do it. The only thing is, I feel bad for you. I know girls live for their wedding day, and because of me, you won't have a proper one."

Mila thought about it for a moment, then she shook her head. "I don't care. I'd rather give up the wedding and the celebration than spend the rest of my life with a man I don't want to be with."

Pitor's face beamed with joy. "That means that you want to be with me, right? Dare I ask this?"

"Ask," she said, smiling.

"So... do you think you could ever love me?"

She giggled. "Don't push your luck."

He laughed, and then he removed his apron and took her hand. "Let's go and see my rabbi friend before someone comes to stop us."

CHAPTER TWELVE

Rabbi Cohen was a secular rabbi who ran a small synagogue on the other side of town. Mila and Pitor boarded a bus, and once they got off, they walked nearly a mile before reaching the synagogue. Pitor held the door for Mila as they entered the building, and then he led her to the main room where services were held. At the front of the room, on a small stage, a handsome young man in a dark suit sat reading a large book.

"Rabbi Cohen," Pitor addressed the young man, who looked up from his book.

Rabbi Cohen recognized Pitor immediately. "Welcome, Pitor. It's been a while since you've been here, but I am glad to have you back," he said cheerfully. "And who is this lovely young lady?"

The rabbi was far younger than the rabbis at the synagogue Mila's family belonged to. He was clean-shaven, with a full head of dark hair and a bright smile. He didn't wear a *payot*, and his hair was cut short. Mila knew that if her father saw Rabbi Cohen, he would say that the man was not a real rabbi. But even though she was terrified by her own actions, she knew she had to take this very different path with her life. If she and Pitor had gone to speak to her father, her father would never have agreed. This was what she wanted. Her father had forced her to do this by giving her no choice in the man she would spend her life with. Mila was defying everything she had grown up believing. Instead, she accepted Rabbi Cohen. She was sure that if Pitor was a member of this secular synagogue, she would join, too, after they were married.

"Rabbi Cohen, this is my betrothed, Mila Zielinsky."

"I didn't know you were engaged, Pitor."

"I wasn't, but I am now. I know in my heart that Mila is my *bashert,* and we have come here because we would like you to marry us."

The rabbi nodded. "Mila," he said, "you come from an Orthodox family?"

"Yes, I do."

"Are you sure that this is what you want? I know your parents would not approve of me performing this wedding. So, I want to be sure you realize all the consequences before we go ahead with this."

"I know the consequences," she said seriously. "But Pitor is right. He is my twin soul, my *bashert.* If I go to my father and ask for his permission or even his blessing, he will forbid this marriage. I want to marry Pitor, and he wants to marry me. This is very hard because I know that I will be forced to give up my sisters and my mother. My father will forbid them from seeing me. He will use them as a punishment for me for defying him. I wish things were different, but they aren't. My father is very stubborn. If he had the chance, he would stop this marriage and force me to marry the man he chose—a man I do not want to spend my life with. So, I have made a decision."

"All right. I'll marry you. Wait here while I go to my office to get my book so we can choose a date."

"Well, that's just it," Pitor said. "I'm afraid that today is the date, and right now is the time."

Mila felt reckless, but there was something about Pitor that made her feel safe even though she was behaving in a way that was foreign to everything she'd been taught.

"I know it sounds crazy, but I met Mila when we were younger, and, somehow, I always knew, even then, that she was my *bashert*. You know how you can just know things, Rabbi?"

The rabbi contemplated what Pitor said and nodded. "Yes, I know." He then looked directly into Pitor's eyes and said, "But what about her family? You will be forcing her to give up her family. Are you sure you want to do this?"

"I don't want to separate her from her family, but I want to marry her, and I can't let them stand in the way."

"Nor can I," Mila said firmly, surprising herself with how bold and outspoken she had become

"Pitor?" the rabbi said skeptically. "What is really happening here? Before you two get married, I think you need to tell me the truth about everything."

Pitor sighed. "I'll tell you whatever you want to know."

"Come into my study where we can talk privately." Rabbi Cohen stood up and began walking. Pitor and Mila followed.

The rabbi's study was a small room with a window that overlooked a well-kept garden.

"Sit down, both of you," Rabbi Cohen said gently, gesturing at two chairs across from a desk.

Both men waited until Mila sat down, and then they sat as well. "Now, go ahead and tell me everything," Rabbi Cohen said.

Pitor sighed, and then he told the rabbi all about his feelings for Mila and how he had spent his entire life hoping that someday she would be his. When he finished, Rabbi Cohen turned to Mila.

"Would you like to tell me how you came to decide that you want to marry Pitor?"

If this had been one of the rabbis that Mila knew from her own synagogue, she would have been very nervous and unable to speak because she knew they would never approve. If she were in her own synagogue right now, she would have looked into the rabbi's eyes and backed down, apologizing profusely for bothering him. When she and Pitor decided to go and speak with Rabbi Cohen, Mila had hoped to be granted permission to marry without explaining every-thing about Anshel to him. There was no doubt in her mind that if she were speaking with any of the rabbis she had grown up with, none of them would ever have approved of this marriage. In fact, she would be running home right now, knowing she and Anshel would be wed just as her father had planned. But Rabbi Cohen was differ-ent. He was easy to talk to, a good listener, and far less judgmental than the religious men she knew. So, she took a breath and looked down at her hands, then began to explain her feelings about her father and Anshel. Finally, red-faced with embarrassment, she told the rabbi that she thought Pitor was correct when he claimed that they were *bashert*, meant for each other.

For a long time, the rabbi didn't say a word. He listened in silence. When she finished, Rabbi Cohen said softly, "I am sure you realize that if you marry Pitor, your father may disown you."

"I do."

"And you want to go through with the marriage anyway?"

"Yes." Her voice was hoarse. "It makes me very sad to know that my father will retaliate, and because of his unwillingness to bend, I will probably lose my family. But I am sure that this is what I want."

Pitor looked at her. "You don't know how happy you made me when you said those words," he said to Mila, looking at her with such love in his eyes that it was as if he forgot the rabbi was there.

She glanced up at him and smiled.

"I will take good care of her, Rabbi. I will be a good husband. I know I have a bad track record when it comes to women, but you have never before heard me say that I wanted to spend my life with someone before. I am saying it now. This is the wife for me. This woman is the other half of my soul. I will never be complete without her. In fact, if we can't marry, I believe neither of us will ever be whole."

"Hmmm," the rabbi said. "That's quite a claim."

"Will you marry us?"

There was a moment of silence, and during that moment, Mila could hear her own heart beating. Then the rabbi said softly, "Yes, I will marry you. God shines His light on people in love."

CHAPTER THIRTEEN

Mila and Pitor were married in Rabbi Cohen's study on that hot summer afternoon. When they walked out of the synagogue as man and wife, Pitor's face was radiant with joy. "Mrs. Barr, my wife," he said as he looked over at Mila with pride.

She smiled, though her lips trembled. "Yes, I am!" she replied. "But now comes the hard part. I have to tell my father... and Anshel."

"I'll go with you."

She knew she should not allow Pitor to go with her to speak to Anshel or to her father. But she was so afraid of what her father would do that she agreed to have Pitor come with her. "My father is going to be difficult," she admitted. "He might hit me."

"He'll have to kill me first," Pitor said, his voice steady. "You are my wife now. No one will lift their hand against you without going through me. Not even your own father. From this day forward, I will protect you with my life."

She smiled, but her lips were still quivering as they walked towards her home. When they arrived, Mila's sisters were outside hanging the freshly washed clothes and sheets on a line. When Ruth saw Mila, she dropped the shirt she was holding and ran to her.

"Mama has been worried about you. Where have you been?" Ruth's eyes flicked between Mila and Pitor. "What are you doing? Who is this strange man? He has no *tallis* or *yarmulke*... is he a goy? And why is he here with you?"

"I need to speak to Papa. And, to Mama, too," Mila said, her voice was quieter now. She closed her eyes for a moment and added, "This is Pitor. He's... my husband."

Sarah was still hanging the last sheet on the clothesline. When she finished, she walked over to where everyone was standing. "Mila? Mama's been looking for you."

"What have you done?" Ruth asked, her hand covering her mouth. "Have you already married this man?"

"Yes," Mila said as bravely as she could.

"Mila?" Sarah's voice wavered. "Papa is going to be furious."

"I know, and I am sorry. But I couldn't marry Anshel. And well... I know this is going to be hard for you two to believe, but I am sure that Pitor is my *bashert*."

"You've gone insane," Ruth said. "Papa will be home any minute, and I feel sick with worry about how he is going to take this. He will be very angry, and when he gets angry, he gets violent."

"It will be alright," Pitor said. "I promise you."

"Don't make promises you have no way of keeping," Ruth snapped. "You don't know or understand our way of life. You know nothing about our ways. This is going to be a very difficult thing for my father to accept. And because I know him, I have a feeling he will not accept it at all." She was angry at this rebellious young man because she believed he had led her sister astray.

"I'll do my best," Pitor said.

Ruth leaned in close to Mila, her voice a harsh whisper. "Have you?"

"Have I what?" Mila knew what Ruth was asking, but she was embarrassed to answer. She hoped that if she pretended not to know, Ruth would be too ashamed to ask a more detailed question, but Ruth did not back down.

"Have you consummated the marriage?" Ruth's face was flushed with shame as she whispered her question.

"No, not yet. But we were married by a rabbi."

"Which one?"

"You don't know him. He's a secular Jewish rabbi. His name is Rabbi Cohen."

"Papa won't accept your marriage. He will never consider it to be legitimate. I promise you that he will say that Rabbi Cohen is not Jewish, so he can't marry you."

"He might say that. In fact, I am sure he will, but what he says no longer matters. Pitor and I are married."

As soon as their father appeared at the end of the walkway, Mila tensed. She glanced at Ruth, who was equally on edge. Sarah, standing close by, shifted nervously, looking to Ruth for guidance. Pitor, however, stood fearlessly. He left the girls standing in the yard and strode toward Mila's father. The older man looked tired and worn out from a long day's work, but he still wore his *tallis* and *kippah* over his simple work clothes.

"Good afternoon, Mr. Zielinsky," Pitor greeted him, standing tall.

"Who are you? And what do you want?" Mr. Zielinsky's eyes narrowed as he looked Pitor up and down. Mila's father was a short man, solid and strong but not nearly as strong as young Pitor, who was tall, muscular, and healthy. However, he radiated authority.

"With all due respect, sir," Pitor said, with his head held high, "I am in love with your daughter."

Mr. Zielinsky's face darkened, his voice rising. "What did you say?"

"I said, sir, that I am in love with your daughter, Mila."

"Well, that's very unfortunate for you. Mila is betrothed to someone else. So, go home."

"I've come to tell you that Mila and I are married. We were married this afternoon in the rabbi's study at a shul in town."

"What?" Mr. Zielinsky's eyes narrowed further. "You must be out of your mind.".

"We are married. Mila loves me too."

"Love? Have you both gone mad? Is that what this is? You are both crazy. I'll have it annulled. You go away forever. You and Mila are never to speak to each other again. Do I make myself clear?"

Mila clung to her sister's arms as she listened closely. Even from where she stood, she could hear the conversation between Pitor and her father.

"I'm sorry, sir, but that is not possible," Pitor said, his voice firm. "Mila and I are husband and wife, and I will make her a good husband. This I promise you."

"You will make her no husband," Mr. Zielinsky barked, "because you will go home and forget about Mila. That's what you will do."

"I can't. And I won't," Pitor said, setting his hands on his hips. He was ready to fight if it was necessary, though he hoped it wouldn't be. He wanted this man to like and accept him for Mila's sake.

Mr. Zielinsky was shaking, and for the first time in his life, he lost control of himself and was physically violent towards someone who was not in his family. With a fierce growl, he swung at Pitor, punching him squarely in the face. Pitor's lip began to bleed, but he didn't flinch. He knew it would be a mistake to hit back, and he hoped he wouldn't have to. Pitor stood staring at Mila's father. There was no doubt in Pitor's mind that he would win in a fight against this old man. But this was his wife's father, and he would take the blow without retaliating. At least not yet.

"Go home!" Mr. Zielinsky roared, his voice reverberating through the yard.

"We will go home," Piotr said evenly. "Mila and I will go home together. We just wanted to come by and tell you what we decided to do. We were hoping for your blessing."

"Mila, come here," her father commanded. Then, turning to Pitor, he snarled, "You will never have my permission or my blessing."

Mila walked over gingerly. She felt as if her knees would buckle. "Yes, Papa," she whispered, choking on the words.

"Tell this man to get out of here. You made a mistake, young lady. A terrible mistake. I am very angry with you, but I am going to have this crazy marriage annulled as soon as possible. You'd better hope that Anshel's family never finds out what you did." His eyes burned into hers. "And I am not going to ask you, but for your sake, I hope that this abomination was not consummated. If you have already lost your virginity to this man, I want you to know that Anshel will be able to tell on your wedding night. He will not tolerate such a thing, and I will be furious with you for ruining your life—and your sisters' chances for good husbands."

"We are married," Pitor said, blood running down his chin. He looked over at Mila. She felt as if she might collapse. "Mila, tell him that you are not going to change your mind. Tell him that we are going home together because we are married."

"We are married, Papa," Mila said. Fear gripped her tightly as she stood there with the late afternoon sun burning her face.

"You defied me," her father growled. He raised his hand to hit her, and in an instant, Pitor changed his mind about not fighting Mr. Zielinski. He didn't care about himself, but he would not allow him to strike Mila.

"Don't you touch her," Pitor warned, his voice low and threatening.

Something in Pitor's voice stopped Mr. Zielinsky. Slowly, he lowered his hand, glaring at his daughter with cold fury. Then, without a word, he tore the lapel of his shirt in a gesture of mourning. "My daughter died today. I am in mourning," he declared before turning and walking into the house.

Mila crumpled to the ground, sobbing. Pitor lifted her gently and took her into his arms as her sisters looked on in horror.

"Don't cry, my darling. Crying never helps anything. We'll go home, and we'll live our lives together. Someday, maybe your papa will come around."

"Of course, she is crying. You've just ruined her life," Ruth spat at

Pitor. Then she glared at him and asked spitefully, "Don't you ever cry?"

"No, I don't," he said softly. "I don't believe in it. Crying doesn't change anything." Then he added, looking at Ruth and Sarah, "I know that you two girls are feeling badly. But you needn't lose your sister. I want you to know that you are always welcome in our home."

"You don't understand. Our papa is going to forbid us from ever seeing Mila again," Sarah cried.

"I can't change that. But please, just know that our door is always open to you both." Then, taking Mila's hand, he led her away.

"That went as badly as I thought it would. But it's not over yet. Now, I must tell Anshel," Mila murmured.

"I'll go with you," Pitor offered.

"No, I should go alone. It's going to hurt his feelings."

"Are you sure that's what you want?"

"I don't want to. But I think it's only fair to him that I do. He's done nothing wrong. I just don't want to marry him, and that's not his fault."

"All right. Where shall I wait for you?"

"Outside his house. I am going to go there now and speak to him."

"All right."

Mila knew exactly how to get to Anshel's home. She and her parents had been there for dinner, but she had never been there alone. Her heart was heavy as she thought about her father, but she knew she'd made the right choice. Mila held Pitor's hand as she led him to the small house that belonged to Anshel's family. It was at the end of a quiet street.

"Wait here," Mila said when they were two houses away. Pitor nodded. Then she made her way to Anshel's home. Slowly, she walked up to the door and knocked.

Mrs. Minsky, Anshel's mother, answered the door. "Mila, what a pleasant surprise! Come in," she said sweetly as she warmly welcomed her future daughter-in-law.

"Good afternoon, Mrs. Minsky," Mila, her voice heavy with emotion. "I need to speak with Anshel. Is he at home?"

"Yes, as a matter of fact, he just got home. He is in his room studying. Come in and sit down. I will get him for you. By the way, can I get you a cup of tea or a piece of cake?"

"No, thank you," Mila said as sweetly as she could, but her voice felt tight. She felt sick because she knew she was about to shatter this woman's image of her as being the perfect young Jewish girl.

Anshel walked out of his room, and when he saw Mila, his face lit up. "Hello," he said, his voice very warm and welcoming. "Sit, please. My mother will get you some tea and maybe something to eat? Yes? Are you hungry?"

Mila could not meet his eyes, but she shook her head. "No, thank you, Anshel." She said, her face flushed, "I came here because I have something I must tell you, and I don't know how to say it."

Anshel tilted his head, concerned. "Please go on."

"I never wanted to hurt you, Anshel. You are a good man, and you will make a wonderful husband for someone. You are smart, and you have so many good traits..."

"Mila? What are you talking about? What are you trying to tell me?"

"I'm sorry." She sighed, then she looked down at the ground, and in a soft voice, she said, "I can't marry you."

Anshel's face softened with understanding. "It's all right, Mila. You're nervous. You're afraid. You are an innocent young woman. The rabbi told us in my wedding class that I might expect something like this from you. He said to be understanding and to make you feel secure. So please, don't worry. Everything will be just fine. So many young couples have gone through this. They have experienced the same feelings of fear and worry as their wedding day grew near. But we'll be just fine. You'll see."

Tears streamed down Mila's cheeks as she shook her head. Then, as firmly as she could, she said, "No, Anshel. I am breaking off the engagement."

He stared at her in disbelief. "But we are so close to the wedding. Perhaps you should go and see the *Rebbetzin*, the rabbi's wife. She will help you to get over your fears."

"No, no, Anshel. I'm sorry. But I am not marrying you." Mila stood up and began to make her way to the door. Then she turned around and softly said, "Goodbye. I really am sorry."

Anshel stared at her with a bewildered look on his face. Then he stood up and placed both hands on the table in front of him. A cold, ominous aura came over the room, and in a low voice that sounded like a growl, Anshel said, "You've made me look like a fool. I can never forgive you for this. I promise you, Mila, you will regret what you have done."

He didn't sound like the Anshel she knew. The threat in his voice was unmistakable, but she forced herself to believe it was only because he was hurt that he acted that way. She hoped, for both their sakes, that time would heal his wounds.

CHAPTER FOURTEEN

Pitor was waiting outside. When Mila walked over to him, he saw she was crying. "Mila," he said softly. "are you all right?"

She nodded.

"I'm sorry you had to do this."

"It was horrible. I hated to hurt Anshel's feelings. It's not his fault that he and I are not suited for each other."

"He'll be fine. He is a scholar. He'll have a new fiancée in a week. You'll see. With the way people gossip, we'll be hearing all about it."

"Oh, I don't know about that. I have a feeling we are both going to be ostracized from now on."

"Are you sorry you did this?" he asked gently.

"Yes, and no. I am sorry that I will have to sneak around to see my mother and my sisters, and that is only if they are willing to go against my father's wishes. But I am not sorry that I didn't marry Anshel."

"And, what about marrying me? Are you sorry about that?"

"I don't think so. I must admit that I am very unsure about everything that happened today."

"I know, I understand. But you'll see. You'll be so happy with me that you will thank the stars that you made this choice today."

They walked slowly back to his modest home, which was within walking distance of the butcher shop. Mila was trembling, nervous, and afraid of what was to come next. "I should go to the *mikveh*, the ritual bath," Mila said softly, "I mean before... well... you know..." She cleared her throat. "But the old lady there is going to ask me a lot of questions, and I don't think I can bear it. She is very nosey, and I am too distraught to explain things to her right now."

"Then don't go."

"But..." she hesitated, trembling, "it's our wedding night."

"I know. It's all right. You don't have to go."

"But I am not clean. I have to go to the *mikveh* so I can be clean for you."

"You are clean enough for me. I don't follow all of this stuff, Mila. I won't stop you from doing whatever you believe is right, but you don't have to do it for me."

She nodded, and she followed him into the small house. For a young bachelor living alone, it was surprisingly orderly. The floors and windows were newly washed, and everything was neatly in its place. The only thing lacking was personal touches—there were no pictures on the walls, and though the bed was made up with spotless blankets, there was no handmade quilt.

"Welcome home, Mila Barr," Pitor said, smiling. "My wife."

She blushed.

"Do you like it? The house, I mean?"

"It's very nice, but it needs a woman's touch."

"You can do whatever you want to with this place. It's your home now. Feel free to change it in any way you like." He smiled warmly. "I'm glad you're here."

Mila looked down at her feet, then she glanced up at him, her voice shaky. "I am scared, Pitor. We've broken all the rules. I wanted to break them—I had to. But now that it's done, I'm so afraid of what the future holds."

He walked over, wrapped his arms around her, and pulled her close. Whispering in her ear, he said, "You never have to be afraid again. We will face everything in life together. I am your *bashert* and your best friend. I will stand by you for the rest of our lives."

"And..." she swallowed hard. "I am ashamed to admit this, but I am very terrified of what we have to do. You know what I am talking about?"

"No? What do we have to do?"

"It's our wedding night. You know... what we have to do," she said, her face burning with shame.

"You mean consummating our marriage?"

She nodded, embarrassed and unable to look at him.

"It's alright. I promise you, it will be fine. In fact, I'll bet that you are going to think that consummating our marriage is the best part of being wed."

"Pitor!" she exclaimed. "I'm so embarrassed."

"You'll see. It's going to be wonderful. Just trust me."

He kissed her gently, and at first, her body was stiff, but when he kissed her again, he guided her to sit down on the sofa. Pitor began rubbing her shoulders, his hands kneading away the tension. Slowly, Mila began to relax under his touch. He sat beside her, kissing her again softly. Though she was still trembling, she allowed him to unbutton her blouse and help her out of it. He turned her around, massaging her back with the same gentle rhythm, easing her nerves. Mila felt her body unwinding as he lifted her from the sofa and led her to the bedroom.

As easily as lifting a baby, Pitor picked Mila up and gently laid her on the bed. He slipped her shoes off, smiling as their eyes met. She smiled back.

When he kissed her, she could feel her body quivering in anticipation. *How can I be afraid and a little excited at the same time?* She wondered. Pitor was in no hurry. He kissed her again, softly, tenderly, and then he removed the rest of her clothes before undressing himself.

Mila stared at his naked body. She had never seen a man without clothes before. Since he'd done physical work all of his life, his body was rippled with muscle. In the light from the moon that filtered through the window, she could see that there was no softness to him. In fact, he resembled the forbidden photographs she'd seen of Michelangelo's *David. He's beautiful, like a sculpture.*

Pitor touched her hair and smiled before climbing into bed beside her, pulling her into his arms. He whispered how beautiful she was and how much she meant to him. He stroked her hair and then told her a funny story about a customer who had come into the butcher shop. Mila laughed, and she felt herself beginning to relax. Then, she told him a funny story about one of the nosey old ladies from her neighborhood. They laughed together. Before she realized it, she was completely calm, and something strange was happening.

The passion began to stir within her. Pitor slowly and gently kissed her lips, her eyes, and her forehead. Then he planted his lips on her neck and her shoulders and then her breasts. She sighed softly. He took his time, and when he finally made love to her, she was ready. It was nothing like she thought it would be. Mila had been expecting something painful, something to endure for the sake of having children. Instead, she found a secret world that was wonderful and magical, something only she and Pitor would ever share.

"My wife," he whispered in her ear when it was over.

"My husband," she replied, her body trembling slightly from the intensity of it all.

CHAPTER FIFTEEN

Mila was happy. Every day was another opportunity to spend time with Pitor. He was loving, and even when she made a mistake or messed something up, he forgave her. One day, she accidentally ruined a stew that she was preparing for dinner by adding too much salt. Not that she had purposely added the salt, but the salt container had slipped from her hand, which was greasy from cutting chicken. Then, it fell into the pot, spilling an abundance of salt. She didn't know what to do. Her hands were shaking. *If only I could ask my mother what to do,* she thought as she stood staring at the pot. *She would know how to fix this.* But, of course, she was forbidden from speaking to her mother or her sisters. So, she stood alone in her kitchen, worried that Pitor would be angry. Most men would have been displeased when they came home from work to find that their dinner was inedible. By the time Pitor arrived home from work late that afternoon, Mila was in tears.

"What's wrong, my love?" he asked, taking her into his arms. "Why are you crying? Shhh, don't cry," he murmured, taking a handkerchief from his pocket and gently wiping her tears.

"I'm afraid that you are going to be angry with me. I did something terrible. Very terrible," Mila said, her voice trembling as she shook.

"Terrible?" His eyebrows shot up. "What did you do?"

She explained what had happened, her words tumbling out in a rush. When she finished, he smiled. "Shhhh, don't cry. It's nothing. You see, I've done that plenty of times. Looks like we just need a new salt container. What do you say? Am I right?" He lifted her chin so their eyes met, still smiling.

She nodded. "But we have nothing to eat for dinner tonight, and it's all my fault."

He chuckled softly. "Watch this." He grabbed a potato from the small pile on the kitchen counter and cut it in half. Then, he put the raw potato into the stew.

"There are potatoes in the stew already," she said, confused.

"I know, but the raw potato will absorb some of the extra salt, and then the stew will be fine," he reassured her, pressing a soft kiss to her lips. "Don't worry about anything. I'm going to go to the bathroom to clean up before dinner. Let that stew boil for a while, but try to keep an eye on it so it doesn't burn. It'll be all right. You'll see. We'll eat soon."

Pitor was right. The stew turned out fine, not too salty, and Mila couldn't help but feel a surge of happiness. She was married to this man who, she suddenly realized, she was hopelessly and joyously in love with.

CHAPTER SIXTEEN

One winter afternoon, Mila's sisters came to see her. She was so excited when she saw them coming up the walk that she ran outside to meet them without her coat. It was cold, but she was so happy to see them that she threw her arms around them one at a time, holding them tightly. "Ruthy, Sarahleh, I'm so glad you both came! Does Papa know you're here?"

"No, of course not," Ruth said. "He would be furious."

"Does Mama know?"

"She knows," Sarah said. "She told us to make sure Papa doesn't find out."

Mila didn't say anything. For a moment, she thought of her mother, and she felt sorry for her having spent her entire life with a man like her father, who was demanding and often impossible to please. Then her thoughts turned to Pitor, and her heart swelled with gratitude. She was so glad that she had married a man who was nothing like her father.

"Mila, are you all right? You look like you're in a daze," Ruth said. "Can we come in? It's freezing out here. You must be freezing! Where is your coat?"

"I forgot to put it on," Mila giggled. "You're right, it *is* cold. Please, both of you, come in. I'm sorry, I was just lost in thought."

Ruth looked at her sister Mila skeptically. "What is it? Is everything all right with you and Pitor?"

"It's better than all right. I am happier than I ever dreamed I could be. Would either of you like some hot tea? I can put some water on to boil. And I have some sweet rolls that Pitor brought home from the market yesterday."

"No thanks. We ate before we came. Mama insisted because she says that your house is not kosher," Ruth admitted, sitting down at the table. "But Believe me, I'm glad you're happy. Sarah and I are both glad. I want you to know that Sarah and I love you very much. You do know that, don't you?"

"Yes, and I love you too."

"But you don't love us enough to think of us before you went and married a man who is not, and never will be, part of our community. Anshel and Mrs. Nusbaum are spreading rumors about you. Anshel is very bitter. He says your husband might as well be a *goy* and that you are living like a *shiksa*. He tells everyone he runs into that you married a man who sells meat that is *treif*, not kosher," Ruth said. "Mrs. Nusbaum has jumped on the bandwagon. She is spreading these terrible rumors about you to everyone. You wouldn't believe the trouble you've caused. And because of what you did, Sarah and I are not getting any offers from good marriage prospects. We are only getting offers from men no one else would want."

"Ruthy is mad at you," Sarah said, shaking her head. "I'm sorry to have to tell you this, but it's true. She and I are having a hard time finding decent husbands because of what you did. Everyone in town, especially Anshel and Mrs. Nusbaum is saying that you are not right in the head. They can't understand how you could throw away a match with someone like Anshel. And now, young men are being warned about us. They are being told to beware of Ruth and me because mental illness supposedly runs in our family."

"Oh, Ruth, I am so sorry. I didn't want to hurt you or Sarah. But I couldn't marry Anshel. Now that Pitor and I have been married for a while and I have gotten to know him better, I am certain that he is my *bashert*."

"So where does that leave us?" Ruth said bitterly. "Can you imagine the kind of suitors who will accept potential wives from a family with mental illness?"

"I'm not mentally ill. None of us are. Not you, not Sarah, not Mama. We are just women who want to be happy. But our community breeds unhappiness. A girl should be able to choose the man with whom she spends the rest of her life. That's too important to leave to her father."

"Have you ever considered that your marriage might be cursed?" Ruth asked.

"What? Cursed? Pitor and I feel blessed to have found each other."

"Well... if you are so blessed, why are you not pregnant?"

"We're in no hurry."

"Don't you think that you might not have conceived because you have made God angry? Mila, face it—you have sinned. Anshel and Mrs. Nusbaum are only speaking the truth about you. You broke God's holy commandments when you married Pitor. You did not honor your parents, and now, you are having a hard time getting pregnant. If your marriage were blessed, you would already be with child."

"Stop it. Don't say that. Please."

"I think we should go home," Sarah said, tugging on Ruth's coat sleeve. "This visit is not going well. Come on, let's go."

"I'm sorry to be the one to tell you these things, Mila. But think about what I've said. I could very well be right," Ruth said as she walked out the door, Sarah at her side.

CHAPTER SEVENTEEN

Mila sank down onto the sofa, her heart heavy. She had been so happy to see her sisters, but now Ruth's words left her devastated. She knew God's Ten Commandments very well, and since Ruth had brought up the fact that she had broken the fifth commandment, Mila couldn't shake the feeling that, deep down, she had always feared she had angered God by defying her father.

Mila was so shaken by Ruth and Sarah's visit that she cut herself when she was trying to peel a potato for that night's dinner. Blood dripped on the floor, bright red against the dark wood. The sight of it made her cry. Grabbing the kitchen rag, she bent down to clean up the mess, then she wrapped her finger in a clean towel. Sitting back at the table, she tried again to peel the potatoes, but her hands were shaking. Mila had never cut herself like this before, even though she had spent her entire youth learning to cook. Her mother had made sure all of her daughters were skilled in the kitchen. But today, Mila could not seem to pull herself together. She was too lost in thought, too terrified of what the future might bring.

I have been too happy, she thought bitterly. *Maybe I've attracted the evil eye, and that's why I haven't gotten pregnant.* She wiped her eyes with the back of her hand. *I have been selfish. I haven't given a single thought to how my marriage would affect my sisters' futures. And now... now I think I might be barren. Ruth could very well be right about all of this. Maybe I should go and see the Rebbetzin. But I doubt she will forgive me. I am afraid she will only reinforce everything Ruth said.*

Mila's thoughts spiraled. *So, what can I do? How can I make this right? Is there any way I can fix it, or are Pitor and I doomed to a childless marriage? Will my sisters be forced to marry men no one else wants because of me? And if Pitor realizes we are cursed, what if he wants a divorce? It's a woman's job to give her husband a family... and I don't know if I am capable.*

The thought of losing Pitor filled her with dread. *I have come to care so much for him. But now, I am pretty sure that I am being punished for my selfish choices.*

CHAPTER EIGHTEEN

When Pitor arrived home that evening, he was in a horrible mood. One of his most loyal customers, a Jewish man who frequented his shop despite the accusations that Pitor did not keep the kosher laws, had come in to buy a chicken and told Pitor that Anshel Minsky had been spreading rumors that his butcher shop was infested with rats. This was completely not true. However, Pitor did not have the influence that Anshel held within the Jewish community. Because of this, Pitor knew these rumors would be detrimental to his business. But when he saw Mila hadn't finished preparing dinner, he put his own worries aside and sat down next to her.

Tears stained her face. Blood was smeared on the floor and soaked into the towel wrapped around her finger. Her hair was disheveled. Pitor took his wife's injured hand in his. Before he said a single word, he kissed her finger. "You hurt yourself," he whispered. "Can I see it? I would like to put some salve on it and then bandage it up."

She nodded. He gently unwrapped the towel and examined the cut. "It's all right; the cut isn't very deep," he said, taking her chin in his hand and raising her face so their eyes met. "I'll take care of it for you." He winked and smiled.

She didn't return his smile.

"My poor love. I know you are hurt, and I hate to see you in pain," he whispered.

"It's not my finger that's bothering me. It's... it's..."

"What is it? Are you feeling ill?"

"No," she shook her head, "my sisters came by this afternoon."

"Are they ill? Is it your parents?"

"Pitor," she said his name, but her voice was not soft and sweet. It was serious. "Have you ever considered that our marriage might be cursed?"

"Cursed? What? Why? That's crazy," he said. "We are so happy. At least, I know that I am. Are you unhappy with me?"

"No, I'm not unhappy. I am very happy, and I love you very much. But Pitor, we have made love many times, and I have not conceived. So far, we are childless even though we have been married for several months. That's a bad sign."

He laughed. "Sweetheart, I didn't think you wanted a baby yet. I thought you might prefer to spend a little bit of time alone together before we had a baby. We are not childless—I've been preventing you from getting pregnant."

"How? Is that even possible?" she asked, her eyes wide.

"It is possible. I've been, well... holding back, I guess you could say."

"I didn't know that could be done."

"Sure, it can. I've been doing it on purpose."

Mila began to weep with relief. "I was so afraid that you weren't going to love me anymore. I was so afraid you would want a divorce when you realized I was barren."

"You're not barren. If you want a baby, we'll have a baby," he said, cupping her face in both hands. "And you should know that no matter what happens, I will never stop loving you. Even if, God forbid, you were barren, I would never divorce you. You are my *bashert*. There is no other woman for me."

Mila leaned forward and kissed him. "You don't know what this means to me."

"Of course I do. I would be heartbroken if I thought I was ever going to lose you. I would never be the same. So, I understand how you feel. And, Mila... thank you for loving me."

They made love on the kitchen floor. When they were finished, Mila sighed. "I don't know what to do. There's nothing for dinner. It's my fault. After I cut myself, I stopped making the soup."

"So what? We'll live on love," he said with a grin.

"Aren't you hungry?"

"Starving," he laughed. "Let me get dressed, and I'll run into town to pick up some bread and cheese. Does that sound all right for dinner?"

She nodded. "Thank you for understanding."

CHAPTER NINETEEN

Every Sunday afternoon, Pitor played soccer in the park with a group of men his age. He had been on an amateur soccer team for several years, and although the other players were not Jewish, no one seemed to mind that Pitor was. They knew him because their families shopped at his butcher shop, and in turn, he shopped at their stores. He bought the furniture he needed from Jan, a boy who was an apprentice carpenter under his father. He purchased his fruit and vegetables from the stand that Anatol's father owned.

Sometimes, Mila would accompany Pitor when he went to the park to play. She would sit among the other women who had come to watch their husbands play. It was the first time she had been in such close contact with non-Jewish women. Although their ways of dressing and speaking were different from what she had grown up with, Mila liked them and enjoyed their company. They told each other jokes and laughed. They didn't cover their heads, and she longed to let her own hair blow freely in the wind.

CHAPTER TWENTY

Over the next week, Mila decided she wanted to get pregnant, so she mentioned it to Pitor. He said he didn't mind if this was what she wanted. He would be happy to be a father. And so, they made up their minds to stop any form of prevention.

It took less than three months for Mila to miss her period. Since she had always been very regular, she took this as a good sign, but she waited an additional month to be sure before she told Pitor.

It was after dinner one night as they were sitting in the living room reading. Mila put her book down and said, "I have some good news."

"What is it?" Pitor asked, looking up from his book.

"I've missed my menses for the last two months. I am pretty sure I am pregnant."

He stood up, swept her into his arms, and kissed her. "Are you happy?"

"Very happy," she smiled.

And they were. But the following week, Mila's mother came to see her. Mila was beaming when her mother arrived. She was excited to tell her mother about her pregnancy. However, before she could say anything, her mother said, "Your father had a very hard time, but he has finally made matches for your sisters. They will both be getting married soon."

"That's good. I'm glad to hear it," Mila replied. "Can I get you something to eat or drink?"

Her mother ignored the question. "Don't you want to know who the boys are? Or don't you even care?"

"Of course, I care. Who are they?"

"Twins, the Finkelstein twins. They're nice boys and polite, but unfortunately, they don't own businesses, and from what I can tell, they are not good providers. This would be fine if they were scholars like Anshel was, but they aren't." Her mother shook her head and sighed. "Oh, Mila, what did you do with your life? You had it good. You had a scholar who wanted to marry you, and that's only because you were always so pretty. It seems that your beauty actually hurt you in the end. It tainted you, Mila."

Her mother sighed deeply. "*Oy*, Mila, what you did to yourself is unbelievable. That was some match your papa made for you. And now Anshel is engaged to someone else. I am sure she appreciates him in a way you never did." Her mother spat on the floor. "You've turned out to be such an ungrateful girl, and it surprises me, Mila. I never took you for a selfish girl. I don't know what I did wrong in raising you. I never expected such terrible behavior from you. I just never expected it."

Mila fought the tears welling in her eyes. She hated her mother at that moment and didn't want to give her the satisfaction of seeing her cry. Steeling herself, Mila said, "I am very happy with my husband, Mother."

"Yes, I am sure you are. But what about your sisters? Will they be happy? Or will they end up settling for these second-rate husbands because you didn't think about how your actions would affect them when you soiled our family name? You've made such a *shanda*—a disgrace—in our little town. Everyone spits when they say your name. Do you know why? Because they don't want their children to turn out like you. And I have to admit, I don't blame them."

She no longer wanted to tell her mother that she was pregnant. She no longer wanted to share her joy with her family. In fact, she wished she could throw her mother out of her house. *Pitor is my family now. And we are happy.* But Mila knew that if she told her mother to leave, she would feel guilty for the rest of her life. So, all she could do was sit and listen to her mother's endless criticism. Finally, after a full hour of demeaning comments, her mother stood up to leave. "I'm going home now. I've said what I had to say. My heart is heavy, Mila. Even if you want to change things, it's too late. You've consummated this marriage, and no decent man would want you now. Besides, like I told you, Anshel is getting married. And what a lucky girl his *kallah*, his bride, will be. Do you want to know who it is?"

"It doesn't matter," Mila replied.

Her mother ignored her. "It's your old friend, Esther Titlebaum. She has always been sneaky. Her parents were always sneaky, too. She was never a real friend to you, but of course, you know that. That girl is no good. She waited like a snake until you ruined your life, and then her parents swooped in and made a match for her with Anshel. Now, she is destined to live a good life, not you. You spoiled it for yourself and for everyone else. But I can't blame Esther. She saw a good thing and grabbed it. Any one of your other girlfriends would have done the same. They were all jealous when you caught Anshel. What girl in her right mind wouldn't do anything to get a man like that? You tell me, Mila. Don't you think Fanny or Sophie would have done the same, even though they are your *good* friends? Anshel's a catch, and everyone knows it—everyone but you. You thought you were too good, and now you've lost him."

With that, her mother turned and walked out the front door.

As Mila watched her mother leave, she whispered softly, "Congratulations, Esther. I wish you and Anshel all the happiness in the world."

When Pitor arrived home that night, Mila told him about her mother's visit.

"Any regrets?" he asked.

"None. I am no longer sorry that I can't visit my parents' home. Seeing my sisters and my mother is no pleasure. I still feel bad for my sisters—guilty, I suppose—but I guess they are right. I must be selfish because I wouldn't change a thing. I would marry you all over again."

He kissed her. "My sweet love. I am glad."

CHAPTER TWENTY-ONE

By the time Mila entered her fifth month of pregnancy, her stomach was like a large and rounded ball that stuck out in front of her. She often patted or rubbed her tummy and spoke softly to the baby growing inside her. Then, a miracle happened that left Mila in awe. She had been lying in bed beside Pitor, waiting to fall asleep, when, for the first time, she felt the baby move. She gasped, and then she smiled in the darkness.

"Give me your hand," she whispered to Pitor.

He gave her his hand, which she placed on her belly. For a few minutes, there was no movement. Then she felt the baby stirring inside of her.

Pitor's hand began to tremble a little. "I can feel the baby," he said excitedly. "Our little son or daughter is moving."

"I know." Mila smiled in the darkness.

He reached over to her and pulled her into his arms. Then he held her close to him. "I want to make love to you so badly, but I would never do anything that might endanger our baby. So, I'll control myself."

"We can hug and kiss," she suggested.

"That makes the longing even worse," he croaked. But even though it made his desire stronger, he still held her and kissed her until they both fell asleep.

Mila was always tired lately, so Pitor took to getting up early to prepare breakfast for her. She usually woke up ravenous, at least that was since the nausea she'd experienced in the early days of her pregnancy had gone away. But this morning, she was not hungry. In fact, she was sick to her stomach.

"What's wrong?" Pitor asked when Mila couldn't eat.

"I don't know. It feels like the nausea is coming back. But it feels a little different than it was in the beginning. I have a headache, and my stomach is hurting. When I was first pregnant, and I felt sick, it was only nausea. I didn't have any pain, but what I am feeling now feels like strong menstrual cramps."

"I could close the store and stay home with you today," he suggested.

"No, your customers will be very upset if they walk all the way into town to go to your butcher shop and find that it's closed when they get there. My guess is that they will go to the kosher butcher around the corner, and you might lose them for good. We can't risk losing customers, especially in this economy. I'm all right. I'm sure I'll feel better as soon as I get up and start doing things. I'm sure it will go away as the day goes on. That's the way it would be with the nausea I felt in the beginning."

Pitor got up and dressed. Once he was ready to leave, he paused, staring at Mila, who was still in bed. "Are you sure I should go and leave you alone here? I'm worried."

"I'm sure," she smiled. "You'll see. I'll be just fine." She got up and walked him to the door. After kissing her several times, Pitor stepped outside and closed the door behind him.

As soon as Pitor left, Mila lay back down on the bed. She was exhausted, so she thought that if she slept, she might wake up to find her stomach pain and nausea gone. Closing her eyes, she quickly drifted off to sleep. But a sharp pain, like a bullet shooting through her lower belly, woke her with a start. Her legs and bottom felt wet. Fear gripped her as she sat up and then looked down. There was blood. A lot of blood—on her nightgown, on the sheets, and running down her legs.

Dear God, help me. I have to get to Pitor.

She was weak, but she forced herself to put on fresh panties and a rag to catch the blood. Then she dressed in an old housedress and made her way to the butcher shop.

When Pitor first saw her, his face lit up, but then it turned pale with fear. "Mila, what's going on? You don't look good."

"I'm bleeding," she whispered. "I need a doctor or a midwife quickly. I am in a lot of pain."

Pitor didn't bother to close the butcher shop. Grabbing Mila's hand, he held her elbow and helped her walk to the doctor's office. The waiting room was crowded with people waiting for their turns to see the doctor, but Pitor didn't care. He ran up to the front desk. "My wife is pregnant. She is bleeding, and she needs to see the doctor right away."

"So do all the others waiting here," the middle-aged woman at the front desk replied coldly, adjusting the white nurse's cap on her wiry gray hair, said. "She'll have to wait her turn. Sit down, and I'll get you in as soon as I can."

Pitor helped Mila into a chair. She was breathing heavily, and he could see that she was suffering. This drove him crazy. He watched the woman at the desk, who was paying no attention to Mila at all. Finally, unable to stand it any longer, Pitor stood and pushed on the door to the doctor's examination room. It was locked.

"Sit down, sir," the woman at the desk warned. "You're going to have to wait your turn. If you don't, I am going to be forced to ask you to leave."

"My wife is having a baby! She started bleeding this morning, and she's in a lot of pain!" he thundered. Pitor was distressed, and his usual calm was completely gone.

"I will get you in as soon as I can. Everyone in this waiting room needs the doctor. He is only one person. He'll get to you as soon as possible," she said in a frustratingly calm manner.

Her indifference infuriated Pitor. Mila was the love of his life, and she was in pain. If she didn't see the doctor soon, she might lose the baby, or worse, she could die. Nothing else but Mila mattered to him. Pitor had always been a strong man, but now his strength was fueled by desperation. He didn't speak to the nurse again. Instead, he looked at Mila and then marched to the door that separated him from the examining room. With all of his might, he kicked the door. The lock broke, and the door flung open.

"You must leave right now!" the nurse shouted. She was loud and agitated now.

"Shut your mouth," Pitor hissed. It was not like him to be rude, especially to women, but he was beside himself. "I need the doctor now!" He started screaming as he entered the area with the examining rooms. He was sure he would find a doctor in one of these examining rooms taking care of other patients. Pitor was determined as he pushed each door open until he found the doctor.

There was a hint of fear in the doctor's eyes when he looked at Pitor. "Who are you? What are you doing back here?"

"Please," Pitor pleaded, his voice raw with emotion. "You must help me. My wife. She needs you. She's bleeding. She's five months pregnant, and she's in pain. Help me, please. I don't mean to be so insistent, but I am afraid she might lose the baby or worse. Please. I am begging you to help us."

The doctor stared at Pitor. He was a middle-aged man with thick gray hair that seemed to be uncombed. For a moment, time seemed to stand still, but Pitor felt a small sense of relief when he looked into the doctor's eyes and saw compassion.

"Where is she?" the doctor asked.

"In the waiting room."

"Lead me to her," the doctor said. Then he stood up and followed Pitor.

Mila sat quietly, but the red bloodstain on her skirt and the pool of blood on the floor beneath her were growing.

As soon as the doctor saw Mila, he turned sharply to the nurse at the front desk. "This girl is hemorrhaging. Can't you see how pale she is? What is the matter with you? She doesn't have a minute to spare. Get her into one of the examining rooms right away and get her prepared. I'll be in in a minute."

"But look at this waiting room, doctor," the nurse protested. "All of these patients are waiting for you. Some of them arrived before this man and his wife. I was only trying to be fair."

"Stop talking and trying to argue with me. Just do what I tell you to do!" The doctor commanded, his voice stern.

The nurse shook her head, but she stood up, clearly displeased. "Yes, doctor," she muttered before turning to Pitor and Mila. "Follow me," she instructed.

Pitor was shaking as he helped Mila to her feet. "Can you walk, or should I carry you?"

"I'm able to walk," she said, but her voice was hoarse and weak.

Holding her arm tightly so she wouldn't fall, Pitor walked alongside his beloved until the nurse showed them to an open examination room.

"Give me a minute," the nurse said as she laid a blanket down on the table. Then she turned to Mila, "Get undressed from the waist down and cover yourself with this blanket." Glancing at Pitor, she added, "You can wait in the waiting room."

Pitor's eyes narrowed as he glared at the nurse. "I'm not leaving my wife," he growled.

The nurse shook her head. "Do as you please. I give up," she spat as she left the room.

It was only a few minutes before the doctor entered. "It's highly unusual for the husband to be in the room during an examination," he said gently.

"I can't go, doctor. Please let me stay with my wife."

"Is it all right with you?" the doctor asked Mila.

She nodded. "Yes, please let him stay."

Pitor held Mila's hand as the doctor moved the blanket to examine her. "I'm sorry to say that there is a lot of blood."

"Will she be all right?" Pitor asked, his voice cracking in panic.

"I hope so. But I'm afraid she's already lost the baby."

"Oh no," Mila groaned. "What did I do wrong? Why is this happening." Tears began to slide down her pale cheeks. Pitor took Mila's hand. Then he lay his head beside hers as he stood next to the examining table.

"You didn't do anything wrong. These things just happen sometimes. It's nature's way."

"I don't understand."

"Well," the doctor said, "sometimes there is something wrong with the baby, and so nature aborts it for its own good."

Mila let out several loud sobs of anguish.

"Shh, it's all right, my love," Pitor whispered in her ear. "We'll have more children. As long as you're alright, everything will work out."

But she couldn't stop crying.

"I'm going to have to do an emergency surgery to stop the bleeding," the doctor said. "She can't afford to lose any more blood."

Pitor nodded. He was terrified of losing her. She was his whole life. Since the day he'd married her, nothing else had been as important to him. He felt like crying, but he refused to give in to it. After he lost his mother, he had wept for days. But then, one morning, he woke up and realized that all of his weeping had done nothing to change his situation. His mother was gone. It was then that Pitor vowed to himself that no matter what happened for the rest of his life, he would never cry. *Tears are worthless. They don't help in any way.* He remembered how he had stood rigidly hiding any emotions when his father died. Everyone had asked him if he was all right. And he just nodded. But he wasn't all right, and he wouldn't be for a long time. But if he knew one thing for sure, he knew that crying wouldn't help.

When his mother got sick, he begged God to let her recover, but she never did. After that, he lost faith in God. Even so, when his father got sick, he prayed again, but this time, he wasn't surprised that God didn't answer his prayers. His father died anyway. Then, when his aunt and uncle lay on their deathbeds, he didn't bother to pray. By then, he was done believing in God.

That was when he realized that nothing he did would matter in the end. He had never been religious, but he had gone through the motions of living a life aligned with the traditions and expectations of his community. After his mother's death, he stopped keeping kosher and going to *shul*. He was convinced that if God did exist, He didn't care for Pitor. *If God truly loved me, Pitor thought, He would have known how much I adored my mother and would never have taken her so soon.* Pitor had no siblings either. All he had was the butcher shop and the house that his aunt and uncle had left him. That was until he married Mila. Once he and Mila were married, Pitor found true happiness.

Pitor didn't want to pray. He didn't trust God. He felt God was cruel and hated Pitor. Pitor's prayers had never done a thing to change God's mind. If God wanted Mila to die, there was nothing Pitor could do to stop it. The thought sent Pitor into a panic.

The doctor turned to Pitor and said, "You should wait in the waiting room. It will be better for her." This brought Pitor out of his thoughts and back to the situation at hand. "Really, son, it will be easier for both of you this way." The doctor tried to insist. His tone was warm and caring. "It's for your own good."

"I don't care about my own good," Pitor growled. "I want Mila to know that I am right here with her. I will not leave her alone."

Pitor was a large, imposing man who was tall and muscular. By the look of madness in Pitor's eyes, the doctor felt it was best not to argue with him.

"Please, Pitor, do as the doctor says," Mila whispered.

"Are you sure you want me to go?"

"He thinks it's best. So, please wait for me in the waiting room."

"Promise me, Mila. Promise me you will be here when I come back. Please, Mila. Promise me you won't die."

She touched his arm. "I won't die," she whispered.

CHAPTER TWENTY-TWO

Pitor paced the floor in the waiting room for several hours before the doctor came out and called his name. Wiping the sweat from his brow, Pitor trembled as he walked over to the doctor.

"Good news. I was able to stop the bleeding. She should be all right in a couple of weeks. But right now, she's very weak. Let her rest and make sure she eats," the doctor said.

"Can I see her?" Pitor asked, his voice shaky.

"You can look in on her. She's asleep, so don't wake her. She needs the rest. For now, you need to make arrangements to take her home. She won't be able to walk that far."

Pitor nodded. "I will make arrangements. Thank you, Doctor." He paid the nurse at the front desk, and then he looked in on Mila. She was fast asleep, but her face was not strained, and Pitor was relieved to see she was not in pain anymore. Then he left the office and went to visit one of his friends, a used junk seller who he knew had a horse and buggy.

"I need to borrow your horse and buggy. I promise you I will return it tomorrow," Pitor said, desperation in his voice.

"Pitor. That horse and buggy are my only livelihood. I need them. I can't lend them to you."

"I'm begging you, Finn. My wife just miscarried, and she almost died. I know how important the horse and buggy are to you, and I swear I will take good care of them. But you must help me. I am begging you."

Finn nodded. "Take them. But please, be careful."

"You know I will," Pitor promised. Then he rode the buggy back to the doctor's office, where Mila was awake and waiting to go home.

She was exhausted. Pitor lifted Mila into his arms. She felt so light that it scared him, but he didn't let her see his fear. Carefully, he placed her in the buggy, then walked around to the other side and got in beside her. After glancing over to make sure she was comfortable, he snapped the whip, and the horse began to move. Before he knew it, he and Mila were at home.

For the first forty-eight hours, Mila slept. When she finally awoke, Pitor was sitting in a chair beside her bed. "I made soup and bread. You should eat."

"I'm not hungry," she replied, her voice weak.

"I know. You've been through a lot. But please, eat. I did all of this cooking for you." He smiled at her and gently brushed her hair out of her eyes.

"All right," she agreed.

"I'll be back in a minute," he said, trying to cheer her up. Then, with a playful tone, he added, "I just can't wait to hear what you have to say about my cooking."

It worked—Mila smiled faintly. But as soon as he left the room, she began to cry again. His kindness towards her only made her feel worse. When he returned carrying the bread and soup, she was still weeping.

"What is it, love? Is it that you are afraid to eat my cooking?" he winked, trying to make a joke. But she could see that she was breaking his heart.

"I'm sorry, Pitor. I am just so sad."

"I know, love. Me too. But I promise you, we'll try again. And we'll keep trying until we have a healthy baby."

She nodded. Pitor picked up a spoonful of soup and blew it on to cool it down. But before he put it into her mouth, he tested it on his own lips. "It's not too hot. Try it," he said gently.

She opened her mouth and allowed him to feed her. After she ate the spoonful of soup, he asked, "What do you think?"

"It's good," she said, managing a small smile. "You're a good cook."

Pitor tried to pretend the compliment made him happy, but he couldn't feel joy while she was so sad.

"Pitor," she whispered, "I'm afraid."

"Of what? Are you afraid I'll take over your role as chief cook," he teased, forcing a smile though he felt helpless. He didn't know what to do or say to make her feel better.

"I'm serious. What if we really are cursed for breaking the commandments?"

"Nonsense. We are not cursed. We are blessed to have each other and share the love that we feel. Now, listen to me, please. You heard the doctor. He said this just happens sometimes."

"He said that it happens when the baby is deformed. Maybe our child was deformed as punishment for what we did."

Pitor shook his head and bent down to kiss her forehead. "No, we are not cursed, and this was not a punishment. It was just something that happened. I promise you we will have a child. You just have to trust me."

Mila nodded as Pitor fed her another spoonful of potato soup. She swallowed it slowly. "That's a good girl," he said, smiling. "You need to eat to build up your strength, so you'll be healthy and strong when we're ready to try again."

CHAPTER TWENTY-THREE

Mila loved Pitor, and he loved her. She was happier than she had ever dreamed possible, yet still, in the back of her mind, she was afraid that they had sinned and were being punished. But to Mila's surprise and delight, two months later, she missed her period again. *Maybe the doctor was right. Maybe it was just something that happened. And now, we will have a child.* She knew she should wait until she was sure she was pregnant before telling Pitor, but her excitement got the better of her. She couldn't hold back and told him immediately. He was elated.

But the following month, to their dismay, Mila woke up to see her monthly period had arrived.

"It's all right," Pitor reassured her. "It will all be fine. And if we don't have children, that will be all right, too."

"But it won't be. If we don't have children, that will mean that I am not a good wife to you."

"You are the only wife for me, whether we have a child or not. I love you, and I am grateful for what we have," he said. "So don't worry about disappointing me because you could never disappoint me even if you tried."

Six months passed, and each month, her period arrived on time. At first, she wept when she saw the blood, but soon, she began to resign herself to the idea that she might never have a child. She stopped knitting baby sweaters and forced herself to give up on the dream of having a baby.

One day, Mila went to the market to buy some flour, and as she was waiting in line to pay, she overheard two women she knew from her village. They saw her, but neither of them said hello. They were busy discussing her sisters' weddings. It hurt Mila to know that she and Pitor had not been invited to either of the weddings, but she had to admit that she had expected that. Her father would never allow her sisters to invite her and Pitor. In his eyes, they were both dead. Though she was not permitted to speak to any of her family members, she silently wished them all well—even her papa.

The following month, Mila missed her period. She longed to tell Pitor, but this time, she kept silent. There was no need to disappoint him again if it was another false alarm. But she was feeling tired, and often, she was nauseated enough to vomit. Even though she was very uncomfortable, she assured herself that these were good signs and that she was very hopeful that she would be pregnant this time. Another three months passed, and Mila still did not bleed. She was sure now and bursting with the news; it was flowing like a river of joy out of every pore in her body, but she still didn't tell her husband. Then her belly began to swell, and she was finally one hundred percent certain that she was with child. Mila finally planned a special dinner to share the good news with Pitor. To sweeten the already wonderful news, Mila went to the store and bought everything she needed to bake a cake.

Pitor had brought a chicken home the night before. When Mila returned from town, she put the chicken into a pot with cut-up carrots, celery, and parsnip and added an onion. Then she began to make her cake. Mila sang softly to herself as she prepared the batter. Once the cake was in the oven, she said a prayer of thanks to God and sat down on the sofa. She was so tired that she could hardly keep her eyes open, but she couldn't leave the cake in the oven without watching it. So, she forced herself to stay awake. But exhaustion took over, and she drifted off to sleep.

The cake rose and spilled out of its pan, creating a mess in the oven. If Pitor hadn't come home early from work, there could easily have been a fire, and Mila might have been killed. All day, he had been feeling under the weather, so he closed the store early and went home. When he approached the house, he smelled the burning cake and sensed something was wrong. He ran inside, finding the kitchen filled with black smoke. The chicken soup was boiling over on the stove, and the cake was charred in the oven. He quickly turned everything off and rushed into the living room to search for Mila. He was overcome with fear and worry—this was not like her.

When Pitor saw she was asleep in the smoky living room, he lifted her into his arms and carried her outside. He left the door open to air the house. Then he laid Mila gently on the grass. She opened her eyes and looked around her, dazed and confused. But Pitor didn't have time to explain. He ran back inside, coughing as he opened all the windows. Then he returned to Mila, sitting beside her on the grass.

"What happened?" she asked, still in a daze.

"You fell asleep," he said, his voice tinged with anger. "I guess you were baking a cake because it spilled out of the pan and all over the oven. There was a lot of smoke. And it could have started a fire."

"I'm sorry," she whispered. "I don't know how I fell asleep."

"Mila, you need to grow up. I can't trust you alone in the house. I know you're young and that you were very sheltered all of your life. But Mila, it's time for you to be responsible. You could have been killed!" His voice was raised, frustration and fear blending into anger. Mila had never heard him speak to her like this before, and the harshness in his tone brought tears to her eyes.

"I'm not irresponsible, Pitor. My mother taught me to cook. I was just so tired..." She looked at him, her voice breaking as she blurted, "I'm pregnant."

This was not how she planned to tell him. She had envisioned a lovely dinner—his favorite chicken soup with matzo balls and a spice cake for dessert. But now, everything was ruined.

PITOR LOOKED AT MILA, and then she saw he was no longer angry. The love and gentleness returned to his eyes. He pulled her towards him. "It's just that I love you so damn much. I couldn't bear to lose you. I'm sorry I yelled at you. I didn't mean to be so harsh with you. Did you say that you're pregnant?"

"Yes, I am pretty sure that I am."

"Oh, my love," he said, holding her close to him, "I didn't mean to yell at you. But when I think of anything happening to you, it makes me crazy. I guess... I just got crazy? Forgive me?" He smiled hopefully.

She smiled. "Of course I forgive you. Oh Pitor, I was planning to make your favorite dinner and a cake too. I just got so tired. I didn't even realize that I had fallen asleep."

"I have an idea," he said. "You realize we can't let this happen again, now, can we?"

She shook her head.

"How about you come to the shop and help me every day. You can work the front counter. Then we will go home and prepare dinner together. Or we'll pick something up at the market—or if you'd like, we can even go out to a restaurant. What do you think?"

"But Pitor, if I don't cook for you, I won't be a proper wife."

"That's silly, of course you will. I need help at my store. Who else would I turn to but my wife? Who else could I trust as much as I trust you. Now, being a good wife, you will come and help me," he said with a grin.

She smiled again, her heart full. She knew Pitor was asking her to come to the store so she'd be safe, but he had also found a way to make her feel important and needed. *What a fortunate woman I am to have such a good husband.*

CHAPTER TWENTY-FOUR

Mila started working at the butcher shop the next day. Pitor refused to allow her to do much because he didn't want to risk her losing the baby. He found small things to keep her occupied. She mostly talked with female customers while Pitor put their orders together. So far, Mila saw that none of Pitor's customers were a part of the ultra-orthodox Jewish community where she grew up. The ones who were Jewish were secular, and the others were not Jewish at all. This was the first time in Mila's life that she had actually met and socialized with people outside her small, ultra-Orthodox world. Her community had forbidden it, but now she found she enjoyed learning about other cultures, and she began to look forward to going to work each day.

When she was at the butcher shop, she was with Pitor, and she loved being with him. When the store was empty, he often told her stories about his customers that made her laugh. She decided that she truly enjoyed being busy and being around people rather than sitting alone in her house.

The months passed quickly, and then, like a wonderful miracle, Mila and Pitor were working at the store when she felt the baby move. She ran over to Pitor, where he stood cutting up a chicken.

Then she took his hand and placed it on her stomach so he could feel it, too. "Our child," Pitor said softly but with pride.

"Yes," she answered, "our baby."

He bent down and kissed her.

After that, there were many times when she and Pitor would fall asleep with his hand resting on her belly. Sometimes, when they were sitting in the living room, and she was busy reading her book, Pitor would lie down and put his head on her belly. Then, in a soft voice, he sang lullabies to the child who was growing inside.

Mila was growing larger every day. Some of the women who came into the butcher shop regularly tried to predict whether the baby would be a boy or a girl. Although Mila smiled and let them talk, she knew that the sex of the child didn't really matter to her or Pitor. As long as the baby was healthy, that was all they cared about.

CHAPTER TWENTY-FIVE

1938

Stomach cramps awoke Mila in the middle of the night, and she knew she was going into labor. She'd been nervous about giving birth for a long time. Since the day she learned she was pregnant, Mila had been praying every day that her child would be healthy, but she had also been secretly worried about what it would be like to give birth. She remembered a conversation with her mother from when they were still on good terms.

"Is it as painful as everyone says, Mama?" she had asked.

Her mother had replied, "It's painful. I won't lie to you and tell you it's not. But the strangest thing happened to me—once my children were born and I held them in my arms for the first time, I could not remember what the pain felt like."

"Was it like that every time you gave birth?"

"Yes, actually, it was. Even now, with all of you grown, I still couldn't describe it if I tried."

The cramps subsided, and Mila let out a breath of relief. She closed her eyes and thought of her mother. She knew her parents hadn't forgiven her, and they probably never would. She knew she had no choice; she had to accept their rejection of her. It had been her decision to marry Pitor, and she didn't regret it. But right now, as she lay in bed wondering if this was just a cramp or if she was really going into labor, she longed for her mother to be at her side.

A little while later, the cramps began again—stronger and more painful this time. Mila was scared. *I know Pitor is tired. Today was such a busy day at the butcher shop. I wish I could let him sleep a little longer. But I can't. I am sure now that this is it. I am in labor, so I must awaken Pitor. He will have to get the doctor as soon as possible.*

She placed her hand on Pitor's shoulder and gently nudged him. "Pitor. It's time," she whispered.

He had been waiting for this moment, and even though he was sleeping deeply when he heard Mila's words, he was awake in an instant. "Are you all right?"

"Yes. But I think we should get the doctor."

"Right. I'll get dressed and go immediately." Pitor jumped out of bed and was dressed and out the door in less than ten minutes.

Mila leaned back on the pillows, gritting her teeth as another pain seized her body. *This is the worst time to be alone. I'm so scared. I wish I had my sisters or someone from my family here with me. But I know that no one from my family will come here. My father has forbidden it, and they won't dare to defy him the way I did. I suppose they don't want to end up like me, alone and giving birth.*

Another sharp cramp shook her, but she reminded herself that Pitor would be back soon. *He will bring the doctor. I have to be brave while Pitor is gone.*

Pitor returned with the doctor a half-hour later. As soon as he entered the house, he ran to Mila's side. "We're here," he said. "How are you?"

"I'm all right. The pains are coming more frequently now."

He nodded, guilt in his eyes. "I'm so sorry to have been gone for so long. When I got to his office, the doctor was with a patient. I tried to get him to leave, but he insisted on finishing first. But don't you worry, he's here now, and he's going to help you. You're going to be fine," Pitor said as he took her hand and kissed it.

"Hello, Mila," the doctor said gently. "I'm going to need to examine you. So, Pitor will have to wait in the living room. Would that be all right with you?"

"Yes," Mila whispered.

"Are you sure?" Pitor asked, concerned. "Because I won't leave you if you don't want me to."

"Pitor. I've been delivering babies for a long time now," the doctor interjected kindly. "I've found that it's best if we do it this way. I promise you, I'll take good care of your wife."

Mila nodded. "It's all right, Pitor. I'll be fine. Go into the living room like the doctor said."

Pitor left the room, closing the door quietly behind him. He sat down for a minute, but his nerves wouldn't allow him to stay still. He got up and began to pace. Hours passed, and the night turned into day. Pitor thought he would go mad as he listened to Mila's grunts and screams coming from their bedroom. He wanted to burst through the door, take her in his arms, and pull the pain out of her, even if it meant he would have had the pain instead of her. But none of this was possible. Women bore the children, and men waited anxiously—especially when they loved the woman the way Pitor loved Mila.

Finally, after three long days of hard labor, the hearty cry of an infant broke through the house, bringing joy and relief to Pitor. In an instant, Pitor was at the bedroom door. He opened the door and rushed to Mila's side.

"You have a son," the doctor announced, placing the tiny infant in Mila's arms. "Just look at him. He's such a strong, healthy boy."

Mila gazed down at the baby, then up at Pitor. "We have a child. I can't believe it. I didn't think it was possible, but I am so happy."

"God rewarded our love," Pitor said simply.

"I thought you didn't believe in God," Mila said, surprised.

"I never said that, my love. What I have always said was that I don't believe in organized religion. That's not the same thing as God," Pitor replied gently.

A single tear fell from her eye onto the baby's tiny hand. "May he be blessed," she whispered.

"Yes, may he be blessed," Pitor repeated.

The doctor smiled, but then he turned to Pitor. "May I speak with you alone?"

Pitor nodded. Mila gave Pitor a look of concern, but he reassured her, "It's all right, love. You rest with the baby; I'll be right back." He followed the doctor out of the room.

Pitor towered over the doctor as they stood in the hallway. "What is it? What's wrong?"

"Pitor, your wife had a hard time giving birth. I am happy to say that you have a healthy son, but I don't recommend that the two of you have any more children. Mila lost a lot of blood and... well... it just isn't a good idea."

Pitor nodded, his face serious. "I understand," he said, then he paid the doctor and thanked him.

CHAPTER TWENTY-SIX

After the doctor left the house, Pitor returned to the bedroom, where Mila lay with their baby cradled in her arms. He dreaded telling her what the doctor had told him, but he knew he had to. "Love," he whispered.

"What did he want to tell you?" she asked, sensing something serious.

"Well, the doctor congratulated us on having a strong, healthy son," Pitor said, forcing a smile.

Mila smiled, but then her eyes narrowed. "He wouldn't have called you out into the hallway just to say that. What did he really say?"

"Mila..." Pitor hesitated, then sighed. "The doctor said that we shouldn't try to have any more children."

To his surprise, she didn't cry. She just nodded. "I knew it. My labor was very hard," she said, squeezing his hand.

"We have a son, and I'm so grateful for that. And we have each other. I would never put you at risk, Mila—you mean too much to me. I am happy with this small family. We don't need more children," Pitor said sincerely.

CHAPTER TWENTY-SEVEN

They named the baby Jakup after Pitor's maternal grandmother, Joasia. Pitor knew that naming the baby for his grandmother would have made his mother very happy. Jakup was a quiet baby, only crying when his needs went unmet—and that was rare. His parents doted on him, so it was unusual for him to sit with a dirty diaper for very long or to feel hungry for more than a few minutes. Many times, when Mila would awaken in the middle of the night to feed Jakup, she would notice Pitor's side of the bed was empty. So she would go into the baby's room, where she found Pitor holding his son and looking out the window.

Mila still helped Pitor in the store, but it was less often than before. When she did, she brought Jakup with her, and all the customers "oohed" and "ahhed" when they saw him. He was a handsome infant with short blond curls like his father and bright blue eyes. Although Pitor didn't want to bring up the fire that had almost cost him his wife, he was still uncomfortable with Mila being alone in the house. So, he insisted on hiring a girl to help around the house, allowing Mila to devote all of her time to Jakup.

At first, Mila protested, but when she saw how much it meant to

Pitor, she agreed. Agata was a twelve-year-old Polish girl, not very pretty. Her hair was thin and not quite blonde or brown, and her face was pockmarked. Pitor told Mila that Agata came from a very poor family who had been shopping at his butcher shop for as long as he could remember. Her mother would come in and buy scraps or bones, and knowing she had five children to feed and very little money to do it with, Pitor often took pity and added extra meat into her package. When Pitor suggested that Agata come and work for them, Agata's mother was thrilled. Agata had already been forced to quit school to help support her family and was working at a factory on a dangerous machine. "She will be happy to have a job that is not so dangerous," her mother had told Pitor.

Not only did Agata prove to be a big help, but she was also Mila's instant friend. They prepared the evening meal together each day, and often, Mila insisted on making extra food for Agata to take home to her family. Every other day, they cleaned the house and did the laundry together while Jakup napped.

Pitor wasn't just a butcher by trade; he was also a skilled fisherman. Sometimes, he would take his family, including Agata, on a picnic by the water. They brought sandwiches and cookies, and the three of them would have lunch on a blanket in the grass while Jakup slept. Once they finished, Mila and Agata would lie on their backs on the blanket and gaze up at the sky while Pitor went fishing. If he caught an extra fish or two, he would send it home with Agata for her family.

CHAPTER TWENTY-EIGHT

September 1, 1939

It was a Friday, the first of September, when the whistles blew, waking up Poland from her slumber in the summer heat. Germany had invaded her, breaking the non-aggression pact, and marched through her streets without hesitation. With every footstep, they crushed the dreams of the Jewish people.

People spoke of what was happening in Germany and how it was affecting the Jews, but Pitor and Mila were too busy running a business and raising their lively one-year-old to give much thought to the politics unfolding. They lived in Poland and rarely paid attention to politics, even within their own country, let alone another. It had been years since there had been a pogrom, and they lived in a village where Jews were accepted. To them, there seemed to be no reason to worry.

Little did they know, on a chilly November night the previous year, something happened in Germany that would change the lives of all the Jews in Europe. Mila and Pitor, too busy to read the newspaper, didn't know about the pogrom that had swept through Germany —a pogrom that would come to be known as Kristallnacht, the night of broken glass. And now that pogrom was knocking on Poland's door, yet they remained blissfully blind to the fact that someday soon, their lives would be shattered.

CHAPTER TWENTY-NINE

1939 started out as a wonderful year, and Jakup's birthday was quite a celebration. Mila baked him a special cake, and Pitor brought him a Jack-in-the-box he had made. There was no family to invite to the little boy's birthday party. Pitor had no family, and no one from Mila's family would attend, but none of that mattered. When Jakup giggled with joy, his parents' eyes lit up with love, and at that moment, nothing else was needed.

Everything in Mila's life seems to have fallen into place. She and Pitor were far from wealthy. Pitor worked long hours, and many times, his generosity towards others came at a cost. Mila knew that if someone came to Pitor hungry and without money, he would always give them something to eat, even if it was part of his own lunch. His heart was big, and he was generous. As long as his family's needs were met, he couldn't bear to see other people go without. If he had been less generous, they might have been wealthy, but Mila didn't mind. It was her parents' dream that she had a wealthy husband, not hers. And she couldn't have been prouder of her husband's big heart.

But in the wee hours of the morning after Jakup's birthday, as Mila and Jakup slept and Pitor prepared for work, Hitler, the chancellor of Germany, was making plans that would change their lives forever.

When the first bomb fell upon the unsuspecting people of Poland, the earth-shattering sound reverberated through the little house. Jakup was jolted awake by the noise and let out a piercing scream. Within seconds, Mila was out of bed. She was frightened by the roar of the explosion but ran to her son's side and picked him up in her arms. Mila held a screaming Jakup close to her bosom as she ran into the bathroom because it was the smallest and safest room she could think of. Pitor, already out of bed, followed his family into the bathroom, his mind reeling but focused on keeping them safe.

"What is this? What was that sound? Is it an earthquake?" Mila asked, her voice trembling.

Pitor did not have a chance to answer her question before another bomb fell, the deafening explosion drowning out everything else. She wouldn't have been able to hear him anyway because Jakup was screaming too loudly. Mila gently rocked her son in her arms, but she could not quiet him. Then, another bomb fell. Jakup was inconsolable. His tiny body shook with terror, and Mila, without realizing it, began to cry.

For a moment, Pitor stood silently, watching them both. Then he whispered, "Hush, both of you. Don't cry; everything will be alright. I am going to find out what is happening." He reached for his son, and Mila handed Jakup to him. Pitor held Jakup close, the little boy resting his head against his father's chest, slowly quieting. With his other arm, Pitor embraced Mila. "You'll be all right," he promised softly.

But the bombs continued to rain down on Poland.

"I'm going outside to see what's happening," Pitor said to Mila. "You and Jakup stay right here."

"No, Pitor, don't go out. Stay here with us. We'll go out when this stops," Mila said.

"I must go and see what this is. Please, Mila, just stay here with Jakup, I'll be right back."

Mila clutched her son, rocking him gently, but each time there was a loud crash, Jakup let out a piercing scream. It seemed like forever, but it was only about fifteen minutes before Pitor returned.

He hugged Mila and Jakup tightly.

"Did you find out anything?" Mila asked, her voice full of worry.

"Yes, I did. We are being bombed."

"Bombed? But why? Who is doing this? Who is bombing us?"

"Everyone's saying that it is Germany. They are saying that it's that crazy chancellor."

"Really? Germany? But why? I mean, are you sure it's them?"

Another bomb fell, shaking the house. Jakup cried out loudly, his little fists clenched as if he were angry and ready to fight. Pitor reached for the boy and took him from Mila. In Pitor's embrace, Jakup began to quiet.

"I'm not positive," Pitor admitted, "but everyone in the neighborhood seems to think so. They are saying that they don't think that the bombs are meant for us directly—Hitler, that crazy bastard, is probably aiming for Warsaw."

"But why would he do this? I thought he had made a peace treaty between Germany and Poland."

"He did, I mean, we do have a peace treaty. But I don't think he respects it. Lately, a lot of my customers, people who come into the butcher shop regularly, have said that they were anticipating trouble with Germany because of this chancellor. I must admit I wasn't paying attention to what they were saying. I was just hoping they were wrong, and until now, I suppose I didn't want to believe it. I just didn't want to know or believe that we were going to go to war," Pitor said, his voice heavy.

"Who is this German chancellor? Is Adolf Hitler his name?" Mila asked, shaking her head in disbelief.

"Yes," Pitor said. "So you've heard of him too?"

"You know I take Jakup to the park almost every day. It gives him a chance to play with other children. Well, lately, several of the women in the park have mentioned Adolf Hitler, and they said that there was going to be trouble with him. I must admit, I never paid much attention either. I took Jakup to the park to play—I didn't want to listen to political gossip. To be honest, it scared me, so I ignored it."

Another bomb exploded, and Mila trembled.

"I understand," Pitor said, his voice steady despite the chaos. "I felt the same way. But now, with the sound of all of these bombs falling, I'm afraid Germany is going to take over Poland."

"How will that affect our family," Mila asked, trying to hold back tears.

"I don't know yet. No one knows."

"Do you think it will affect us? Or will it just be another government change?" she asked hopefully.

"I hope that's all it will be," Pitor said.

Mila nodded, but she was still shaking. The bombing seemed to stop for some time, so she went into the kitchen to prepare some porridge for their breakfast. Pitor sat down on the sofa and tried to put Jakup beside him, but the child was terrified and clung to his father, refusing to let go. Pitor was nervous. He wanted to pace the room and think, but he couldn't. He knew Jakup needed him, so he kept the boy on his lap and rocked him slowly.

"Don't be afraid, boychik," Pitor whispered softly. "Your papa's here. I'll protect you and your mama with my life if I have to."

Jakup put his thumb in his mouth and laid his head against his father's chest. *I have been hearing terrible things about how Germany is treating its Jewish citizens. I hope the same things are not in store for us.* Pitor thought, but he didn't want to share his thoughts with Mila. *Perhaps it won't be like that here. Maybe they won't bother us.* He was trying hard to stay optimistic. He didn't want to scare her unnecessarily.

"Come," Mila called from the kitchen. "Eat before it gets cold."

Pitor carried his precious son into the kitchen and then sat him in his chair at the table.

Pitor gave Mila a reassuring smile. "Porridge looks good! Looks like you've perfected it. I don't see a single lump."

She smiled back, and he winked at her before starting to eat heartily, pretending not to worry about everything happening around them. He hid his fears so his family could feel secure and not frightened. After Jakup finished eating, he sat down on the floor and began to play with one of his puzzles. Pitor smiled at his son, who was still right beside him. He leaned down and gently ruffled Jakup's hair, but he could see that Mila was watching him closely. He knew pretending that everything was all right was not working on her. He could see in her eyes that she knew he was doing his best to hide his fears.

"I'm going to stay home with the two of you today. How does that sound?" Pitor asked.

Jakup giggled and hugged his father's leg before returning to playing with his puzzle. Though the bombs still fell sporadically outside, the boy was comforted. He was happy to have his father home.

"I'm glad you'll be home with us today," Mila said, wiping a tear from her cheek. "We need you. I couldn't bear to listen to these bombs alone with Jakup, without you here."

"I'm sure everyone in the village feels the same way," Pitor said. "There probably wouldn't be much business anyway. And honestly, there's nothing I enjoy more than a day at home with my family."

Mila leaned down and kissed him warmly.

Pitor smiled. "Don't worry too much, my love. I'm sure the bombs are meant for Warsaw. This little village is so small, the Germans probably don't even recognize it."

"So, what will happen if they don't recognize us? Does that mean that they will leave us alone?"

"I wish I could answer that. I wish we had the money to put the three of us on a boat that would take us far away from here," Pitor said.

"Far away from here? Where would we go? This little village is our home. Everyone we know and everything we own is here. You built a good business here. You've worked at that store since you were very young. Little by little, we put our home together. I would hate to leave all of this behind."

"I know. It doesn't matter because we don't have enough money for passage on a ship anyway. Eh, it's probably my fault. I never ask people to pay back the money they owe me. I know they don't have it, and I hate to see them go without eating. I probably should have asked, but I didn't. Maybe we could have had enough money if I had been shrewder. But I guess I have been satisfied to live a simple life. We've always had a roof over our heads and enough to eat. And, of course, most importantly, we've had each other, which has been my greatest joy. So, I never wanted for more."

"Me too," Mila admitted. "But, with things being the way they are right now, I'm wondering if you should try to collect some of the money people owe you. Just in case we need to get out of here."

"I would do that, my love. I would do anything for our family. But the people who owe me money—they don't have it. They were struggling when they borrowed it, and they're probably struggling even more now."

"So what can we do? If Germany takes over Poland, what exactly will that mean for us? We can only hope it will be just another government change. Maybe it won't affect us at all."

"That's what I'm hoping for," Pitor said. Though he wouldn't tell Mila what he was thinking, he was haunted by the things he'd heard about how the Jews were being treated in Germany. *Well, from what I am told, the Nazi party has made it clear that they hate Jews and that they blame us for losing the Great War. They have made the hatred of Jews acceptable. I don't like it, however, it's nothing that hasn't happened to us before. We Jews have weathered many pogroms throughout history. I have a feeling this one will be the same. I am assuming they will boycott our stores. But even if they do, I don't believe my Polish customers will stop coming to my butcher shop. They know that even though I was born a Jew, Mila and I have lived a very secular life. If I had been a good Jew, I would have insisted that Jakup be circumcised, but I didn't care if he was or not. The idea of cutting our baby upset Mila so much that, rather than seeing her upset, I never insisted. Now I'm glad we didn't, just in case Jakup ever needs to pose as a Christian. I just don't know what all of this is going to bring. But I am worried.*

Mila never paid much attention to politics, but she knew that by bombing Poland, Hitler had broken his promise. She had heard bits and pieces of talk about how bad it was in Germany for the Jews, and the thought frightened her. If Hitler could break his promise to Poland so easily, what else could he have in store for the Polish people and Poland's Jews?

CHAPTER THIRTY

For the next 26 days, Poland fought valiantly against Hitler's invading armies. But on September 27th, Poland could no longer hold out and was forced to surrender. Germany took 140,000 soldiers as prisoners. The bombings stopped, but Poland was left in peril. And an eerie silence settled over the streets of the little village where Mila, Jakup, and Pitor lived.

Once Germany had defeated Poland, a law was put into place requiring that all citizens of Poland who were of Jewish descent wear a Star of David on their coats and their clothes so they could be easily identified as Jewish.

Then, in November of the following year, the Warsaw Ghetto was established.

CHAPTER THIRTY-ONE

Spring 1940

Germany's influence had overtaken Poland, but the small village where Pitor and his family lived had been spared for the time being. Jakup was big for his age. He was a strong, hearty little boy who looked just like Pitor, with a full head of thick blond curly hair, and striking blue eyes. Like his father, he was brave, and often got hurt trying to do things he was too young to do. Even though he required constant attention, his parents adored him. Pitor could never find it in his heart to scold his son. The child was so fearless and spirited that everything he did made Pitor laugh.

One afternoon, Pitor went to the library and took out a book on kite making. He wanted to surprise Mila and his son with an afternoon devoted to flying a kite. Pitor knew Mila would enjoy it, and Jakup would be enthralled. In order to keep the project a surprise, Pitor began building the kite in the back of the butcher shop between serving customers. It was not as easy as he'd imagined, but he was determined. After two weeks of effort, Pitor finally had a kite he was fairly certain would fly.

The following Sunday, Pitor forfeited his usual soccer game and told Mila to pack a lunch. "We're going on a picnic. I have a surprise for you and for Jakup," he said.

Mila put her arms around Pitor and kissed him. "I love you more every day," she said

"Me too. I love you more than life itself."

Mila packed sandwiches, and the three of them walked to the park. Pitor carried the kite, which was wrapped in brown paper so Mila could not tell what it was.

"Is that the surprise?" Mila asked, eyeing the package Pitor carried.

Pitor winked. "You bet it is."

"What is it?" she asked playfully.

"Nope, I can't tell you. If I did, it wouldn't be a surprise. Besides, you'll know very soon," he teased.

Mila pretended to be upset, but then she laughed. "All right," she said.

After lunch, Pitor began to assemble the kite. Jakup watched him, wide-eyed, bursting with excitement. Meanwhile, Mila had to hold their son back so that Pitor could put everything together undisturbed. It wasn't easy to control Jakup when he was so excited. He was determined to help his father put the kite together, and he could barely be contained.

Jakup squirmed in his mother's arms. He was a strong boy, but Mila held on. Finally, Pitor stood up, ready to fly the kite. "It's all right. Let him go," Pitor said with a smile.

Jakup ran to take his father's side, and Mila followed closely. Pitor knelt down and said, "Stay here with Mama and watch while I get the kite in the air. Then you can help me fly it, all right?"

Jakup nodded eagerly. He stood beside Mila and watched as Pitor ran with the kite, and it was suddenly soaring up into the heavens. Once it was flying, Jakup squealed with delight.

"Let him come to me," Pitor called, and Mila released Jakup, who ran as fast as his little legs could carry him. Mila sat down on the grass, and her heart swelled with love as she watched Pitor play with their son. *He must have worked very hard to build that kite for Jakup. And just look, Jakup is thrilled.* She was beaming.

"Look, son," Pitor said with pride, "it's your kite. It's flying for you."

It was a perfect day. For the rest of her life, whenever things became difficult, she would close her eyes and remember this day. She would picture the colorful kite dancing in the Wedgewood blue sky, hear her son's laughter, and feel the warmth of Pitor's kind, loving words.

CHAPTER THIRTY-TWO

Nᴏᴠᴇᴍʙᴇʀ 1940

The winter was upon them, and it was far too cold for Jakup to go outside for long. Each day, Mila bundled him up in a coat, a hat, and a wool scarf, which she made for him. Then, she would take him out for a short walk. Once, on a day that was a little less frigid, they built a small snowman. It brought back memories to Mila of a time long ago when she and her sisters made a snowman. A terrible sense of loss gripped her, and she almost began to cry. But then she looked over at Jakup, his cheeks bright red from the cold, and realized that they had been outside for over an hour. Mila was trying hard to hide her sadness. *Between the cold and my memories, it's probably best we go inside for the rest of the day.*

"Come on, little man, how about some lunch?" she said, her voice gentle. "Would you like some hot soup and, for dessert, some hot chocolate?"

"Chocolate!" Jakup said, his face lighting up. "I want the chocolate."

"Yes, you can have the hot chocolate," Mila laughed. "But you'll have to eat some soup first."

"All right, Mama." He was so sweet and agreeable, just like his father.

Mila couldn't complain about Jakup's eating habits. He had a hearty appetite and ate well. He was hungry from playing outside all morning. So, he quickly gobbled up his soup. Then Mila gave him a cookie with some hot chocolate, which made him smile.

Once they finished lunch, Mila sat down on the sofa with Jakup beside her. Pitor was at work and wouldn't be home for a few hours. Mila planned to read to Jakup until he fell asleep. Then she would put him in his bed, and she hoped he would nap until dinner. If he fell asleep, that would give her time to clean the house and wash some clothes.

As Mila read from a book of fairy tales, Jakup's eyelids grew heavy, and soon he drifted off to sleep. But just as she was about to put him to bed, there was a knock on the door.

Mila stood up quietly, careful not to wake Jakup, and went to the door.

CHAPTER THIRTY-THREE

Sarah, Mila's youngest sister, stood shivering in the doorway. Snowflakes still lingered in her hair and on her eyelashes.

"Come in," Mila said. "But be as quiet as you can. Jakup is asleep."

Sarah glanced at the little boy. "This is the first time I have ever seen my nephew. He's beautiful."

"He looks just like his father," Mila said, smiling. Then, softening her voice, she added, "Sarah, won't you please sit down? Can I get you a cup of tea to warm up?"

"No, it's all right. I won't stay longer than a few minutes." Sarah nodded, hesitating for a moment. "I want you to know that it took a lot of courage for me to come here," she blurted out. "When I told Mama and Ruth, they both forbade it."

"I'm glad you came," Mila said, her tone gentle.

"I came because I have something very important. I have to tell you. It's not good news, I am afraid, but I thought it's only right that you know what is happening."

"What is it? Please, Sarah, just tell me already. If you have bad news, then tell me quickly. All of this dancing around the subject is only making things worse."

"It's Papa. He's very sick—it's his heart."

"I had no idea," Mila gasped.

"I know you didn't know. How could you? No one will tell you anything. But I came because the doctor thinks he is dying." Sarah's voice cracked as she began to cry. "I thought you should know. I realize that everything has gone wrong with you and Papa, but I thought perhaps you might want to see him. I mean... you might want to say goodbye."

"Goodbye?" The very thought of that made Mila shiver. "Yes, of course, I want to see him. I will come tonight when Pitor is home and can stay with Jakup."

"I think you should bring Jakup with you," Sarah suggested softly.

"I don't know," Mila hesitated. "I hate to scare or upset Jakup. But to be honest, he doesn't even know his grandfather. They've never met."

"And if you don't bring him to the house tonight, they will probably never meet. I think Papa should see his grandson, even though he has been stubborn about your marriage. Maybe if he sees Jakup, he will change his mind. It can't hurt anyway."

"Perhaps you're right," Mila said, her heart heavy.

"I will see you tonight then," Sarah stood up and walked to the door. Quietly, she opened it and slipped back out into the cold. Mila watched her sister disappear into the falling snow. Mila could still see Sarah's silhouette as Sarah wrapped her scarf tighter around her neck, turned the corner, and headed back to their old neighborhood.

Once alone, Mila burst into tears. *Papa, why did you force this separation between me, Mama, and my sisters? Why is your damn pride so important to you—so important that you have been willing to push me and my family out of your life? I hope you will let us back in when we come to the house tonight.*

CHAPTER THIRTY-FOUR

When Pitor arrived home from work that evening, Mila was sitting on the sofa staring out the window, and Jakup was playing with his toys on the floor. But when Pitor saw Mila's face, he knew she had been crying.

"What is it?" he asked, sitting down beside her and taking her hand. "Are you all right?"

"My sister, Sarah, came by the house today. She came to tell me that my father is dying. I must go and say goodbye to him. I don't know if he will see me, but I must try," Mila said quietly.

"Of course," Pitor said, squeezing her hand. "Don't worry, you won't go alone. I'll go with you."

"I want to bring Jakup, too. I want my father to see him at least once."

"Yes, I agree with you. Get ready, and we'll go," Pitor said.

"I have some soup for you. Do you want to eat first?" Mila asked.

"No, let's go now. We can try to return before it gets dark."

Mila dressed Jakup in his warmest clothes, then bundled herself up as well. The three of them set out towards Mila's childhood home. It had been years since she had been in the old neighborhood, and as she passed the familiar buildings, Mila felt a single tear of nostalgia run down her cheek.

"It's hard for me to believe that I used to live here. I used to be a part of this community," Mila murmured.

"Do you miss it, love?" Pitor asked.

"Actually, no. I miss the memories of growing up with my sisters, but I am not sorry I chose the life I did. I am glad I married you, and we have a wonderful, healthy son."

"Me too," he smiled, his heart swelling with pride.

When they arrived at her parents' home, Mila knocked on the door. Her mother answered. When she saw Mila, her mother shook her head. "You shouldn't have come here. Your papa won't be pleased."

"Mama, please. It's very cold outside. Can we come in?"

Mila saw her mother's eyes shift to Jakup and then soften. "Yes, come. Come in," she said. They stepped inside, and Mila picked Jakup up into her arms as Pitor followed behind them. "Sit down, all of you, please," her mother said. They sat.

"Your father is very sick. I suppose you know that. I'm assuming that Sarah went to see you today, and she told you everything. That's why you're here, isn't it?"

"Yes, Mama. But I have wanted to come many times before. I was afraid Papa would not want to see me," Mila said.

"I asked him a few days ago if he would like to see you," her mother said. "He said no, but I am going to let you go into his room anyway. Take the baby with you. Let him see his grandson. I don't know if he will speak to you, but at least your father will have seen his grandchild before he dies."

Pitor put his hand on Mila's arm, offering her strength. She nodded, then gently lifted Jakup into her arms. He was surprisingly quiet, as though he sensed this was not the time to be fussy or demanding.

"Are you all right?" Pitor whispered to Mila.

"Yes, I'm all right," she replied, her voice steady.

"Then let's go into your papa's room."

They followed Mila's mother into the bedroom, where Mila's father lay on the bed. When he saw Mila and Jakup, his eyes lit up for a moment. But then he remembered his anger, and he turned away. Mila felt the tears welling in her eyes.

"Papa," she said in a small voice, "Papa, please. Please. Don't send us away. Please, just for a moment, take a look at my little boy. This is Jakup—he's your grandson."

Mila's father did not turn his head. He would not look at Mila or Jakup. Mila reached over and touched her father's arm. "Papa, please. Please look at us. We have walked here in the snow and ice to see you."

Slowly, her father turned his head and studied Mila for a long moment before sighing. "I'm dying."

"No, Papa. No," Mila said, her voice trembling. "You are ill, but you won't die. You can't die."

He nodded. "Yes, I am ill. And I am afraid it's true I am dying."

There was a moment of silence. A single tear ran down Mila's cheek. Pitor put his hand on her shoulder. "It's all right, love," he whispered.

"He's a good man?" her father asked Mila, his voice hoarse.

"You mean Pitor?"

"Of course, who else would I be talking about?" her father answered.

"Yes, Papa. Pitor is a very good man. He is a good husband and a wonderful father."

"You know, sometimes in life, a man has to admit that maybe he was wrong," her father sighed. Then he went on, "Well, this is my time to admit that I might have been wrong about Pitor. It's time for me to accept that maybe you made the right choice."

"I know, I did. Pitor is my *bashert*, Papa."

"I see he is here at your side. He came here with you, knowing that I did not accept him. But even so, he did not let you come alone. I can see how he loves you. I see it in his eyes."

"I do love your daughter with all my heart," Pitor said earnestly.

Her father nodded. "Yes. And that is good. It's good because I know you will take care of her and your child. I must tell you again that your marriage was not what I wanted. I wanted a scholar for my Mila. But it wasn't meant to be. And from what I hear about your butcher shop, it's not kosher, but you are a good provider."

"I do my best. It's a humble business, but it keeps us going," Pitor said.

"Good. That's a lucrative business. Now let me see this little man who you have brought here to my bedside to meet me," Mila's father said. He was looking at Jakup.

Pitor gently placed Jakup on the bed next to his grandfather. "Jakup, this is your *Zede*, your grandpa. Can you say *Zede*?"

"*Zede*," Jakup repeated.

When he heard the child's voice calling him *Zede*, Mila's father's eyes softened, and within seconds, they were wet with tears. The hardness born from years of hard work seemed to wash away from the old man's face, and now the tears ran down his cheeks. Jakup reached out his hand to his *Zede*, who took the little boy into his arms. Mila began to cry, and Pitor pulled her close to him.

Mila's father looked up at Mila and smiled, then at Pitor. "Nu?" he said. "It's difficult for an old man to admit he doesn't know everything. But I can see that I was wrong about you, Pitor. It seems you turned out to be a good man after all."

Then he turned to Mila. "Call your mother in here."

Mila stepped out of the room and called for her mother. She entered quietly and stood by the door.

"Now, listen to me," Mila's father said to his wife, his voice growing weaker. "After I am gone, you must look to Pitor for advice and for help. Do you understand me?"

"Yes, I understand," she said. "But what about Ruth or Sarah's husband?"

"They are not strong like Pitor. He is strong. I didn't want him in the beginning, but now I see that all of the women in this family are going to need a strong man. And so, I give my blessing to Pitor and Mila's marriage."

"Thank you, Papa. You don't know what this means to me. All I have ever wanted was your love and your blessing."

"You have it now," he said softly. "You should only be happy, *mine kind*, my child." He hugged the little boy and ruffled his hair. Then he smiled. "I'm tired now. Go home, *Zie gesunt*—be well. I want to go to sleep now."

"Yes, Papa," Mila said. "And Papa, I love you,".

"I love you too," he whispered.

Mila lifted Jakup into her arms, and then the three of them left the room. Mila's mother stayed behind, sitting quietly by her husband's side.

That night, Mila's father passed away.

CHAPTER THIRTY-FIVE

Now that Pitor was accepted as a member of Mila's family, he offered to help make all the arrangements for his father-in-law's funeral. He held no grudge against Mila's father or anyone else in her family. For years, they had shunned him, but it didn't matter to him. He was glad that Mila was able to reconcile with her father before he passed away. But when ten men came from the synagogue to form a *minyan* and say *Kaddish* for Mila's father, Pitor was not permitted to join them.

Anshel was there. He had grown up, and he looked smart and very handsome in his dark suit. When he glanced over at Mila, his gaze was sharp, and she was certain she saw hatred and resentment simmering in his eyes. *I hurt his pride by breaking our engagement, and even though he is married now, I don't think he will ever forgive me.*

Pitor sat *shiva* at his mother-in-law's home with his beloved Mila and their son for seven days following the funeral. Two of Mila's mother's friends set up the food for the *shiva*. They covered the mirrors and put a jug of water and a towel outside the front door—a symbolic gesture to wash away death so it would not enter the house. Those returning from the cemetery used it to cleanse their hands.

Everyone waited patiently to eat, as the mourners were to eat first. But Mila had no appetite.

Pitor brought her a plate of food and coaxed her to eat a little. "I missed so many years with my father because he was stubborn," Mila whispered to Pitor as she, her mother, and her sisters all sat on hard wooden boxes, as tradition required. They wore no shoes, and all the mirrors in the house were covered.

"Yes, I know," Pitor said softly. "But at least, in the end, you were able to tell him you loved him."

"Yes, I really am happy for that. I'm glad you came with me. Thank you," Mila said, managing a small, bittersweet smile.

"You don't need to ever thank me. I love you, and I would do anything I could to make you happy."

Mila's mother was so busy with her friends and neighbors that she had little time to grieve, although she would burst into tears every so often.

When Anshel came to pay his respects, Mila couldn't bring herself to look at him. He had caused her so much grief.

"Make sure you eat something sweet before you leave the house," Mila overheard her mother tell two of her friends who had come to pay their respects to the grieving family.

This is the purpose of the shiva, Mila thought. *Everyone comes to help the mourners with their grief. They are here to be a distraction so they can make the transition less painful.*

As Jakup sat quietly on the sofa, Mila prepared a small plate for him. She brought it to him and began to feed him when Anshel walked over to her. "He's a good-looking little boy," he said.

"Thank you," Mila replied curtly.

"Mila, I heard that you never had him circumcised. Is that true?"

"Anshel, that's really not your concern."

"Oh? I believe it is. After all, that should have been my son. You should have been my wife. And when I see what has become of you, I am ashamed for you."

"Well, don't be. Pitor and I are happy together. I hope you are happy in your marriage, too."

"I'm glad you have found happiness living like *goyim*, non-Jews. But abandoning God and Judaism is a sin."

"We haven't abandoned God," Mila said calmly. "And we practice some Judaism for the sake of my family, but we are just not as religious as you are."

"He ruined you, Mila. Pitor ruined you, and you don't even know it," Anshel said, shaking his head as he walked away.

That night, when Mila and Pitor returned home, she sat in the living room in the dark and wept. Pitor found her there and sat down beside her. He put his arms around her and held her for a long time.

"How is it, Pitor, that no matter what happens, you never cry," she asked softly.

"It doesn't do any good," he whispered into her hair.

"But I can't help it," Mila said, her voice quivering.

"Then cry. I'll hold you and support you. Let the pain out, love. Let it go."

"If you ever needed me to support you, I would do the same for you," she said.

"If I ever need to cry, I promise you I will," Pitor said, kissing the top of her head.

"And then I can be your strength, the way you are always my strength," she said, nestling into his embrace.

"You are my strength. And... my weakness," he said, kissing her softly on the forehead.

Even though Mila's father had finally accepted her husband and their son, the scars left by Anshel's gossip and disdain still lingered. Mila's sisters were still cold towards her. She wished she knew what to do or say to bring things back to the way they were when the girls were just children. But it seemed impossible. Her sisters were against the idea of accepting Pitor. He would never be a part of their ultra-religious world. And because of this, they shunned their sister. When she tried to talk to them, they were polite, but it was obvious they were hurt by all the gossip, and so they were not welcoming to Mila.

CHAPTER THIRTY-SIX

From that day forward, Mila and Pitor brought Jakup to Mila's mother's house to visit with his grandmother at least once a week. They invited her to come to their home for Shabbat dinner on Friday night, but she always refused. Mila knew it was because her mother was religious and didn't feel that Pitor's home was kosher enough for her. This was never openly discussed after Mila's father's death, but Mila understood her mother's unspoken reasons.

Despite this, Pitor was kind to his mother-in-law. He could see her loneliness—she had never lived alone before, and the weight of that solitude was clear. He took a chance and offered Mila's mother an invitation to come and live with them. She said she couldn't leave her community. She explained that she had friends who lived in her neighborhood.

But Pitor and Mila could see her sadness. The poor old woman was unable to adjust to the loss of her spouse. Since her husband's passing, she seemed to age rapidly. Where she had once been the matriarch of a family with cooking, housework, and laundry to do, she was now all alone, with nothing to do. It was easy to see that Mila's mother enjoyed the visits. She adored Jakup, so Pitor thought she would accept his offer because if she lived with them, she would be able to spend more time with Jakup. However, she was stubborn and refused to leave her home. She probably would have accepted an offer like this if it had come from one of her other daughters who still lived in their Orthodox community. But no such offer ever came from either of her other children, so the old woman lived alone.

The winter was cold and dark and unforgiving. The color of the sky ranged from dove gray to deep charcoal. Snow fell and lined the walkway almost every day. However, during the week, while Pitor was working and if the weather wasn't too bad, Mila would dress Jakup warmly and then take him to visit with his grandmother. But every time Mila went to see her mother, she saw that the old woman seemed to grow more and more forgetful.

"You really shouldn't be living alone, Mama. You should really consider moving in with us. Pitor is very kind, and he would be very good to you."

Her mother just shook her head. Jakup was affectionate towards his grandmother. He often sat beside her on the sofa and laid his head on her lap. Sometimes, she stroked his hair and told him she loved him, but she never put her arms around him or cuddled him. Mila knew that even though her father had accepted Pitor in the end, her mother still had not. Unfortunately, because she was stubborn, she was missing out on the physical affection she might share with her grandson. What hurt most was that Mila's mother was not cold with Ruth or Sarah's children. She allowed herself to cuddle and openly love them. Mila hoped Jakup was too young to notice the difference in the way his grandmother treated him compared to his cousins.

Even though Mila didn't always like her mother as a person, and she knew her mother could be stubborn, she still loved her. This was her mother, after all—the only mother she had ever known. Mila wished she were different, less stubborn and rigid, but she couldn't help worrying about her. The winter seemed endless, and during the cold and dark months, the old woman had grown very thin and frail. She no longer went to the synagogue on Friday night. She no longer went to visit her lady friends who lived in the neighborhood. After her husband's death, a part of Mila's mother had died too. She lost her motivation to do anything, even the charity work she had enjoyed in her earlier years.

Many times, Mila would go to visit her mother and find there was no food in her mother's house. "What are you going to eat tonight?" Mila would ask her mother gently.

"Perhaps Ruth will bring me something," her mother would reply. "Or maybe Sarah will."

From then on, Mila began bringing food to her mother, but her mother would not eat it. The next day, when Mila came to visit, she would find the food she'd brought the previous day rotting and uneaten. *It's not kosher enough for her. She'd rather die of starvation than eat the food I bring,* Mila thought bitterly. *My mother refuses to eat it because it's not up to her standards. But what have those standards ever done for her? Nothing. However, she will not even bend an inch.*

Mila considered speaking to her sisters. They should know about their mother's decline, as the old woman might have accepted help from them. But they never invited Mila to visit, and when she invited them to her home, they refused. So, she never had an opportunity to speak to them. *Even though my papa finally accepted my marriage to Pitor, the rest of my family still does not.*

Then, on a particularly cold winter morning—too cold to leave the house—Mila awakened from a terrible dream about her mother. There was no reason for the dream. She had experienced nightmares before and found they disappeared in the morning light. But not this one. It was gnawing at her. When Pitor came home from work that night, she told him about it. "I am feeling uneasy about my mother," Mila confessed. "I had a bad dream about her, and it won't go away."

"It's too late for us to go to her house tonight," Pitor said, glancing at the window, where the snow was falling heavily in the darkness. "And the roads are dangerous."

"I know. I thought about taking Jakup to see Mama this morning, but when I walked outside, it was just too cold. Icicles have formed on the trees and windowsills. I am sure there is a layer of ice hiding under the snow. I was afraid for Jakup."

Pitor studied her anxious face and then nodded. "Why don't I go to your mother's house? I'll go and check on her to make sure she is all right, and I'll be back as soon as I can."

"Would you, Pitor?"

She knew he was tired. *How could he be anything but exhausted?* He'd worked all day and had come home later than usual. Besides that, the freezing cold was taking its toll on him, too. But Pitor loved Mila, and he would never disappoint his wife. "Of course, I will go," he said, smiling gently.

"Are you sure? I know the roads are treacherous when they get icy like this."

"That's true. But don't worry about me. I'll be fine," he said, squeezing her hand before bundling up for the cold.

CHAPTER THIRTY-SEVEN

FEBRUARY 1941

Pitor slipped on his heavy winter coat, hat, scarf, gloves, and boots. Then he kissed Mila and Jakup and made his way outside. The snow was falling harder now, and he wished he could just go home and get some rest. But Mila was worried about her mother, and he would do anything for her.

As Pitor walked through town on his way to the Jewish sector where his mother-in-law lived, he noticed two young women walking together. *They shouldn't be out alone after dark,* he thought. He felt he should probably be a gentleman and escort them safely to their destination. But when they saw him looking at them, they both smiled fetchingly. At that point, Pitor was sure they were prostitutes, and he decided it was best not to get involved with strange women. He was happily married, and he didn't want them to think he was interested even though he was always willing to help. *I have no romantic interest in any other woman. I know I never will because I am so fortunate to be married to my bashert, and we are blessed with a beautiful son. He is healthy and strong. What a precious little man he is. God is good to me.*

When Pitor reached his mother-in-law's house, he knocked, but there was no response. He knocked again, harder this time, but still, no one answered. A cold dread settled over him. He tried to open the door, but it was locked. Pitor knew the lock was flimsy, so he pushed the door open with his shoulder. A gust of icy wind and snow followed him inside. Pitor looked around the meticulously clean house. His mother-in-law was a much better housekeeper than her daughter. Mila often didn't feel like cleaning, so Pitor would help her. Sometimes, she wouldn't do the wash for a week, and he had to wear dirty clothes. He didn't mind. He hadn't married her to be his maid. He married her because he loved her, so he never complained about her lack of housekeeping skills.

There was an eerie quiet in his mother-in-law's house, and Pitor had always been a little intuitive, so he was pretty sure that he knew what he was going to find. *She's gone,* he thought, his heart sinking. *How am I ever going to tell Mila? She is going to be heartbroken.*

He walked into the bedroom and found his mother-in-law lying on the bed. She looked peaceful, but when Pitor put his hand on her neck, he found her skin to be cold. Pitor wanted to curse because he knew how hard the *shiva* for her father had been on Mila, and now they would have to go through it all again.

Before heading home, Pitor walked down the street to the house where Ruth, Mila's sister, lived with her husband and child. Pitor knocked on the door, and Ruth's husband opened it. He looked appalled at seeing Pitor. He just stood there looking dumbfounded, and he didn't invite Pitor inside.

"What are you doing here? What do you want?" Ruth's husband asked curtly.

Pitor stood outside, snow falling heavier, chilling him to the bone. "My wife sent me to check on our mother-in-law. I went to the house and found that the old woman had passed away. I came here to let you and Ruth know that her mother is dead."

Hearing her name, Ruth appeared at the door. She stared at Pitor, surprised he'd had the nerve to come to their home. And she didn't invite Pitor inside either.

Pitor stood outside the door with the snow falling in his hair.

They think they are so much better than me because they are very religious. He thought. Then he said, "Hello, Ruth. I am sorry to have to be the one to tell you this, but your mother has passed away. I would appreciate it if you would let Sarah know, too. I'd rather not go to her house and have another experience like this one. It's too cold outside to stand out here and deliver news to the both of you."

"What? Are you sure?" Ruth asked, shock clouding her features.

"Yes," Pitor confirmed softly. "I'm sorry."

Neither Ruth nor her husband spoke, and no invitation to come inside was offered. With the cold wind biting his face, Pitor said, "I have nothing more to say to you. So, I'm leaving." As he turned to go, Ruth's husband closed the door behind him.

Pitor walked home, the snow now a heavy blanket falling around him. When he arrived, Jakup was already asleep. He entered the house, wet from the snow, but the fire was burning, and the house was warm. Mila helped him out of his coat and boots. Pitor sat down by the fireplace, and Mila went into the kitchen and returned with a bowl of hot soup for Pitor. She knelt by his side. "Did you see my mother?" she asked, her eyes wide with hope and worry.

Even though Pitor was starving and would have enjoyed a few minutes of peace before telling Mila about her mother, he stood up. Then he walked into the kitchen, where he put the bowl of soup down on the table. Mila followed him, a shadow of fear passing over her face. Pitor wrapped his arms around her and said softly, "Love, I am so sorry. Your mother passed away. I found her in her bed."

"Do you know what happened?" Mila asked, trembling. He wished he could say or do something to help her, but there was nothing else to say.

"I don't think she suffered at all. It appears that she died in her sleep."

"Oh... oh... Pitor," Mila said, burying her face in his shoulder. He could feel by the way she shook that she was crying, but there was nothing he could say. He just held her until he finally put her to bed. Then he got in beside her and began stroking her hair. He sang softly to her as if she were a child until she drifted off to sleep.

In the kitchen, Pitor's untouched bowl of soup grew cold on the table.

CHAPTER THIRTY-EIGHT

Just like when Mila's father died, Pitor was again excluded from being one of the ten men in the *minyan* for Mila's mother. Her two other sons-in-law didn't approve of Pitor. They snubbed him openly. Once again, Anshel appeared, this time with his wife, to pay his respects, but Pitor didn't know who he was. If he had known Anshel, he might have thrown him out of the house because of all the problems he had caused Mila. But Pitor had never met Anshel, and so he didn't realize who Anshel was. Ruth and Sarah's husbands recited the *minyan,* but they remained silent otherwise, not speaking a single word to Mila, Pitor, or even little Jakup. Mila didn't care; she was glad that they didn't say anything insulting.

Mila watched as her sisters, their husbands, and Anshel with his wife huddled together, talking softly among themselves. In their own way, they were trying to let Pitor know he was not accepted and would never be a part of their world. Her sisters did not allow Jakup to play with their children. They never said anything unkind, but they took their children away when they started talking to Jakup, leaving Jakup sitting on the floor playing all alone. *Once this shiva is over, I will probably never see my sisters again,* Mila thought. *They have decided that they don't want us in their lives, and I am tired of it all. I am tired of their laws and the way they treat me and my family, and honestly, I am giving up on them. I just don't care anymore.*

The seven days of *shiva* dragged on slowly. Mila was sad about losing her mother, but in truth, they had not been close in a long time. She had chosen Pitor over her family, and she never once regretted her decision. He was her best friend and her *bashert*. She knew it for sure now that they had been together for several years. Whether her sisters and their husbands acknowledged this truth made very little difference to her.

In the beginning, she had wished her sisters would accept her husband. She had longed to be close to them again. In fact, she'd often fantasized about what holidays might be like if they were a close family. However, she knew these daydreams were little more than fantasies because her sisters and their husbands would never eat in Pitor's house or allow Jakup to play with their children.

CHAPTER THIRTY-NINE

Mila was right about her sisters and their families. Time passed following her mother's death, and during that time, she did not see her sisters even once. It was as if they, too, had died when her parents died. She would always feel that it was a shame that they were all so divided. It would have been nice to have a united family, but this was what Sarah and Ruth wanted, so Mila accepted it and stopped trying to visit them.

To make matters worse, when Pitor finally rebuilt his business after Anshel's rumors about the rats, Anshel struck again. This time, Mila was the one to hear the rumor, and it hit her hard because Anshel claimed that Mila's mother had become ill and died due to eating food that came from Pitor's butcher shop. Once again, Anshel lied, and once again, the Jewish community believed him.

Jakup was a curious little boy. He was smart and busy, always taking things apart and then trying to put them back together. This made his father laugh, and although Jakup's antics were often annoying and exhausting, Mila laughed, too. It was almost uncanny how much Jakup resembled his father. Mila often teased Pitor, telling him that Jakup was his tiny twin. Sometimes, when Jakup did something that she knew he had learned from Pitor—like the way he buttoned his shirt or the way he ate his porridge—she would ruffle his curly blond hair and laugh. Then, picking him up with a smile, she would say, "You are your papa's little twin."

When Agata turned thirteen, she ran away with one of the boys who lived in her neighborhood. Before she left, she confided in Mila that she had fallen in love and was planning to marry. "My parents tried to break us up. They say we are too young, but Antoni is almost seventeen, and we are in love. So, Antoni and I are going to leave this little village and move to Warsaw, where he can find work," she said. "I will miss your family. It has been so wonderful working for you and Pitor. And, of course, I love Jakup, but I must do this. I hope you understand."

"Of course I do," Mila said as she hugged Agata. "Just remember that if you ever want to come back, there will always be a job here waiting for you."

Pitor adored his son, but he also knew that Jakup was a handful, often getting into mischief because he was bored. So, Pitor spent most of his free time making imaginative toys for Jakup, special things that he knew would keep the child's interest. Jakup didn't like carved animals. He enjoyed puzzles that challenged him. His mind was active, and he was always in need of entertainment. But Mila knew that deep inside, he was a good boy. But Jakup, like his father when he was young, sometimes got into trouble when he wasn't occupied. Mila was often exhausted because she had to keep an eye on him all the time. She missed Agata terribly. The only time she got a break was when Jakup took a nap, which he resisted until he was so worn out that he fell asleep mid-play. She would wait and hope for these moments, and once he was sleeping, she quietly carried him to his bed, careful not to wake him up.

But he never slept for very long, and his mother was always behind on both her sleep and her housework. The house was usually a mess, the laundry rarely done, and Mila was always tired—but she was happy. Life was good. Pitor was not only very handsome, but he was a hard worker and a good provider. Most importantly, he and Mila adored each other, and they both doted on their precocious little boy. The family always had enough to eat. Their home was warm, and although it was not luxurious, Pitor made sure that his family wanted for nothing. Most of all, Mila and Pitor's home was filled with laughter and love.

Pitor could be very serious. He was responsible and willing to work long, tedious hours, but he also had a lighthearted and funny side. Often, when he came home from work, he told stories or jokes about his day that made Mila laugh. He was proving to be a wonderful papa. He could turn an angry weeping child who was frustrated because he wasn't getting his own way into a laughing little boy. But Jakup was too fascinated by the world around him to be quiet and content for very long. Soon, he needed attention again and someone to play with him. Since Pitor was at work most of the time, keeping Jakup entertained fell to Mila. Despite being worn out from Jakup, Mila was content. She had everything and more than she had ever dreamed possible.

Sometimes, when Pitor was at work, and Jakup was taking a nap, her thoughts traveled back to the days when her parents had been trying to arrange her marriage. She would think about the young men her father brought home for dinner and how judgmental they were of her. Even now, she knew Anshel was spreading demeaning rumors about her. In fact, when she went into the Jewish sector of town to go to her favorite bakery, she couldn't help but notice how people looked at her in disgust. Mila stopped going into her old neighborhood, but she often wondered how Anshel could call himself a religious man and still spend so much of his time trying to ruin her reputation and her life. *For a religious man, he is so very vindictive.*

Then she would think of Pitor and how he had known from the first time they met that they were meant to be together. She was his *bashert*. He knew it all along, and she was glad that she had not listened to her parents even though it had cost her dearly. In the end, it was worth everything.

CHAPTER FORTY

MARCH 1941

When the Nazis arrived in an open-air truck one bitterly cold winter morning, it came as a shock and a terrible surprise to the small village on the outskirts of Warsaw. The air was frigid, and many of the residents were too poor to own a heavy coat, but the Germans wore long wool coats on top of their well-made uniforms. They carried guns, and as soon as they jumped down from their truck, they began to round up all the Jews in the village.

There had been no prior warning of what was to come that day. Pitor had a family to support. So, although the country was in turmoil, he went to work that morning. Someone must have told the German soldiers that Pitor was a strong man who would fight back because when they came to arrest Pitor, they arrived in force. Four heavily armed soldiers, along with two sneaky-looking SS officers in long black leather coats, entered Pitor's butcher shop. These SS officers were a part of Hitler's Secret Service. Their appearance alone was intimidating. They stood in a line, blocking the door so no one could leave. Then, they pointed their guns at the customers in the store, and in a firm, loud voice, one of the SS asked the customers, "Who here is Jewish?"

No one answered, but an old woman who had been waiting patiently to purchase some bones for soup fainted. She was a skinny lady who collapsed like a rag doll onto the floor. The two SS officers laughed at the old woman as if they had just seen something that was very funny. None of the customers laughed. Pitor went over to the old woman. He was pretending not to be afraid or intimidated as he helped the old woman to stand up. Pitor stood beside her and held onto her shoulder as she looked around in a daze.

"Get out of my store," Pitor hissed at the Nazis.

Both of the SS officers laughed. "Your store, is it?" one sneered.

"Yes, I'm the owner of this butcher shop, and you are not welcome here. Now get out."

"He's funny. Look at this. We have a regular comedian who is also a butcher," one of the SS officers said to the other one. "Don't you think he's hilarious?"

"Oh, he is funny, alright. But not because he wants to be. He's funny because he's so stupid. This poor fool has no idea how powerful we are, but he's about to find out," the SS officer said, then he turned to Pitor. "This may have been your store up until 5 minutes ago. But now, well... things have changed." He smiled manically.

Pitor's fists clenched. *You lousy coward, you wouldn't be so brave if you were here up against me alone, without all these men to back you.*

"You're coming with us, and until we see fit to change things here, your butcher shop will be closed. Now, that's enough talking, let's go." One of the soldiers nudged Pitor with his rifle butt. For a moment, Pitor could not move. His thoughts were of his wife and son. *I must find a way to protect them,* he thought, and he knew if he put up a fight, these men would think nothing of killing him. He wasn't afraid to die, but he knew that if he was dead, there would be no one to protect his wife and child. Therefore, he held back and swallowed his anger. Pitor hated these men and would have liked to destroy them. Instead, he did as he was told.

When Pitor got outside, he saw several open-air trucks and at least ten soldiers and SS officers standing around and yelling, "Get in line, you filthy pigs." Pitor would have loved to kill one of them, but he knew he couldn't, at least not yet. So, he took his place at the end of a line that the Nazis had formed in the middle of the street. As he stood in the line, he recognized several people who lived in the village, including children and elderly people. Not all of them had warm clothes to brave the weather, but every one of them wore the Star of David on their clothes. *They've come for us Jews. I have been afraid this was going to happen. I am strong, but I am only one man. I can't fight them alone.*

Some of the people in line were crying, but Pitor was silent. His thoughts were consumed by his wife and son. He prayed they were safe because they were at home, and their house was on the outskirts of town. And he wished he could go home and protect them. There was chaos in the streets, even though the Nazis did their best to keep order. The children were terrified. They screamed and cried as they clung to their mothers. The elderly stood outside, shaking from the cold. Many of them stooped and were unable to stand upright. Those who were of working age looked confused and frightened. Pitor felt a tug at his pants leg. He looked down and froze—Jakup was there, alone, his small face contorted with fear. Pitor was immediately terrified.

How could Jakup be in town alone without Mila? *Dear God, he thought, let Mila be all right.* Pitor tried to keep his voice calm as he asked his son, "Where is your mother?" But, of course, he knew the little boy was too young to answer. Poor Jakup began to cry. Pitor took his son into his arms and looked around desperately for Mila. When he saw her, she was frantically searching for Jakup, her eyes wild with fear. "Mila," Pitor cried out. Mila spun around, and when she saw Pitor, a look of relief spread over her face. This made him feel a little better.

Mila ran to Pitor, who was still holding Jakup. "These frightening men knocked on the door of our house," Mila said. She was gasping for breath, her face pale and blotchy with fright. "I tried to ignore them. I wasn't going to let them in. There were soldiers and men in those long black coats. Even when I was in the house, I could hear them yelling. I was so shaken, and then one of them kicked our front door in. Jakup was so scared he began screaming, and I was terrified. So when one of the soldiers said we had to get into a line and follow them, we did. That's how we got here. The soldiers brought us here with lots of other people. I was going out of my mind until I saw you."

He nodded. "Come here," he said, putting one of his arms around her and holding his son with his other arm.

"What are we going to do, Pitor? What do these Germans want from us, and where are they taking us?" Mila asked frantically.

"Shhh," Pitor whispered, hoping to calm her. "I don't know what they want or where they're taking us, or even why. But I'm glad you found me and that we are all together."

"Jakup found you," Mila said.

Jakup was sucking his thumb, still nestled in his father's arms. Mila reached out and rubbed her son's back. Jakup nuzzled even deeper into his father's chest and sucked on his thumb hard enough to make a sucking noise. "I am so glad he found you."

Pitor tried to give his wife and son an encouraging smile. He was doing his best to hide his fears, but it was difficult because he had heard so many horrible things about the treatment of Jews in Germany. Now, things looked very bleak as the Germans were rounding up the Jews in Poland.

"All of you, listen to me!" one of the soldiers bellowed. "Just quiet down and do exactly what we tell you to do. As long as you cooperate with us, none of you will get hurt." The murmur of frightened voices quieted. The cold air seemed to hold its breath.

"Where are we going? When can we go home?" a woman called out from somewhere in the crowd of nervous, frightened Jews. "Please tell us what is in store for us?"

"How dare you. It's not for you to ask questions. Just shut your mouth and march."

"But please, can't you tell us where you're taking us?" another woman asked.

This time, one of the SS officers answered her. "Didn't the soldier tell you to shut your mouth? How dare you disrespect him and speak." The SS officer pulled her out of the crowd. Pitor could see that her hands were shaking. He did not know the woman, but he wished he could help her. Then he looked down at the little boy who was trembling in his arms and into the eyes of the woman who owned his heart. He knew their safety was more important to him than anything else in the entire world. So, instead of standing up to the Germans and possibly getting himself killed, Pitor remained quiet.

CHAPTER FORTY-ONE

Once the open-air trucks were full, the Nazis ordered the rest of the people to walk. It was a long, grueling march to the train station. The soldiers and the SS guards walked along with the group, keeping their guns pointed at the Jews. The Jewish people who lived in this small Polish Village had never caused any trouble with the police or the government. They had always kept to themselves.

Late in the afternoon, they arrived in Warsaw. Warsaw was still a heavily populated city. However, it was not the same city that Pitor remembered. This city had suffered heavy bombing attacks, and many of the buildings were reduced to rubble. Mila could not speak for a few moments. She was feeling nervous and displaced. She squeezed Pitor's arm. "Look at what they did to this city," she whispered as the entire group approached an iron gate.

Pitor nodded because he didn't know what to say. Lost in his own thoughts, he was worried about how he was going to protect his family because he was certain that the Germans had something terrible in store for them. He desperately wished he knew what they were planning. *If I only knew more about where we were going, I might have found a way to escape. The only problem is running while carrying a small child, which will be very difficult. In fact, it would probably be impossible to get away from the gunfire fast enough. If I were alone, I would try, but I can't risk it with Mila and Jakup. I am sure that if they catch us, the Germans would make a spectacle of murdering us. They would use my family as an example of what happens if someone tries to defy them. Someday, I'll make them pay. But not now—not yet.*

Since Pitor was very tall, he was able to see over the heads of the crowd. Mila asked him what was going on, but he did not tell her what he was seeing. Pitor didn't want to scare her. He couldn't help but notice that the gates were topped with barbed wire. This sent a shiver down his spine as he watched the SS officers at the front of the line. One of the SS officers walked to the opening at the front of the gate, and Pitor was feeling anxious. A guard from inside the gate greeted the SS officer with a strange salute that Pitor had never seen before. The two Nazis spoke for a few moments, but Pitor was too far away to hear what they said. Still, Pitor continued to watch as the gate was lifted and the Jewish captives were forced to enter this strange part of the city. Pitor and his family followed the line as they entered the gate. Broken-down buildings loomed over them, and lots of people wearing the yellow Star of David walked on the streets. Pitor was not sure what this place was or why they were there. Still, this area was a part of Warsaw. Although he'd never been here before, it seemed as if the Nazis had built a city for the Jews where they could live and not encounter any Aryans.

A short, dark-haired SS officer spoke loudly enough to be heard by everyone in the group, "Quiet all you swine. Listen to me. I do not intend to repeat these orders."

The terrified people from that small village turned their fearful but hopeful faces towards this SS officer. They quickly grew quiet. Silence hung in the air like a dark rain cloud, ready to erupt into a tornado.

"Our generous Führer built this area especially for all of you. I hope you appreciate the time and effort we put into this. We call this lovely area the Warsaw Ghetto. It's a ghetto because it will be the home to all of you displaced Jews. Now that you are here, you will need to find a place to live," he took a breath and looked around to make sure that no one was planning to resist. Once he was sure they weren't, he continued to speak, "In order to be assigned an apartment, you must get in line to speak with the Judenrat—the Jewish Council. These are Jewish people who we have been selected to help you communicate better with the German guards. So, hurry up and get in line to see them. The better accommodations go to those who move quickly."

Once the SS officer finished speaking, Pitor turned to Mila, who was trying to soothe a fussy Jakup. Pitor touched Jakup's head gently, hoping to settle him down a little. Then Pitor spoke to Mila in a soft but confident voice, "Why don't you sit down here on this rock and hold on to Jakup. I will get in line to speak with the Judenrat. I'll do my best to get us a decent place."

"Pitor..." Mila looked as if she might start crying. "Pitor," she repeated his name and found that even though she was smiling, tears were running down her cheeks. "Are we ever going to be allowed to go home? I don't want to live here. I want to go home to our house. I want to make dinner in our kitchen. I want to sleep in our beds. How can they say that this place is our home? I don't want to live here. This place is not our home."

"It's all right, it's all right," Pitor said, pulling her close. "I don't know what they plan to do with us, but my guess is they'll keep us here for a few days. After a few days, those of us who are not criminals and those of us who have not been openly opposed to Nazi rule will be allowed to leave here and return home."

"I hope you're right."

"I hope so, too. Now, listen to me. I'm going to get into the line to see the Judenrat. My guess is that you don't want to stand in line. I am sure it's easier for you to wait here with Jakup. Try and rock him to sleep. If he will just sleep, we can do what we need to do."

"I hope he will sleep. He's just a child, and he's scared. But I am not a child, and I am scared too. My family, everyone I love, is here," her hands were trembling as she stroked Jakup's head. "Anyway, I will wait here while you speak to the Judenrat. But please return as quickly as you can. Jakup and I need you."

"Don't be afraid, darling," Pitor said, pressing his forehead to hers. "I will protect you and our son. I committed myself to caring for you and our children on the day I married you. and I promise to uphold my promise to keep you safe."

Mila kissed her husband, then adjusted Jakup on her lap as she watched Pitor join the line to speak to the Judenrat.

CHAPTER FORTY-TWO

Jakup was fussy. He was hungry, tired, and too nervous to sleep, so he missed his nap. This made him cranky. Mila had spent the last 6 months toilet-training her son. He had learned to use the toilet and to ask for it when he needed to go, but there was no public toilet near the rock where Mila and Jakup sat waiting for Pitor to return. Jakup complained to Mila for half an hour that he needed to go to the bathroom, but Mila was afraid to leave the area in case Pitor came back looking for them. When Mila did not take him to the toilet, he wet his pants. She was very frustrated, but she could not blame him. It was her fault.

Mila had a small suitcase with a few items of clothing. Earlier, when the Nazis came to her house, they gave her 10 minutes to pack a bag. She could hardly remember what she packed; though she'd left her home that same day, it seemed like a lifetime ago.

Inside the small suitcase, Mila found clothes to change Jakup in, and she did so right in the middle of the square. This was something she would not normally do, and it felt strange. But these were extenuating circumstances, and so she did what she had to do and decided that it had been the right choice because at least her son was warm and dry.

It was dusk when Pitor returned. He carried a paper in his hand as he walked quickly over to Mila, "I'm sorry it's so late, but the line was very long."

Mila nodded, eager to reach the apartment where they would be staying. She longed to wash up and clean Jakup before he developed a rash. Though she wasn't happy to be here in this place called the Warsaw Ghetto, it would be nice to be in an apartment away from the middle of the square where they would have some privacy.

"Did you get us a place to stay?"

"Yes," he breathed, but the look on his face told Mila something wasn't right.

"What's wrong?" she asked him.

"I'm sorry," he said. "I did the best I could, but we're sharing an apartment with another family."

"Couldn't you offer to pay someone off so we could get something more private?"

"There is nothing available that is more private. This Warsaw Ghetto is overcrowded. People are living on top of each other. The family we are living with has two children. Our apartment is not so bad. Some of the other families who are living together have at least five or six children."

"I'm tired," Mila said. "Where is this apartment? Do you have any idea how to get there?"

"Yes, I do. The Judenrat gave me directions," Pitor said, but he didn't tell her that Anshel was the Judenrat that he had spoken with. He didn't mention that they were being sent to an overcrowded, dilapidated apartment, the worst Anshel could assign out of spite. Pitor assumed that most of the apartments were dirty and cramped, but Anshel had made it clear he was giving them one of the worst. Pitor sighed. He could understand why Anshel was still bitter about losing Mila. In Pitor's estimation, Mila was the most desirable woman on earth.

Jakup was tired of walking. He plopped down on the ground and refused to move. "Come on, little man." Mila tried to lift him up and put him back on his feet, but Jakup just sank back down.

"He's tired. This has been a long day for him. He's just a child. It's all right. I'll carry him," Pitor said as he picked Jakup up and hoisted the little boy onto his shoulders. Jakup giggled. Pitor knew how much Jakup enjoyed riding on his shoulders. Mila walked in silence at Pitor's side. It wasn't much further, only two blocks more from the center of town. When they came upon a tall brick building desperately needing repairs, Pitor knew that this was the apartment that Anshel had assigned them. He quickly checked the address written on the paper in his pocket against the address on the building, and to his chagrin, he was right. *This is it. Because of Anshel, this old run-down building will be our home until the Nazis see fit to let us go back to our house. I'd like to kill him. He's such a weakling that I could do it with one punch. But if I did, it would give the Nazis a reason to shoot me. Where would that leave my family?*

Mila didn't say anything, but Pitor could see that she was not pleased as they walked up three flights of rickety wooden stairs. The banister was broken in several places, and climbing up was very dangerous. A strong and terrible odor of old food and urine permeated the entire building. Jakup gagged from the smell, and Pitor was afraid the child might vomit. "Here, tuck your face into my shoulder," he whispered to Jakup. "Come on. It will be all right." Jakup did as Pitor suggested. As they continued on their way, neither Mila nor Pitor said a word to each other. At the top of the stairs, they headed down a long hallway until they came to a door marked 325.

"This is it," Pitor said, not looking at Mila because he was ashamed that she was going to have to live in such squalor. The paint on the door was chipping, and the walls were filthy. A spider sat on the ceiling, waiting for some unfortunate insect to enter her web. *Damn that Anshel,* Pitor thought. *He's such a selfish bastard. I don't care that he did this to me. I don't matter—I can survive anything. But if he ever really cared for Mila, how could he do this to her? And to*

Jakup? He calls himself a religious man. Would a man of God do such a thing to a child?

Mila cleared her throat and asked, "Did the fellow you spoke with from the Jewish Council say how long we would have to be here?"

"No, love, he didn't say. I don't think he knows. The Judenrat are just puppets for the Nazis." Pitor didn't want to tell her what Anshel said when he asked how long they were going to be in this place.

Pitor closed his eyes as he remembered Anshel's answer. "We will be here until the Germans decide what to do with us."

Then things went wrong. Pitor had lost control. He'd become angry. After all, he had been standing in line for hours waiting for his turn to get to the front where he might get answers to his questions.

He remembered how he'd felt some relief when he finally reached the front of the line. "What is your name? And how many are in your family," the young Judenrat asked. He was wearing a long black coat and long sideburns that showed that he was an Orthodox Jew. He did not look up at Pitor as he shuffled through a pile of papers.

"Barr, my name is Pitor Barr. There are three of us in my family. My wife, myself, and my three-year-old son," Pitor said. He didn't recognize the Judenrat, but the Judenrat recognized him. It was Anshel, the man who Mila had once been engaged to. Anshel smiled at Pitor. It wasn't a warm smile; it was a malicious smile. Pitor saw the malice behind the smile, and he wasn't sure what to make of it. But Anshel looked at him with such hatred that Pitor knew that there was more to this.

Anshel had won; he was in control of Mila's fate, and he was determined to make sure she was miserable with her secular husband.

"Let me see what we have available," Anshel said.

Pitor was annoyed. He wasn't sure what was going on here, but he was frustrated, and his frustration was growing into anger. He knew it was best if he tried to curtail his anger. In a soft voice, he asked, "How long are we expected to remain in this place?"

The young, handsome Judenrat looked into Pitor's eyes. Then he said, "Until the Germans say otherwise. They make all the decisions. We just carry them out, and so far, they have been fair with us."

Pitor was livid now. He glared at the Judenrat, and then anger overtook him. *How could this stupid man be such a pawn for the Nazis? How could he sell out his own people for them?* Pitor was so angry that he didn't notice the young Nazi guard who sat a few feet away from the table where the four Judenrats sat.

"You don't know who I am, do you?" Anshel asked. There was a look of pleasure on his face that Pitor could not yet understand.

"Should I know you?" Pitor said.

"Oh yes, you certainly should."

Pitor shrugged. "I'm sorry, but I don't recognize you." He was trying to keep his anger at bay. He knew that any confrontation would not be good for him or for Mila and Jakup. "Perhaps you're a customer at my butcher shop?"

Anshel let out a laugh. "Do you think I would ever eat the *traif,* non-Kosher meat you sell? No good Jew would shop at your butcher shop."

Pitor nodded. He was angry. It was obvious that this Judenrat was baiting him, but Pitor couldn't figure out why. "All right, so what is it? Where do I know you from? I am too tired to play games with you. Just tell me how you and I know each other and how this is going to affect me and my family."

Anshel shook his head. "You certainly are stupid."

Pitor almost punched him, but he forced himself to be quiet and not start a fight. *All I need from this crazy fellow is a decent apartment. If I fight with him, he won't give us one.*

"Let me give you a little clue. My name is Anshel Minsky. I was engaged to Mila until you stepped in with your secular, sinful ways and ruined everything." He smiled again. This time, Anshel reminded Pitor of the wolf from Red Riding Hood, an old fairy tale that Pitor's mother had often told him when he was a child.

"I'm sorry," Pitor forced himself to remain calm. "Neither Mila nor I ever wanted to hurt you."

"You didn't hurt me, you fool. You shamed me. Both of you shamed me. And I promise you that now that I have the power to help or hurt you, I plan to make your life and the lives of your wife and child a living hell."

Pitor could no longer contain himself, and he was physically very strong. In an instant, he grabbed Anshel by his shirt collar, and with one hand, he lifted him out of the chair.

Then in a deep and menacing voice, Pitor said, "I don't need the Nazis to figure out where I should go or what I should do. My wife, my child, and I own a home. We don't need the Germans telling us what we should and shouldn't do."

And that was when the Nazi guard put his gun to Pitor's head and whispered in a menacing voice, "Drop him Jew, or his face will be the last thing you will ever see."

For a single moment, Pitor was blinded by anger, but then he remembered Mila and Jakup waiting for him outside. *What would become of them if I was shot dead right here, right now? They would be on their own with no one to protect them.* Pitor drew a ragged breath, closed his eyes, and regained his composure. He dropped the Judenrat and glanced over at the Nazi guard, and nodded his head.

The Nazi answered Pitor, "You used to own a home. Not anymore. Now your house belongs to Germany. And from now on, if you want to live, you will do whatever any German tells you to do." Then the Nazi turned to Anshel and said, "Give him his housing assignment and make sure it's one of the worst ones here, you swine."

"Here's your housing assignment, Barr. You'll be living in one of our nicest buildings," Anshel said in a tone dripping with sarcasm. "And to add to your comfortable surroundings, you will be sharing your two-room apartment with another family." Then Anshel let out a short laugh and tossed Pitor's living assignment papers and his key at Pitor. Pitor was shocked that Anshel, who was a Jewish Council member that was supposed to be there to help his fellow Jews, seemed almost friendly with the Nazis. In Pitor's mind, Anshel showed a lack of self-respect. Anshel had not even become angry when the Nazi guard called him swine. It was almost as if he expected to be called that. Pitor didn't say another word. He just took the housing assignment papers and walked outside. As he made his way back to where he left Mila and Jakup, he thought, *I hope losing my temper won't make things worse for my family. This place looks bad enough. What the hell did that lousy Nazi mean when he said my house belongs to them? I will not mention anything about this to Mila. At least not yet, not until I know more. Why would I upset her if I could help it?*

Now, as Pitor was looking over the building where he and his family would live, he could see that Anshel had given him one of the worst living quarters available. Not that he had seen any of the others, but he couldn't imagine that they were as bad as this. Pitor was not looking forward to entering the apartment. The building was bad enough, but he knew that procrastinating would not change things. So, he sucked in a deep breath and then put Jakup down on his feet. Next, he found the key Anshel had given him and put the key in the lock. The handle squeaked as he turned it, and the door creaked loudly when he pushed it open. Two little girls who sat on a small cot that was covered with a stained, threadbare sheet looked up when Pitor and his family entered. They looked scared. They had been playing with a doll that was worn and decrepit. For a moment, Pitor observed the children. If he had to guess their age, he would have thought they were about eight. They were small for their age, and in reality, they were both twelve years old.

"Hello," Mila said softly. "Don't be afraid of us. I am Mila, and this is my husband, Pitor." Then she smiled and said, "And this little fellow is our son, Jakup."

The two girls smiled at Mila.

Pitor stole a glance at Mila, and the look on her face broke his heart. All he had ever wanted was to keep her happy. He had worked hard to give her the best life he could, and now the Germans had taken everything away from them. *Someday I will find a way to make these Nazis pay for this. They have no idea what kind of man they're dealing with.*

Pitor was lost in thought when a young woman walked over to them. Her long, dark curly hair was uncombed, and the housedress she wore was fraying at the sleeves.

"Who are you? And what are you doing here?" the young woman asked Mila.

Before Mila could answer, Pitor walked over to the woman and said, "I spoke with someone at the Jewish Council today. He assigned us this apartment."

"Well, there is not enough room here for another family. I have two children. They share a room. My husband and I have the other room. So, as you can see, there is no place for another family. You will have to go back and tell them that they need to find you another apartment."

"I can see that this apartment is already full, but this is where we were sent. I am not going back there. If you want our living quarters changed, you are going to have to go and speak with a Jewish Council member," Pitor said, "otherwise, we'll all just have to make the best of it for now."

"The Jewish Council never helps with anything. You'll learn that quick enough," the woman said. "They do whatever the Germans tell them to do because they think it will make their lives better. In the end, I doubt it will. Anyway, I'm sorry if I seem rude. It's just that I wasn't expecting another family to move in here. This place is just so small."

"I understand. No offense taken," Pitor said. Then he glanced over at Mila. And he was immediately sorry he had looked over at her because her expression told him she was horrified.

"Believe me, my family and I would prefer a place of our own," Mila said, "and I don't expect that we are going to be here very long. I don't know what all of this is about, but what I do know is that my husband and I own a house, which we plan to return to as soon as possible."

The young woman shook her head. "I don't think any of us are ever leaving here alive."

"What do you mean by that? That's just not possible," Mila replied, her voice trembling. "My husband and I own our own home, and we plan to return to it as soon as we can." Pitor could see that her hands were shaking.

"A lot of us had our own homes before we were arrested. Don't think you are so special. I am sorry to have to be the one to tell you this, but what you don't realize is that the Nazis have stolen everything we have. If, by some miracle, we ever get out of here, I would bet that our homes would be occupied by Germans."

"Please, Pitor, tell me she's crazy. She doesn't understand," Mila pleaded, her voice breaking. "You must explain to her that there is some mistake. Tell her that we have done nothing wrong. We shouldn't have been arrested. We don't belong here." She was shaking uncontrollably, tears streaming down her face. She was almost hysterical as she turned to the woman and said, "You don't understand, but you will see. We will be going home very soon. These Nazis can't just take our house. They can't just steal our belongings. There are laws to protect us."

Pitor took his wife into his arms and held her close to him. He couldn't lie to her and promise her they would soon be free to return home. So, he was silent.

"I am sorry for you, but you are a poor little fool," the young woman said, shaking her head. "Germany has conquered Poland. We have no rights anymore. Our laws are meaningless now. Whatever you owned before you were arrested is gone now. Nothing belongs to you anymore. You see, things are far worse for us because we are not only Poles, but we are also Jews. You'll soon understand that the Nazis hate Jews more than anything in the world. So, I am sure they are planning to make our lives even more miserable than they already are."

"Must we stay here, Pitor?" Mila asked.

Pitor nodded in defeat. "I am afraid so. At least for now." He looked down at the ground, ashamed. He wished he had killed Anshel and that Nazi who held the gun to his head. *I have no doubt that if I had tried to fight him, he would have shot me.* Pitor reminded himself. He had always been strong and capable. Never had he backed down from a fight, and now he felt like he looked weak in Mila's eyes. And there was nothing he could say or do at this moment to change the way Mila was looking at him.

"I am sorry. I really didn't mean to be rude," the woman said. "I don't want to be mean either. However, this is hard on all of us. My husband and I had a house too. We lost our home as well. I know what you are feeling, and I don't blame you." Her voice was much gentler now. Then, with a sad but sincere smile, she added, "I suppose if you're going to stay here with us, I should introduce myself. My name is Miriam Chapman. My husband is out right now, but he will return shortly. His name is Hymie. And the two little girls who were playing on the bed when you walked in here are our daughters, Lena and Anna."

Mila nodded. "It's nice to meet you," she said, but she still wasn't sure how she felt about this woman. Even so, she decided it was best to be cordial. She wanted to believe that Miriam Chapman was wrong and that she and Pitor would soon be permitted to take their son and return to their home. "My name is Mila. This is my husband Pitor and my son Jakup."

"We'll make room. My two girls will move into the bedroom with Hymie and me. "And the three of you can have this room," Miriam said.

"But there is only one cot in this room. Where will we all sleep?" Mila asked.

"I don't know. I am afraid you will have to figure that out. I didn't make it any better for my own family than I did for yours. We have the same amount of space in the bedroom. There is only one small bed, so I am going to put our two girls on the floor to sleep because we don't have any other place for them. Then Hymie will have to build a Partition to give him and me some privacy.

"As you can see, this entire ghetto is overcrowded. Hymie and I have been lucky to have had this apartment all to ourselves for a while. However, once you start talking to other people, you will find that most people are living with at least one other family. I was just hoping that wouldn't happen to us. It's nothing against you, and I'm sorry if I was rude, but this place, this Jewish ghetto, is getting to me. And the longer you're here, the more it will get to you, too," Miriam said.

Mila didn't answer. She set her suitcase down in the corner and sat on the edge of the dirty cot. "I'd like to wash these sheets," she said quietly.

Miriam nodded. "Soap is hard to come by. Don't waste it. Don't use it if you don't have to."

Mila didn't know what to say, so she shrugged.

"It's all right. My two girls were the only ones who ever slept in that bed, and they're both healthy. So, you have nothing to worry about."

Mila frowned but remained silent.

"You are going to find that there is a lot of disease going around here in the ghetto," Miriam continued. "It's filthy, and people are always getting sick. Sadly, there are a lot of deaths, too."

Pitor nodded. He could see how upset Mila was, and he wished Miriam would stop talking.

"I will tell you this," Miriam went on, "just wait and see how many talented and famous Jews are living here in the Warsaw Ghetto. The Nazis failed to see their worth, so they arrested them along with all the rest of us. As bad as it gets here, we always have entertainment. We have music, art, and live theater. That part of being confined here in this ghetto isn't bad, but everything else is a nightmare. The Germans have cut our food rations so low that we're always hungry. My husband, like yours, is a large man. The rations they allot us are hardly ever enough for him. My children are still growing, so I cannot take food from them to give to my husband. Instead, I have to supplement his rations with mine."

It wasn't until Miriam mentioned sharing her rations that Mila actually studied Miriam. She had avoided looking at Miriam before because she felt ashamed about having to move into this apartment, which she knew was going to inconvenience Miriam and her family. But now, as she looked more closely at Miriam, Mila was shocked at how thin Miriam was.

In a defeated voice, Miriam said, "I'm sorry if I was rude. I didn't mean to be. It's just that it's so hard here in this place. The truth is, my husband and I never owned a house. I'm sorry I lied to you about that. But before we were arrested, we lived in an apartment in Warsaw. It wasn't a big place, but of course, it was bigger and nicer than this place. We had lived there for several years, and even though we were renting, we felt like it was ours. I always believed my children would grow up with all of the children who were living in our neighborhood. We had known all of them since their birth, and before that, we knew their parents. So, my husband and I were very upset when we were sent here to this Warsaw ghetto. Nothing worked out the way we planned. And now, we are here, and we have no idea what has happened to our friends or family. Everyone from our community is scattered. My parents did not live in Warsaw or even in the outskirts, and so they are not here with us in the ghetto. I don't know where they are. I pray every day that they're safe, but I don't know if they are. Not knowing... it's unbearable, you know?"

"Yes, I do know," Mila said softly. "I was estranged from my sisters before we were arrested. I looked for them when we got off the train, but I didn't see either of them. They would be easy to spot because they are always together. I don't know for sure if they are as close as they were before I left the community, but I am assuming they are. Even though we do not speak, I pray that they are both all right."

Miriam looked like she might start to cry, and Mila wouldn't have known what to say or how to comfort her. So, she hoped Miriam wouldn't start weeping.

"Try not to feel bad. Just stay hopeful about your sisters. The truth is that none of us know where our loved ones are. At least Hymie and I are fortunate that my husband's parents are living in an apartment a few streets away from us. If I had known that another family would be moving in here, I would have asked the Judenrats if my in-laws could move in. I don't mean to insult you, but my children love their *Bubbie* and *Zede*."

Mila felt sorry for Miriam. She had already forgiven her for being rude. Moving into this tiny apartment and sharing it with strangers was no easier for Miriam than it was for her. Mila managed to smile warmly. Then she said, "Well, let's hope we can be friends. You and I. We are forced to live together, so things might be easier for both of us if we are friends."

"Yes," Miriam said as she wiped a tear from her cheek.

Pitor was watching and listening, but he couldn't speak. He couldn't believe what was happening. He had spent his entire life building his business. Pitor had a large clientele who adored him and came to his butcher shop to buy meat every week. He owned a house and nice furniture. In fact, Pitor had spent his life preparing in every way for his family to live a comfortable life. And... in an instant, everything he'd worked for had been stolen from him. This made him crazy with rage. He wanted to fight and kill some of those Nazis. He would have taken them on if the Nazis were fair. Pitor would gladly have fought them if they fought with fists instead of guns. But the Nazis were weak, and the use of weapons was the only way the Nazis had to control the Jews, especially Pitor. Pitor was certain that the day would come when he could show these lousy Nazis just how strong he was. When the time was right, he would do just that. However, he knew he still had to be careful because they had guns, and the largest and strongest man in the world was still no match for a man with a gun. For now, he would have to swallow his anger, and it had a terribly bitter taste. He will be watching and waiting for an opportunity to get revenge.

"Did they give you your ration cards when they assigned you this place?" Miriam asked.

"I'm not sure. I waited outside with my son while my husband went in to see the Jewish Council to get our housing assignment. So, if we receive any ration cards, he will have them."

"You probably got them. Be very careful with your ration cards, Mila, and you must never lose track of them. Ration cards are worth more than gold here. That's because food is so scarce. Sometimes Hymie tries to buy food on the black market, but it's dangerous. The Nazis are always watching. Besides that, the prices of anything on the black market are just too high for Hymie and me. Worse, I have to admit, the food we purchased through the black market turned out to be old. The black market is run by children who can get in and out of the ghetto. However, they don't know when food is not fresh. My two girls have both gotten sick from eating it."

Pitor's jaw tightened, irritation flickering in his eyes. Miriam seemed to have a way of making things worse than they were before, and Pitor couldn't bear to listen to her talk. "I'm going outside to sit in the courtyard," he said to Mila, forcing a calm tone. "I need some fresh air. Would you like me to take Jakup with me?" Jakup seemed to understand what his father said, and he lifted his arms, eager to be picked up. "Looks like he wants to go with me. Is it all right with you if I take him?"

"Of course. It will give us girls a chance to talk and get to know each other," Mila tried to smile, but her lips quivered. Pitor knew that unless the conversation took a turn, his wife was going to cry. He couldn't bear her tears right now. When she cried, it made him feel helpless, and right now, there was nothing he could do to make her feel better.

"Come on, little fella," Pitor said as he scooped Jakup up into his arms and put him on his shoulders. "Let's go explore the outside of this building."

After Pitor and Jakup left, Miriam filled a kettle with water and put it on the stove. While the water was heating, Miriam sat down at a small kitchen table and motioned for Mila to join her. Mila sat, feeling the exhaustion settle over her. Miriam sighed, "Believe it or not, it's tougher on the men here. They feel so helpless. My husband was never a drinker, but now he turns to alcohol whenever he can find a little extra money. I'm embarrassed to tell you that there have been times when he has spent our food money on drinking. Although I was terribly ashamed, I had no choice but to go and ask his mother if she could spare a few rations so I could feed the children. Plenty of nights I have gone to bed hungry."

Mila didn't know what to say. She had been cut off from her family for marrying Pitor. It had been years since she had been a part of their circle, but now all of their fighting meant nothing to her. Each night, right before she fell asleep, Mila said a silent prayer for her sisters and their families. But even as she prayed, she knew they would never allow her and her family into their world. The day she married Pitor, they removed her from their lives. Although she had not known that they were going to be sent to this ghetto, she had made her choice, and she wasn't sorry. Not even now.

The piercing whistle of the kettle jolted her back to the present. It was only then she realized Miriam had been talking to her the entire time they were sitting there, and she hadn't even heard a single word.

"I have some ersatz coffee," Miriam said, pouring the hot water into two chipped mugs. "It's not the most delicious coffee you'll ever have, but it's hot, and it's better than nothing."

"I'm sure I will enjoy it. Thank you. This is very kind of you," Mila said, cradling the warm mug in her hands.

Miriam managed a faint smile. "I try to remember my manners, but it's hard to have nice manners here. In this ghetto, it's a dog-eat-dog world."

"I understand," Mila replied quietly.

CHAPTER FORTY-THREE

Hymie stumbled home late that afternoon, reeking of alcohol, his words slurring. As soon as Miriam saw her husband's condition, a loud, angry argument erupted between them. Even though they were in their bedroom with the door closed, the shouting and foul language filled the apartment. Mila and her family couldn't help but hear every word. Miriam hated exposing her children to this, but she had no choice. Both of her daughters sat on the dirty cot together, holding hands. They heard every word that Miriam and Hymie said, and she was relieved that they didn't ask any questions.

Pitor and Mila looked at each other, and then they both looked over at Jakup, who was sitting quietly on their cot, playing with one of his puzzles. Mila and Pitor didn't fight a lot, but on the rare occasions when they did, they were careful not to argue in front of their son. Now Jakup was listening carefully to Hymie and Miriam fight. His eyes were wide, and the look on Jakup's face told his parents that he was frightened.

Mila picked her son up and cradled him in her arms. "Everything is going to be alright. you'll see. It won't be so bad here," she was whispering softly to Jakup. Pitor overheard Mila trying to comfort their child, and his heart sank. He wished there was something he could do to reassure his family that all of this would pass, but he wasn't sure that this was only temporary. In fact, right now, he wasn't sure of anything at all. The only thing he felt sure of was that there was nothing he could do to improve their situation. This left him feeling angry, weak, and powerless, and he knew he must try his best not to take his anger out on his loved ones.

Just then, Mila reached over and squeezed his upper arm gently. "It will be alright, Pitor," she whispered in her soothing, steady voice. "You'll see. We'll make the best of it until we are permitted to return to our home."

He looked into her eyes, and he knew she was trying her best to be strong for his sake. Once again, he was thankful that he'd found his bashert.

CHAPTER FORTY-FOUR

Because Pitor had a trade, he was able to find a job working under another butcher. Within a week, Pitor's boss learned that his new employee was quite capable and that any job he was given was performed quickly and with perfection. Yet, instead of being glad to have found someone who was an excellent butcher, Pitor's new boss grew jealous, and he refused to acknowledge how good Pitor was at his job. With each passing day, he was more and more threatened by Pitor's competence, and he began struggling to keep Pitor from outshining him.

Mostly, Pitor ignored his boss. He didn't care what his boss said or did to him. Pitor was not himself. He knew he was depressed, and that was why none of this petty nonsense really mattered to him. He was an excellent butcher, but there was hardly any meat to cut. So, most of the day, he stood around the shop looking for things that needed to be done. That was until the Nazis decided they would bring the whole carcasses of animals they had hunted and killed to the butcher shop where Pitor worked. This was because they'd heard he was clean, efficient, and capable of butchering and wrapping their meat. As for Pitor, he saw this as a bit of good luck because it gave him an opportunity to steal bits and pieces of the meat that would not be missed. His boss remained oblivious, and Pitor made sure he didn't find out. He was certain that if he had, he would have said that since it was his shop, he was entitled to the stolen meat. And Pitor was not willing to risk this. It wasn't much food, just bits and pieces of meat, but it helped to keep his family alive.

Meanwhile, the crowded apartment made Mila want to get out for a few hours a day. She begged Pitor to allow her to get a job. At first, he refused adamantly, but Mila was insistent. Pitor hated to argue with her, so he finally agreed. However, he never told Mila how much of a blow it was to his masculinity. Since he and his family had been imprisoned in the ghetto, Pitor felt weak and incapable of protecting them.

It was more difficult for Mila to find work, and that was because Jakup was too young to be left alone. So when Pitor finally relented, they both decided that she would need a job where she was able to bring Jakup along. Mila knew everyone was trying to find work, and having to bring Jakup with her was going to be a deterrent for anyone who might consider hiring her. Still, she had to try. Mila walked up and down the streets in the ghetto, where she applied for work at a bakery, a general store, and a restaurant. Not only did she have no work experience, but none of the potential employers were willing to allow her to bring her son to work with her.

She was about to give up when a neighbor suggested that Mila apply to work at the school. The school was very overcrowded, and they were desperate for help. Even though Mila had no teaching experience, the headmaster decided to give her a chance. He said that Mila could bring Jakup with her, even though he was still too young to start classes. The headmaster made it clear that Jakup must be quiet and never disrupt the classes, and if he turned out to be a problem, Mila would be asked to leave. Mila was worried that Jakup would become fussy because he was bored, but he wasn't. In fact, Jakup was very well-behaved because he enjoyed the school and was fascinated by the opportunity to be surrounded by so many other children.

It turned out that Miriam was telling the truth about the small rations that the Jews were given. Rations were very tiny, but because both Mila and Pitor were working, they had a little extra money. And it just so happened that a few days after Mila started working, Pitor was approached by a man who, for a hefty price, was willing to sell him food acquired on the black market. Pitor knew that if they were caught by the Nazi guards, both he and the seller would be executed, but he had to take the chance anyway. Carefully, he started buying a few extra supplies each week, gambling with his life to keep his family fed.

Pitor and Mila didn't discuss it, but they both knew that the ghetto was a run-down and terrible place. It was filled with hunger and disease.

There were lots of young couples who were close to the same age as Mila and Pitor. Many of them had children Jakup's age, so he had other young people to play with. Pitor and Mila gradually made new friends, but not all the imprisoned Jews were friendly; some of them were Ultra-Orthodox and Hasidic Jews, and they refused to accept Pitor and Mila as friends. They kept to themselves and refused to have any contact with secular Jews, who they did not believe were Jewish at all. Pitor found their coldness irritating, but for Mila, the disapproving stares and harsh snubs were deeply hurtful. Once or twice, she had wept because they snubbed her and Jakup. It was particularly painful when, one afternoon at the park, a Hasidic woman pulled her two children away, refusing to let them play with Jakup. The ghetto was a harsh and terrible place to live, and Mila was often unnerved by the cruelty she saw in the streets, the cruelty inflicted by Jewish people and Nazi guards.

Within weeks of their arrival, Mila learned the Nazis had no respect for life, especially when it came to Jews. Sometimes when she was out shopping for food or on her way to work at the school, she would witness a Nazi beating up a Jewish person in broad daylight, right on the street, or in a shop. Most of the time, no one came to his aid, not because no one cared, but because they knew that if they helped, they might be killed. So, ordinary people who were appalled by this violence kept their mouths shut. They caught glimpses of blood and often of death as they walked quickly by these beatings with their heads down. Usually, they would pass by and silently pray for the victim. When Mila saw these heinous acts, she wished she could help the victim, but each day, Pitor stressed how dangerous it was for her to say or do anything. She knew he was worried about her safety, and so he made her promise not to get involved no matter what she saw when she was outside the apartment.

One afternoon, as she and Jakup were returning from the school where Mila worked, a sudden gunshot shattered the air. Mila froze, her eyes widening as she saw a Nazi guard shoot a young woman in the street. Her body crumpled, and blood pooled on the pavement. Her heart raced as she picked Jakup up and began to run towards home. The Nazi was too busy with his recent kill to notice Mila, and she was glad. She knew she should have just kept walking with her head down, but her feet seemed to have a mind of their own, and she ran as fast as she could.

Even when she was several streets away, she was still trembling. Sweat poured down her cheeks. For a moment, she leaned against the building, trying to steady herself. Jakup was clutched tightly to her chest, his small body trembling. She knew he had seen the woman get shot, and although he was silent, she knew Jakup was terrified. Closing her eyes for a moment, she hoped to find peace, but it was impossible to get the sight of the woman bleeding to death on the sidewalk out of her mind. *That could have been us.* She thought about Jakup being shot, and bile rose in her throat. She quickly set Jakup down, but the boy, terrified, began to cry, his arms outstretched, desperate for her comfort. She couldn't because she was so sick to her stomach that she vomited in the alley.

CHAPTER FORTY-FIVE

Pitor's depression turned to anger. He hated the Nazis, but even more than the Nazis, he hated any Jew who collaborated with them. He tried to keep his hatred and anger inside, but sometimes, after work, he went to a bar, and after a few drinks, he found himself saying things that were far too bold. This could have resulted in Pitor's demise, but God was with him, and instead, he found many like-minded men. These men and Pitor shared common enemies, and from this, they became friends instantly.

Those who were like Pitor formed groups that met in each other's apartments in strict rotation each week. They longed to fight back and reclaim their lives, but first, they needed a plan. Invitations to these gatherings were given with great caution. If the Nazis ever found out about this, they would execute all of them. After the resistance groups were formed, some of the wives began to attend the meetings with their husbands. Mila asked Pitor if she could go with him. At first, he refused. He told her it was dangerous and that she should stay at home with Jakup. But she begged him, and finally, he allowed her and Jakup to attend.

It was hard for Mila to hear about all the terrible things the Nazis had done to these people and even harder for her to listen to them discussing plans about how to retaliate. At the end of the evening, when Mila and Pitor were in bed, and Jakup was fast asleep, Mila turned to her husband and said, "You were right not to bring us to these meetings. It was far too horrible for me to go with you again."

"It's all right, love," he whispered into her hair. "You stay here at the apartment with Jakup. If and when there is anything you should know, I will make sure to tell you."

"I love you, Pitor."

"I know, and I love you too. And I promise you, I will do whatever I must do to free you from this place."

Mila kissed him softly, and then she glanced over at Jakup. "He's sound asleep," she said, her voice tender.

Pitor looked at Jakup, a small smile softening his face. "So he is," he replied. Then they smiled at each other and quietly made love.

CHAPTER FORTY-SIX

Miriam and her husband were coarse, but Mila decided that for Jakup's sake, she would get along with them. Even though they were living in hell, Mila's disposition was often light and hopeful. When Miriam's daughter, Anna, had a birthday, Mila shared her rations with Miriam so she would have enough to bake a cake. It was a tiny cake, but after Miriam gave her children, her husband, and herself a tiny slice, she shared the rest with Mila and her family. Each person got a small slice. But Mila lied, claiming she was too full from dinner to eat another bite. She insisted that Jakup and Pitor share her portion. Pitor gave her a knowing look. Then he took his fork and gently put a small amount of cake into her mouth. "But I'm really not hungry," she protested, but he just shook his head, finishing the extra cake, which made her smile.

Early one morning, Mila got up and dressed as she always did. However, Jakup had tried to dress himself. So, she stood by to help him as needed. Once they had breakfast, Pitor, Mila, and Jakup left the apartment and walked to the school where she worked. When they arrived, she was surprised to find the door locked. A note was taped to it, reading:

"Closed due to a typhoid epidemic."

Someone at school must have come down with typhoid, Mila thought, her heart racing. Like everyone else in the ghetto, she was terrified of typhoid. It was a horrible disease, and she had heard of many people who died from it. She was worried about herself, but she was more worried about her son and about Pitor if they brought this terrible illness into the apartment. For a moment, she thought of Miriam and her family, and she felt bad for them, too. *Jakup and I have been exposed.* The thought left her petrified. The outcome of this could easily leave them all dead. Then she looked down at her little boy whose hand was in hers, and she wanted to cry out, "Help me! Somebody, please help us. Please get my family out of here. I want to go home." But she didn't say a word out loud. Instead, her mind echoed the one terrible thought: *Jakup had been exposed.*

Mila picked Jakup up and held him in her arms. He wriggled in her arms, struggling to get down because, lately, he loved to walk. Much like his father, he loved to be independent, but she had no patience for that right now. She had to get back to the apartment, so she carried him, practically running all the way. When she got home, she ran into the apartment and immediately locked the door behind her. Out of breath and with tears in her eyes, she sank onto the worn sofa, feeling foolish. It wasn't as if she could lock the door to the apartment and just keep typhoid out of their lives.

Jakup, unaware of any danger, sat down on the floor and began playing with a toy that Pitor had made for him. The child was so innocent. It hurt her heart to watch him play. He was still so young, and Mila wished she could protect him, but she knew it was impossible. Only God could protect him. Jakup giggled, oblivious to the danger he and his family were facing. Mila leaned her head back on the sofa and let the tears fall. *I am so stupid. Why didn't I think about something like this happening before I took this job at the school?*

I was yearning for normalcy. I wanted to pretend we were not here in this place. I tried to make the school a safe haven for all the children who had been forced to live in this squalor. I meant well, but it turns out that I am a fool. I should have listened to Pitor when he told me to stay home and not go to work. Now, because of me and my selfishness, my son and my husband are at risk. In fact, everyone in this apartment is at risk, and it's my fault. Miriam, her husband, and their two little girls didn't deserve this. The truth of the matter is that I deserve whatever happens to me. I didn't have to work.

Pitor was providing well enough. I was just bored and selfish. I didn't want to sit in this apartment all day, every day. I felt that as long as I was stuck here in this ghetto, the least I could do was try to make things better for the children. A school where I could bring Jakup with me to work seemed ideal. I was happy about the idea that Jakup would have the opportunity to play with other children his age. But what seemed like an excellent idea has now backfired on me. Just look at what I've done. I don't even know how long the gestation period is. I do not know how long I must wait before I can relax and know that everyone here is going to be alright. What should I do? I don't know what is best. Should I tell Miriam? There is a chance that no one here will come down with the disease. I pray that is what happens. Maybe I shouldn't alarm Miriam. Perhaps it is better to just keep this to myself and pray that no one comes down with the disease.

Mila knew that there were no answers to her questions. Only time would tell whether she and those she loved would be afflicted. Anxious and frightened, lost and alone, Mila felt tremendous guilt and fear each time someone in the apartment coughed or sneezed. Although she tried to keep her fears to herself, she couldn't. She needed someone to lean on, and for Mila, that someone was always Pitor. He would never judge her or think badly of her, no matter what she told him. Even though she doubted he would know what to do, at least he would listen and relieve some of the burden she was carrying. Perhaps he might even know of some way of preventing the spread of this disease. All afternoon, she prayed silently as she went about her housekeeping chores. And each time she looked at her son, she felt like she might cry. *What have I done to my family and to these poor people who are living with us? They didn't deserve to be exposed to this disease.*

Most afternoons, after they were both finished with their chores for the day, Mila and Miriam would sit down and share a cup of tea. It was a relaxing ritual that they had developed, but that day, Mila could not bear to look at Miriam directly in the eyes. Her guilt was too overpowering. So, instead, she made herself look too busy to stop for a break. Miriam accepted this without question. Even though Mila was avoiding Miriam, she knew she could not avoid her forever. They lived in such close quarters it would be impossible. She closed her eyes and said a prayer for her family and then one for Miriam's family. If Anna or Lena got sick with typhoid, Mila knew she would never forgive herself. Even worse, if anything happened to Jakup or Pitor, she would be unable to live with herself.

Pitor returned to the apartment after he finished work at the usual time. Mila decided to wait and let him have his dinner before she spoke with him about the typhoid epidemic at the school. Pitor was always famished when he first got home from work, and although she'd been waiting all day to talk to him and lean on him for support, she curtailed her own needs until later.

As always, Pitor went to kiss Mila when he entered the apartment, but she turned away. He looked at her suspiciously, but she said nothing as she poured him a bowl of hot cabbage and potato soup. "Did I do something wrong?" Pitor asked, his brow furrowed.

She shook her head but still avoided his eyes. "Eat," she said quietly.

It had been a long day, and he hadn't eaten anything since breakfast. So, he gobbled up the soup, then cleaned the bowl with a thick slice of bread that Mila had baked. Pitor was so tired and hungry that he failed to notice that Mila had tears in her eyes until he finished. But once he was done, Pitor looked up from his bowl and saw that Mila was crying. He immediately got up from the chair and took her into his arms. "What is it? What's wrong?" he asked frantically. "Did I do something wrong?"

Mila shook her head. She needed to speak to him, but this was a conversation that she chose to have privately with her husband. "I need to talk to you," she whispered, "but not here. There is no privacy in this apartment. Everything we say is heard by Miriam or her family. So, I was hoping you and I might go outside and take a walk. Would that be alright? Miriam and Hymie are not home, but her daughters are, and I don't want to upset them."

"Of course," he said, surprised. "Where is Miriam?" Pitor asked because it was very rare for Miriam to leave the apartment even though Mila was home and would have agreed to watch her daughters.

"She left about an hour ago and said she was going to go visit with one of her friends who lives a few streets away from us. We could leave Jakup with Anna and Lena, but I would prefer to take him with us. He could use the fresh air."

"That's fine, my love. Let's go."

"Come on, big boy," Pitor said as he lifted Jakup into the air and onto his shoulders. Jakup squealed with delight. He loved to play with his father, and he really enjoyed it when Pitor would lift him up onto his shoulders and then carry him around the small apartment. But this time, the three of them left the apartment and went outside. As soon as they were out, Jakup wanted to get down and walk. When Pitor insisted on carrying him, Jakup began to fuss. Mila, who usually had patience with their son, had no patience now. She was nervous, frustrated, and very tense.

"Behave yourself," Mila said to Jakup, her voice sharper than usual.

Jakup, who was not used to being reprimanded by his mother in this tone of voice, began to cry. Pitor took Jakup down from his shoulders and placed him gently on the sidewalk. "It's alright, love," he said as he took Jakup's hand. "I'll walk with him," Mila nodded, taking a deep breath. With Jakup's hand safely in Pitor's, the three of them began to walk, the cool evening air wrapping around them.

"Can we go to the park?" Jakup asked his father.

"Sure, it's fine with me if it's all right with your mother."

"Yes," Mila said. Her voice was gentle as she tried to regain her composure. "The park sounds like a very good idea."

When they arrived at the park, Jakup saw a little girl playing in the sandbox. He pulled his hand away from his father, ran over to the little girl, and plopped down beside her with a delighted grin. Mila watched in horror. *What if Jakup had unknowingly exposed this girl to typhoid?* Mila did not know how the disease spread, but Jakup might have exposed every child who came to play in this sandbox in the future.

For a few minutes, Pitor and Mila sat on the park bench together, holding hands but not speaking. Pitor was patiently waiting for Mila to tell him what was going on. Mila was dreading it. Finally, Pitor asked, "I know something is not right with you. Please, Mila, just tell me what's wrong?"

"Oh, Pitor," she sighed, her voice breaking. "I don't know what we're going to do."

"You are going to have to tell me what's wrong if you want me to help you."

She was breathing heavily, almost panting.

"Mila," he said gently but firmly as he took her hand, brought it to his lips, and kissed it. "You should know that you can tell me anything."

She nodded, acknowledging that she knew she could talk to him. Then she looked down at the ground and blurted out, "When I went to work at the school this morning, the door was locked, and there was a note on the door... it said that the school was closed."

He didn't want to interrupt her, but she could see in his eyes that he wanted her to get to the point of this conversation.

"They closed the school because one of the students recently came down with typhoid. Jakup and I have been exposed. I am sick with worry and guilt," she said. There were a few moments of silence, then in a soft voice, she added, "Just look at him over there playing with that little girl. He's playing so sweetly and gently with her, but I am heartsick to know that she is now exposed to it, too."

Pitor nodded and squeezed her hand, his eyes steady and reassuring.

"I don't know what to do. I'm worried about you and Jakup, as well as Miriam and her family. We are smashed together in that small apartment. So, if one of us comes down with typhoid, it will spread to everyone."

Pitor nodded slowly. "There's nothing we can do, Mila. Typhoid is going around here in the ghetto like mad, and it's not the only disease that's affecting the ghetto. People are coming down with all kinds of diseases. It's happening constantly, and it's not your fault. You were trying to do a good thing by teaching these children. I know you would never hurt anyone on purpose. Disease spreads fast here because it's so overcrowded in this ghetto, and it's filthy. People find it hard to get decent food and clean water, but I'm not telling you anything you don't already know. This is the reason people are getting sick, so please don't blame yourself."

"It's hard not to, Pitor. If I had just stayed at home, we would never have been exposed."

"Of course, we would have. We can't live in a bubble. I work in the marketplace, and I am sure people come into the store sick all the time. They have no choice; they need to buy food. So, I am sure we have been exposed already. We just have to hope and pray that we'll be spared."

"And if we're not, what happens then? If one of us comes down with typhoid, what are we going to do?" she asked, her voice trembling.

"There are doctors here in the ghetto," Pitor said, his tone calm and steady. "Good doctors who were arrested for no reason other than the fact that they are Jewish. If any of us need a doctor, it should be fairly easy to find one."

"Doctors are expensive," Mila said, worry creasing her forehead.

"And if Miriam's family gets sick too… it's my fault. We'll have to help them pay, but money is so tight. We spend everything we get on food from the black market. How will we ever find the money to pay for a doctor?"

"Don't worry. I have been putting money away for a while now. So, I have a little bit for emergencies. If we need it, it's there."

"You do realize that this is my fault? I could have stayed home with Jakup and not tried to do anything else. We would all be safe then. Jakup would be safe."

"We don't know that for certain," Pitor said firmly. "Miriam, her husband, and their children are always going outside. The girls go to school. Miriam goes to the market, and Hymie, well, Hymie spends his time at the tavern. All of them are in contact with other people all the time. So, any one of them could easily bring some illness into the apartment. Even me—I am working at a butcher shop where I am in contact with people all day long. I could unknowingly bring home a disease."

Mila looked away. "I realize all of that, but it wasn't you or Miriam or her family that put us all in jeopardy. It was me and my selfish foolishness,"

"All I know is that you can't blame yourself. You have been doing a wonderful job teaching all those children. Because of you, they will know how to read, add, and subtract. When this war is over, they will be able to find work because of all that you've taught them. So, please stop berating yourself. You are not guilty of any crime, my love. I know you never meant for this to happen."

Pitor always had a way of calming her when she was upset. Somehow, he always knew the right things to say.

They were both quiet for a while as they sat outside holding hands. Then she turned to him and asked in a very serious voice, "Pitor, do you think this will ever end? Do you think that we'll ever get out of here?"

"I hope so, and if I am to keep my sanity, I must force myself to believe that we will be released from this place soon. I want to go home so badly. I want to take you and Jakup back to the safety and peace of our little house. I long to go back to work at my own shop. But, unfortunately, I can't right now. So, each morning, when I get out of bed, I remind myself that I'm lucky to have a job. At least we are able to get a little bit of meat or some bones for soup, occasionally. Most people don't have any way to get their hands on extra food other than the black market. It's very expensive, so very few can afford it."

She nodded, a faint smile forming. "You're right. You usually are," she said. He leaned over and kissed her. Then she said, "I'm grateful for the extra meat you bring home. I truly am. When I look at you and Jakup, I worry because you're both so thin."

"I know. You are skinny, too. We are all undernourished because the rations are so low, but it would be worse if we couldn't get our hands on that little bit of extra meat."

Again, they were quiet, holding hands, each lost in their own thoughts. Then Mila asked, "I don't know how to ask you this."

"You can ask me anything," he said, squeezing her hand gently. "What is it?"

"It's not about the typhoid epidemic."

"That's good because there is no point in discussing that any further. We just have to pray that no one in our apartment is affected."

"Yes. I agree with you."

"So, what did you want to ask me, love?"

"Well," her face was hot, and she knew she was blushing. But Pitor was her husband, and she felt they should be able to talk about anything. "As you know, it's very difficult for you and me to act as man and wife. Making love has become such a luxury," she cleared her throat, then went on. "I know it's because Jakup shares our room. So, I had an idea. I was thinking about asking Miriam if she could watch Jakup for a couple of hours several evenings each week so you and I could be alone together. In exchange, I would offer to watch her two girls if she and Hymie needed some time alone too."

"I think that's a wonderful idea. I certainly have missed making love to you," he said, smiling, and Mila felt confident that everything was going to be alright.

"I'll ask her tonight." She smiled, reassured, then hesitated again. "Do you think I need to tell her about the typhoid at the school? It seems only fair that she should know."

"I don't think you should," Pitor said, shaking his head. "There's no reason to alarm her. If someone in the apartment comes down with this disease, we will deal with it then. But for now, I don't think there is any reason to worry her."

Mila nodded.

CHAPTER FORTY-SEVEN

Miriam was more than happy to watch Jakup for a few hours every other night. In exchange, Mila agreed to look after Lena and Anne on the nights that Miriam and Hymie wanted to be alone.

That night, Hymie was not home as usual, but Miriam and her two daughters played with Jakup while Pitor and Mila slipped into their bedroom. As soon as they were alone, Pitor pulled Mila to him and kissed her with so much passion that her knees buckled. Then he picked her up and laid her gently on the bed. Pitor lay down beside his wife and kissed her cheeks and her forehead and then her lips again. He was so filled with passion that he could hardly contain himself when they made love. It was wild and passionate, but it was over quickly. Embarrassed, Pitor looked away, ashamed.

"I'm so sorry," he murmured, looking down at the ground.

"It's all right," Mila said. "Lie beside me for a while, and then we will try again."

He did as she asked, and they lay on the bed side by side. Mila played with the hair on Pitor's stomach that led down to his manhood, but she didn't touch him. She hoped he would be able to make love again soon. They lay together in each other's arms and declared their love for one another. Pitor reached over to kiss Mila gently on the lips. Then they talked about silly things they had both encountered in this crazy place where they had been forced to live. Pitor told her about some of the customers who came into the butcher shop. "Would you believe that we have Nazis who come in all the time with giant carcasses of animals they've hunted?"

"You have to butcher whole cows?'

"Sometimes they are cows, but often, they are other animals, like wild pigs."

"If the orthodox Jews knew you were butchering pigs, they would never set foot in your shop."

"It doesn't matter. They've never come to shop, and I've survived without their business."

"Yes, you have. And you've done well, even here in this ghetto. That's something to be admired."

Pitor smiled. He had never revealed to her what it was like for him at his job, but now he began to tell her everything. Pitor explained how desperate everyone was to buy bits and pieces of meat that they struggled to afford. He told her how people tried to bargain with the owner of the butcher shop by trading expensive jewelry and treasured housewares for a small, scrawny chicken.

"I should tell you," he added, lowering his voice, "I have sometimes stolen meat from the shop and sold it on the black market. This is how I got the extra money to put away for emergencies."

Mila took his hand. "I understand completely. I know that your heart is pure, and if you have to steal, then I stand behind you. We are all doing what we have to do to survive."

He hugged her. "You are my greatest gift from God. I didn't believe in God, or if I did, I didn't believe he loved me, that is until he gave you to me. You are the love of my life. And if I could, I would indulge your every whim. If we were free, I would work as many hours as I could to buy you jewels and furs. It makes me happy to give you what you want, but right now, I am powerless. However, one day, I hope to be able to fulfill all of your wishes."

He kissed her softly. Then he took the blanket off of her to reveal her naked body and slowly planted soft kisses all over her face and neck. "You are so beautiful," he said as he looked her up and down as if he was seeing her beauty for the first time, even though he'd seen it a thousand times before. Slowly, savoring every single moment, he kissed her entire body until, like a rose in full bloom, she opened to him, and they made love again. The second time was much more satisfying than the first.

Two hours passed quickly. During that time, Pitor had fallen asleep, and Mila wished she could get some sleep too. She was calm and at peace, so she hated to get up and get dressed. She wished she could spend the evening in bed with Pitor, but that wouldn't be fair to Miriam. Mila slid up so she was high enough to kiss Pitor. He awakened and held her close to him. A sigh escaped her lips as she forced herself to rise and get out of bed. Mila smiled at Pitor as she slipped her dress over her head. "I love you," he said.

"I know, and I love you too."

Later that evening, Mila watched over Miriam's two daughters while Miriam and Hymie disappeared into their bedroom. Both Lena and Anna were curious about what their parents might be doing in the bedroom and why they could not go in. Anna asked Mila what was going on. "Why are our parents alone in the bedroom? And why can't we go in?"

"Your parents need some time to talk alone. So, we are giving them a little break," Mila replied, then she did her best to distract them. But the apartment was so small that privacy was almost impossible. Occasionally, Mila heard Miriam moan, and she knew that Lena and Anna had heard it, too, but she was glad that neither of the girls asked any more questions.

Mila hoped they could continue this new arrangement. It was so much better than before. Having a little time alone gave Mila and

Pitor something to look forward to. So, Mila and Pitor were grateful that they got along well with Miriam and her husband. Sometimes, the two women would put some of their rations together and make a big pot of soup for both families. Living like this was not ideal, but they made the best of it.

Several days passed after the school closed, and Mila was relieved that no one in their apartment showed signs of typhoid. The following week, the school reopened. Reluctantly, but with Pitor's support, Mila agreed to return to work. "The children in that school need you," he told her. "When this is all over—and someday, it *will* be over—they will all need to be able to read and write and to do simple arithmetic too in order to survive in the world. So, my love, I believe your work at the school is a *mitzvah*."

Mila took her husband's hand and squeezed it. "Do you think I should return to the school, even with the risk of disease?"

"Well, I don't believe it will make any difference if you are working at the school or not. The disease is here in the ghetto. We can only hope that we are spared. But as for the work itself, it's up to you. You don't have to go back if you don't want to. But like I've said before, I think your work at the school is very important. The Nazis will not be able to remain in power forever, and not only that, but they won't be able to control the Jews forever. You'll see, someday we will be free again. And when that happens, the children who were forced to live in this ghetto will be behind in their education. That is unless someone takes the time to teach them what they need to learn."

Mila raised Pitor's hand to her lips, kissing it softly. "You always know what to say to make me feel better. And I must tell you that I agree with you. These children have been forced out of their homes and their schools. I am glad to be of use to them. I know you say that they need me, but strangely, I have found that I need them too. Teaching has made living in this ghetto a little more tolerable. That's because it has given me a purpose."

"You are wonderful with children," Pitor said with a smile.

"Thank you, Pitor, for your understanding and encouragement."

At that moment, she decided she had to return to her teaching job at the school, regardless of the risks.

Up until now, Lena and Anna had been attending another school. But Miriam really liked Mila, and so she decided to send her daughters to the same school where Mila worked. Miriam felt it was easier and safer for her two girls to walk with Mila and Jakup to the makeshift school each morning. When they first started school, it was difficult to find space, so when one of the rabbis suggested a room in the synagogue, the teachers agreed eagerly. It was set up in a large room, which wasn't a very long walk from Mila's apartment, and Mila had to admit that she enjoyed her job. She found it rewarding to teach children to read and write. They were so curious about the world that each time the children read a book, they were full of questions. Mila also made friends with the mothers of her students. Sometimes, after school was over for the day, they would offer to take her out for a cup of coffee, and if Jakup wasn't too tired, she went. It was good to have friends to talk to, and it was also good to be busy, which allowed her to push aside the constant worry of typhoid, if only for a while.

But one afternoon, Anna came down with a fever. Anna kept quiet about not feeling well, so Mila had no idea that the child was sick until that evening when Anna could not eat anything for dinner.

When Mila asked Miriam why Anna was not at the table with the rest of them, Miriam replied, "I felt her forehead," Miriam said anxiously. "She's burning up. I am very worried because I'm pretty sure she's running a fever. I don't know what's wrong with her, and when I ask her, she says she's fine. As you know, both of my girls have always had healthy appetites, but tonight, Anna says she's not hungry. This is just not like her."

"Can I go into the bedroom to see her?" Mila asked.

Miriam hesitated. "I don't know if you should. Whatever she has could be contagious, and we certainly don't want to spread it to everyone in this apartment."

"No, we don't. But the rooms are so small, and this apartment is so cramped, I don't know how we can avoid it. I have to be honest with you. I really don't think that my going into the bedroom and speaking with Anna will make any difference. If this disease is going to spread, then it will spread," Mila said.

Miriam nodded, defeated. "You're right. Go on in. She's in bed."

Lena had been quiet until now, but when Mila observed her, she thought Lena looked distraught. Before she went into the bedroom to speak with Anna, she walked over to Lena, stood behind her, and massaged her shoulders. "You're worried about your sister. I know," Mila said in a soft, kind voice.

Lena nodded, her voice cracked as she asked, "Is Anna going to die?"

Mila took a deep breath. "I certainly hope not."

"I overheard my parents talking. From what they were saying, they don't have money for a doctor, and without a doctor, it's very possible that Anna will die," Lena said. She was trying to sound very adult, but when she finished her sentence, she began to cry. "I love my sister. She's my best friend. She's been my best friend my entire life. I can't go on living without her."

"Shh, don't cry. Nobody here is talking about death. Maybe it's something she ate. Let me go into the bedroom and talk to her. When I come out, I'll tell you what she says. Don't cry, I'll be right back."

Mila entered the bedroom. The little girl looked very small, lying in the middle of the bed all alone. "Hello, Annie," Mila said in a soft, comforting voice. Anna's family, as well as Mila and her family, often affectionately called Anna 'Annie.' "You didn't eat, and you're lying in bed. Everyone is very concerned about you. Will you tell me, please, what's wrong?"

"I don't feel good. I don't know what's wrong, but I'm very afraid."

"What hurts, sweetheart?"

"My stomach hurts, and I have a terrible headache. Earlier today, I had diarrhea. Do you know what's wrong with me?"

"I don't, sweet girl," Mila said, but she was pretty sure that Annie had typhoid. Mila trembled as she put her hand on the child's forehead. It was very hot. "I'm going to go and talk to your mother. I'll check on you again later, but before I go, would you like me to bring you a bowl of soup. We can use a couple of my books to create a table for you so you can eat in bed."

"That's very kind, but... I'm not hungry."

"It's all right. Just let me know if you change your mind." Mila gave her hand a gentle squeeze and stepped out of the room.

Miriam was standing just outside the bedroom door. She was nervously waiting to speak to Mila. Everyone who lived in the ghetto knew that there was a typhoid epidemic, and everyone, including Mila and Miriam, knew the symptoms.

Mila walked out of the bedroom and found Miriam wringing her hands on the skirt of her old housedress. Her eyes were red from crying when she asked Mila, "It's typhoid, isn't it?"

"I'm not sure, but I hope not. But you should send for a doctor. I will go to his office for you if you want," Mila offered.

"There's no money for a doctor, and they are so busy that I doubt any of them will come to our apartment and treat Anna without payment. Everyone is hungry, and everyone needs money," Miriam said, her face lined with exhaustion. She looked like she had aged ten years since the morning.

Mila didn't say anything else. There was nothing more to say. She knew Miriam was right. In the ghetto, everyone was just trying to survive as best they could. Mila didn't mention the doctor again, but that night, when she went into the bedroom to ask Anna if she needed anything, Anna looked horrible. She was obviously getting worse.

When Pitor returned home from work, Mila was waiting. He had not even taken off his coat when Mila whispered, "Can we go outside in the courtyard? I need to speak to you in private."

"Of course. Where is Jakup?" he asked.

"Taking a nap before we have dinner. I let Miriam, Lena, and Hymie eat their dinner, and we waited for you to get home."

"Alright, just give me a minute to freshen up, and we'll go."

When Pitor returned from the bathroom, his face and hands were scrubbed clean. His hair was damp and combed back neatly away from his face. He had already removed his blood-stained butcher's apron and donned a clean white shirt.

"Are you ready?" Mila asked.

He looked at her, puzzled, but nodded.

"Miriam, can you look after Jakup for a few minutes? He's asleep, but if he wakes up, tell him that his father and I will be right back. We need to go outside for a bit."

"Sure, but please don't be too long. I want to check on Anna before dinner."

Pitor followed Mila out of the apartment, down the stairs, and into the courtyard, where they sat side by side on a bench. Pitor took Mila's hand and held it in his. "What's wrong?" he asked her.

"It looks like Annie has come down with typhoid. I'm afraid that either Jakup or I are carriers and brought it home from the school."

"Anything is possible, but it's highly unlikely. She could have caught it anywhere, even from another child at school. The disease is spreading through the ghetto like wildfire."

"I know, but I can't help blaming myself."

"We've talked about this before, love. You can't blame yourself for everything. This was out of your control." He hesitated for a moment, then asked, "Do you still believe in God?"

"Yes, I do, Pitor"

"Then pray."

"I do, I pray all the time. And I will continue to pray. But right now, Annie needs a doctor, and her parents don't have the money to pay for a doctor."

"That's a shame. I'm sorry to hear it. But if you're asking me for money to give to Annie's parents to pay for a doctor, I have to say no.

I must hold on to this money in case we need it. Our family has to come first."

"But Pitor, have a heart—a little girl is sick. She might die. How can we ignore that when we have enough money to pay for a doctor?"

"Mila, your gentle, generous heart is one of the things I love about you. As you know, there are a million things that I love about you. And I would love to help Anna, but we are living in terrible conditions. Our resources are low, and I must hold on to our money in case you or Jakup need anything."

"So you're saying no?"

"My love, I have to say no. I don't like it, and I would love to help the child. But I have to be strong enough to protect my family. I must put you and Jakup first. I hope you didn't tell Miriam about the money we've saved. I don't want her to beg me, and I don't want her and Hymie to resent us."

"I didn't tell her. I didn't know what you would say, so I kept quiet. But, Pitor, I feel so bad about Annie."

"Believe me, so do I. But not bad enough to put those that I love at risk. I'm sorry, Mila, but we have to hold on to the money we have just in case we need it."

Pitor had always been generous. When they lived in the Jewish sector of the little village where he ran his butcher shop, he did what he could to help the less fortunate. Sometimes, if he had any leftover pieces of meat, he gave them to the needy. This was an unusual thing for a butcher to do because meat or chicken were very hard to come by. Therefore, any meat was considered a luxury. But Pitor had always had a big heart, and he tried to help everyone he could. So, hoarding this money was a side of him that Mila had never seen before. Not that he was cruel or that he didn't care about the child who was suffering. Mila was sure he did. Pitor was thinking of the future and trying to protect his loved ones.

Mila thought of Jakup. In her mind's eye, she saw her little boy smile. Then she realized Pitor was right. *What if Jakup got sick, and they had no money left to pay a doctor? What then? Jakup is the most important thing in our lives, and we need to hold on to the money just in case.*

Meanwhile, over the next couple of days, Annie seemed to fade away. Somehow, every time Mila went into the bedroom, Anna appeared to grow smaller, almost lost in the large bed. Though Annie was very sick and feverish, she did not complain. Every hour, either Mila or Miriam checked on Annie. They both wanted Annie to eat, but most of the time, Annie was asleep.

It was no surprise when Miriam turned over in bed one morning and found Annie had passed away during the night. Annie's life had barely started, but it was cut short in an instant. Miriam told Mila that she and her husband had no money for a funeral. Mila wept, but she did not offer any of the money that she and Pitor had saved. So, Annie was buried in a Pauper's grave.

Lena changed after Annie died. Lena had been very close to her sister, and now she found herself alone. She had always been a good girl doing whatever her parents asked of her, but now she was different. Lena was angry and rebellious, and she was reckless, willing to risk her life to punish those who she felt were responsible for her devastating loss. She blamed the Nazis. She blamed the filthy ghetto, but most of all, she blamed her parents for not having enough money to summon a doctor. Lena began to dress provocatively and stay out all night. Hymie tried to stop her, but she wouldn't listen, and even when he started beating her, she refused to be controlled. Miriam changed, too. She grew sullen. When she wasn't fighting with her husband, she was fighting with her daughter.

One afternoon, when Miriam and Hymie were arguing, he lost his temper and struck her. Then, he began to break things in the kitchen. Dishes and glasses lay shattered on the floor. Neither Hymie nor Miriam swept up the glass. Mila did it because she did not want Jakup to slip and fall or get cut by the broken glass. Mila worked all day and came home to clean up the messes that Miriam and Hymie made while they were fighting. At first, Mila felt sorry for Miriam and Hymie, but when they continued to break things and leave messes for Mila to clean up, she got angry. She was tired of cleaning up after Miriam and Hymie. But she was also furious because the things Miriam and Hymie were breaking were difficult to come by, and they didn't belong to Miriam's family. They belonged to Mila and Pitor. Since they had entered the ghetto, Pitor was very careful about what he and Mila purchased. They both agreed that they must not spend money needlessly.

CHAPTER FORTY-EIGHT

There was no point in trying to keep a butcher shop open. Pitor and his coworkers had nothing to do, and they did not earn any money because there was almost no meat available. The only rations allotted to Jewish prisoners in the ghetto were bread, cabbage, carrots, an occasional egg, and potatoes, and even these things were scarce. Each week, everyone received their ration cards. Each person was given 800 calories a day and no more, regardless of age or body size. The people who were living in the ghetto always seemed to be hungry, and the only available meat had to come through the black market. Most of the things for sale on the black market were obtained by children who were small enough to get through the fencing that surrounded the ghetto.

Although the ghetto was guarded by Jewish policemen on the inside and patrolled by Nazis and Polish police on the outside, food was so scarce that these children still took the risk, finding spots where they could slip through the fencing unnoticed. After dark, they would leave the ghetto and go into the streets of Warsaw, where they had connections and were often able to purchase overpriced food. The children knew the sellers raised their prices for Jewish customers and that they were taking advantage of the terrible situation these children were in. Still, they needed the food, so they paid, knowing their survival depended on it.

Pitor despised the Nazis and the Polish police who collaborated with them, but if anything, he hated the Jewish Council the most. He couldn't understand how the Jewish policemen could turn on their own people just to save their own lives. There was something sinister going on. Pitor knew it when he saw Anshel outside, sending people to board a train bound for an unknown destination. There had been whispers that those who agreed to get on the train were sent to their death. But no one, not even the Judenrat officers, knew for sure where the trains were headed. *Anshel is a real big shot here. He walks around with that clipboard, writing names and pretending to care about the people. I can see that he doesn't care. He thinks that if he collaborates with the Nazis, he will be spared in the end. But I don't believe it. I think that once they no longer need these Judenrats, the Nazis will murder all of them.*

Pitor had never been the kind of man to wait quietly and hope for change. He got up early one morning and turned over in bed to look at his wife, the woman he loved more than life itself. Then he glanced over at Jakup, his son, his little boy who lay sucking his thumb, sleeping quietly, and Pitor felt a pain in his chest. *I'll be damned if I'll let them starve. I won't do it. If it kills me, I'll find a way to get the food they need.*

Pitor knew how the black market worked; it was no secret. Everyone in the ghetto knew who left in the dead of night, risking their lives by finding holes in the walls or in the barbed wire. It drove Pitor crazy to know that children were risking their lives on his behalf. He had always been self-sufficient, and so for the next several nights, Pitor went out and stayed in the shadows where he would not be seen as he followed the children. He discovered how and where the fencing was broken, allowing the children to get in and out of the ghetto. Though far larger than the children, Pitor was determined. He cut his hand on barbed wire as he pulled the fencing apart, creating a wider opening. Then Pitor pushed himself through. As he crawled through the broken fence, he tore his pants leg and then cut his calf on a sharp wire. Now, both his hand and his leg were bleeding. He was afraid that the blood would leave a trail and the Nazis would find him. He wanted to tear off part of his shirt to tie around his leg to stop the bleeding, but there was no time to waste. He had to follow the children to see where they made their connections to the black market. Once he knew who they bought their food from, he could buy from them, too.

Most of the children's faces were familiar to Pitor; he had seen them at the market or in the park. Though some of them were very young, they were a scruffy and rugged lot. They were careful as they watched for the guard in the overhead tower. One wrong move, one mistake, and their young lives would be over. Pitor had once been a child of questionable character, and he knew how tough these boys were as he watched them slip through the shadows as they made their way to an abandoned building that had been destroyed by the bombings. *So, this is where they meet with their sellers.* Pitor had followed them, but not too closely. Just close enough to see where they went and what they brought back to the ghetto with them. He couldn't always see what they had purchased because most of them tucked the food into their clothes before reentering the ghetto. But at least he knew that the next time he left the ghetto, he knew where to go.

The following night, despite the risks, Pitor left the ghetto and went straight to the abandoned building to meet with those who were selling to the children on the black market. At first, the people who were selling to the children were wary of Pitor. He was an adult, and he had blond hair and blue eyes. He could have easily been a spy for the Nazis, but when he told the men who were selling the black market food that he was a Jew who was going to be buying and selling on the black market, one of the sellers agreed to sell to him. There was no doubt about it. The food was overpriced, but he dared not argue or try to negotiate. If he did, he was afraid they would refuse to sell to him. So, without complaining about anything, Pitor bought a chicken and some carrots to take back with him.

Mila was awake when he got back to the apartment. He could see that she was angry. She'd been angry the night before when he'd come home bleeding from his hands and his leg. But until he was sure he could buy on the black market, he didn't admit to leaving the ghetto. Now that he knew where to go and how to buy, he planned to tell Mila everything.

"Where were you? I've been worried about you all night," Mila said. Pitor looked at her, and his heart swelled with love. Even with her hair disheveled and even in a dirty nightgown, she was very beautiful.

"Look what I brought home for us," Pitor said cheerfully. He was hoping Mila would forget how worried she'd been when she saw the chicken.

"Pitor, please don't tell me that you went outside the ghetto," Mila said, her voice trembling. "Do you have any idea what they will do to you if they catch you leaving? Yes, the extra food is nice, and yes, we are hungry, and you're right, we would love some meat, but I don't want to risk losing you. A chicken isn't worth a lifetime without you. I couldn't bear it." She began to cry. "I couldn't go on living if something happened to you. Please, Pitor, I am begging you not to leave the ghetto again. Don't break their rules and give them any reason to hurt you." She moved closer, wrapping her arms around him tightly. He could feel her tears on his chest where his shirt was open.

"I'm sorry I scared you. I didn't mean to. I just want you and Jakup to be healthy. And for that, you need food. You need decent food, not just potatoes and bread. You need vegetables and meat."

"Pitor, I don't care about the food," she replied. "All I care about is keeping our family together and keeping us safe until we can get out of here. Please, I'm begging you to promise me that you won't go out into the city again. Please."

"My darling, my love," he whispered as a lock of her hair fell into her eyes. Gently, as if the strands were made of gold, he placed the hair behind her ear. Then, in a soft voice, he said, "I will do whatever you want. If you don't want me to go, I promise you I won't. We'll do our best to live on the rations they give us."

Mila frowned at him.

In a firm and logical voice, Pitor went on, "Now, if this is what you want, then that's what we'll do. But please consider the consequences. The Nazis give us such small rations that it's almost impossible to live on what they give us. Mila, you are so thin that sometimes it scares me. You need meat and bread."

"I'm fine," she insisted softly.

"What about Jakup? If you don't care about yourself, then what about our son? He is still growing, and he needs good food so his bones and muscles can develop properly. I am his father, and it is my responsibility to provide these things for him. Now, believe me, I promise you I was careful when I left the ghetto, and if you will allow me to continue to leave the ghetto and buy food, I will always be extremely careful. Please, Mila, if not for your sake, then for Jakup's, let me take care of this."

Mila looked into Pitor's eyes and took a deep breath. "You are the best husband and father. I don't want you to do this because I love you too much, but I understand why you feel you must. Jakup is only a child, and he needs our protection," she sighed, shaking her head in defeat. She could not argue with him. He was only doing what was best for their son. "Do what you must, then," Mila said as she put her arms around her husband again and squeezed him even tighter. He put his arms around her and held her. For several moments, neither of them spoke. Then, in a voice barely above a whisper, she said, "Please, please, please, Pitor, be careful."

A few nights later, Pitor returned to the break in the wire fencing he'd found by following the children. The wire had been cut, and it was very sharp, which made it dangerous to go through the small break, but he was determined. After crawling out of the ghetto walls, he continued on his belly until he came to a building. Then he hid in the shadows. Once he felt certain that he was not being watched, he stood up and quickly made his way to the place where he'd met with the Polish food sellers he'd met with a few nights before. It was a dark, moonless night, but Pitor didn't mind the darkness; he found it easier to hide. As he walked through the empty streets, his thoughts turned to Mila and Jakup. *What if I took them with me? What if we escaped the ghetto and tried to blend in with non-Jews in Warsaw? I would like to try, but I can't trust Jakup to be quiet, and if he makes even the slightest noise, the guards could overhear him, and they would think nothing of shooting my entire family.* Pitor forced the thought away. As much as he wanted freedom for himself and his family, his love for them would not allow him to take the risk.

And so, even though he left the confines of the ghetto each night and was free to wander Warsaw as long as he did not get caught, Pitor knew he was still a prisoner. Each morning, he would return to the ghetto, bound by his love for those waiting inside. But still, every night, he searched his mind for ways that he might get his family out safely.

CHAPTER FORTY-NINE

1941

Once Pitor found a way to feed his family, he left the ghetto at least twice a week to buy food on the black market. This should have been enough for him; he was providing the extras that his family needed to live. But he couldn't watch the children who were taking the same risks without feeling sorry for them. They were so young, and they were in constant danger as they slipped through the shadows. So, Pitor spent a week setting up a safer network for them—a way that they could work as a team instead of independently. This was not only better for them, but it was also better for Pitor.

Once Pitor set up the network, which only operated at night, he decided he needed to do something during the day to bring in extra money so he could afford to buy food on the black market. There wasn't a lot of work available in the ghetto, but Pitor got up early one morning and went out looking for a job. He was confident that if he and his family proved to be useful to the Germans, they would be allowed to stay in the ghetto. So, he searched the factories that the Nazis had set up in the ghetto and finally found work at one of the factories that produced ammunition. This job was dangerous. He worked on a machine that had to be monitored every second, but Pitor was smart and careful. He knew the nature of his work, and even though he was often tired from leaving the ghetto at night, he was always alert. Mila tried to convince Pitor to look for something less dangerous, but he told her that his job was a godsend. It gave them the extra money they needed. What he didn't tell Mila was that working at an ammunition factory allowed him to steal a few bullets and also to leave the ghetto occasionally to work at one of the outside factories for a day.

Pitor was busy making connections with people who could sell him guns and ammunition if he ever needed them. On his way home from work one evening when the factory had closed early, Pitor saw a notice in the center of town. When he read it, he felt a shiver go down his spine. It was written in both German and Yiddish, and because it was written in Yiddish, Pitor knew it was posted by the Judenrat. It stated that the ghetto was overcrowded, and it was causing disease to spread uncontrollably. In order to deal with this problem, the Jews were going to be deported to work camps in the east. The notice promised that they would be given more food rations and better living conditions, but Pitor knew better. He didn't trust the Judenrat at all. He never did.

Being part of a group of slave laborers who were doing work that helped the German war effort, Pitor assumed he would be exempt from being forced to board one of the transports. He decided Mila must also work and make herself useful to the Nazis. Since Pitor had made several connections, he began to try to obtain a work card for her.

Mila's friend Ava had a child who was a year younger than Jakup, and Pitor was sure that if they paid her, Ava would watch Jakup if Mila could find work at one of the factories.

CHAPTER FIFTY

SS Main Office, Warsaw

1942

Horst Ackermann was miserable as he sat at his desk smoking a cigarette. He had just left his superior officer, *Obersturmführer* Weaver, who had made it clear to him that he was not happy with Horst's performance lately. "You have been very lax, Ackermann," his superior officer had snapped. Weaver's eyes bore into him. "You should know that *Reichsführer* Himmler has decided that we are just not producing Aryan children fast enough. He would like us to go into the Polish neighborhoods to find and take children who look Aryan. We need more blond-haired, blue-eyed children, and so far, you haven't brought us one child. You aren't even married. You should be married already and have a brood of Aryan children at home. I believe you are over thirty, aren't you?"

"Yes. I'm thirty-one," Horst answered quietly.

"Well, Ackermann, you have failed us miserably. You owe it to your country to find a wife as soon as possible. And while you are looking for your wife, I suggest you start searching the Polish neighborhoods for children who would fit our expectations. When you find them, take them to one of the Lebensborn homes. They will know what to do with them."

"With all due respect, *Obersturmführer*, I have been to the Lebensborn home, and I have spread my seed with several of the women there. I was hoping that would be enough."

"It isn't enough. I know you go to the Lebensborn home often, and I'm sure it's an enjoyable task," Weaver snickered, "but it's not enough. Germany needs more children. We have been forced to start Germanizing Polish children. I personally don't like it because they are not true Aryans, but it seems that we need as many as we can get. Therefore, after work each evening, you are to go into Warsaw to find and take children who are blond and blue-eyed. Not such a difficult task, but you have known about this for almost a month, and so far, you have ignored Himmler's request. Ackermann, you have failed. You have not brought us even one child," the *Obersturmführer* said. "Perhaps you would rather be a guard in the Warsaw Ghetto than move up the ranks? For a while, I thought you were on your way to promotion. You seemed so promising, but maybe I was wrong about you. Perhaps you don't deserve a promotion. Perhaps you would rather spend your days with filthy lice-ridden Jews and risk catching typhoid? What do you think?"

Horst could feel his heart pounding in his chest. It was beating so hard that he felt sick to his stomach. He wanted to say something that would put him back into Weaver's good graces, but the *Obersturm-führer* did not give him a chance to speak. "You are walking a real tightrope here, Ackermann. As a friend, I am telling you that you should take a walk through the ghetto on your way home tonight. Just so you can see how good you have it right now. Have you ever been there? I don't think so."

Horst wanted to lie to him, but it was hopeless. *Obersturm-führer* Weaver seemed to have a sixth sense when it came to the men who were in his charge. He kept a close watch over them. He knew what they did on their days off, and Horst was sure that

Weaver would know if he was lying. "I have not been there," Horst admitted.

"Then make it your business to take a walk through the ghetto on your way home today. I have a feeling that once you see the possibilities of being forced to work in that hell, it will motivate you to try a little harder to do your job as you have been commanded." Obersturmführer Weaver lit a cigarette, then he said, "That's all. You can go now. Make sure you take a walk through the ghetto on your way home. And while you're there, try not to catch typhoid." He laughed a little and raised his hand. "Heil Hitler."

Horst returned the salute, his stomach churning as he left Weaver's office. He went back to his own office and sat down. Then he lit a cigarette, took a bottle of whiskey out of his desk drawer, and took a swig. It calmed his nerves a little. He didn't want to walk through the ghetto. In fact, he wanted nothing to do with the Jews. *They are so dirty, and they carry disease. But I must follow orders because if Weaver should find out that I didn't do what he told me to do, he would make my life a living hell. So, I'll walk through that place as fast as I can and get it over with. Tomorrow, I'll see if I can find a blond-haired, blue-eyed child in Warsaw.* He thought as he put out the cigarette, then slipped on his coat and left the building.

Until now, Horst had purposely avoided the Jewish ghetto. He had always been terrified of disease. Even as a child, he ran away from other children who had runny noses or were coughing. Since he had been transferred from Berlin to Warsaw, he had heard the other officers he worked with talking about the filth and disease in the ghetto. So, he'd avoided it. But now, under Weaver's watchful eye, he knew he had no choice. Tonight, he would walk through the ghetto.

CHAPTER FIFTY-ONE

September 1942

Without warning, the deportations of the Jews in the ghetto suddenly stopped. Mila and Pitor hoped they were over for good. Through the front window of her apartment, Mila could see Anshel walking through the ghetto streets and greeting people like he was some sort of politician. However, one afternoon, when Mila asked him if the deportations were over, he could not give her an answer. Pitor was skeptical. He didn't trust the Judenrat, especially Anshel, who he knew had a personal vendetta towards him and Mila. When he told Mila how he felt, she didn't want to believe it. "Anshel was jealous at first, but I am sure he's over it by now. From what I know of him, he's happily married with several children."

"I still don't trust him, or any of the Judenrat for that matter," Pitor said grimly. "Something is going on here, but I don't know what it is."

Mila just shrugged, trying to stay as calm as possible. She didn't want to think about any additional dangers that might be looming in their future. Instead, she told Pitor that since the deportations had begun, the ghetto had grown less crowded. He just nodded, but Mila knew he was still skeptical.

A week later, Pitor's intuition about Anshel proved to be correct. When he and Mila, with Jakup in her arms, lined up to collect their ration cards from the Judenrat, Anshel claimed they had already collected their cards. Mila insisted that this was not the case. "Then they must have been lost. I'm sorry, Mila," Anshel said in a condescending tone that made Pitor's blood boil.

"You lousy, good-for-nothing snake," Pitor growled in a low, threatening voice. "I could break your skinny little neck for this."

"No, Pitor," Mila whispered urgently, her grip tightening on his arm. "The guards are right outside. If you hit him, they will shoot you. Please don't. Please, think of me and Jakup."

Pitor reached across the table and grabbed Anshel by his shirt collar. "I am going to kill you one day," he said. Jakup, sensing the tension, began to cry. Pitor glared at Anshel, then he let Anshel's shirt collar drop from his hands, and he took Mila's hand, and they left.

"Don't worry," Pitor said to Mila, "I can buy us food on the black market to help us get through until next week."

IT WAS GETTING COLDER OUTSIDE every day, and Mila had still not been able to find work. So, each afternoon before Pitor got home from work, she took Jakup outside for a little while. The air in the building where they lived was smelly and dust-filled. Jakup was still a child, and a child needed fresh air. Over the years, Mila became good friends with Ava, one of the other mothers who lived in the building. Ava had a precocious 3-year-old little girl. Her name was Chaya, and since she was only a year younger than Jakup, they played well together. Chaya was a beautiful child. Chaya, with her long black curls and dark eyes, looked more like Mila than Jakup, whose blond hair and blue eyes mirrored Pitor's. Mila smiled when she thought of her husband and son, and every time Mila looked at Jakup, her heart swelled with love for her family.

One afternoon, while Jakup and Chaya played in the courtyard of their building, Mila and Ava sat on the bench watching them.

"Can you keep an eye on Jakup for a minute while I go upstairs and check on the soup I am making for dinner?" Mila asked Ava.

"Of course, go ahead. I'll be right here."

Mila smiled. "I'll be very quick," she said as she got up and went inside the building.

Ava watched the children gather bunches of leaves. It made her sad to know that they were growing up in this terrible place with so much uncertainty about their future. She remembered her own childhood. Her father was a shoemaker. He earned a very modest living, and anyone who knew them would have considered her family to be poor. But Ava and her older brother Zeb never knew it. When they were very young, it seemed that there was always plenty to eat and more than enough love to go around. Especially on Friday mornings before *Shabbos* when her *bubbie* came over very early, and Ava could help make challah. Her brother was outside playing with his friends, but there was no place in the world that she would rather have been.

Her *bubbie* sang songs in Yiddish while her mother braided the dough. At night, when Ava's father returned home from work, the family gathered around the small table in the dining room. Ava's mother covered her eyes as she lit the Shabbat candles. These were Ava's most precious memories. They made her smile and then cry because she missed them so much. Both of her parents were gone now. They had suffered, and that made her feel sick. She couldn't bear to remember her father being beaten to death by a group of young Nazis or her mother's suicide that followed. Then Zeb ran away. He said he was going to find a group of resistance fighters and pay the Nazis back for all they'd taken from him. And because Ava's mother was Ava's bubbie's favorite child, Ava's bubbie lost the will to live and went to sleep one night but never woke up in the morning. The doctor said it was a heart attack, but Ava knew it was a broken heart. Ava was sure that she, too, would have died if it had not been for her daughter and her husband. She could not leave them alone to face the fate that the Nazis had in store for them. Ava knew her child would need her, so she forced herself to get out of bed each morning to eat and to smile, at least for Chaya's sake. Then, when what was left of her family was forced to leave their home and come to this terrible ghetto, Ava was glad that Chaya was only three years old and had no idea how bad things really were. She did everything in her power to protect her little girl and to soften the blow for her husband, who was devastated by his own losses.

Ava had never trusted the Judenrat. These were Jews who were chosen because of their high standing in the community. For the most part, they were wealthy and influential men, but Ava had her doubts from the beginning. They tried to convince everyone in the ghetto that they were put in place as liaisons between the Jews and the Nazis and that they were there to help the Jews to better communicate their needs. But Ava knew better. She knew the Judenrat were of no help to their fellow Jews. They had taken these jobs to help themselves, and if it meant selling their fellow Jews out to the Nazis, they would do so.

Until recently, the Judenrat had been telling their fellow Jews that it was to their benefit to board trains that would take them to specially designed work camps. Once they were working in these camps, the Judenrat assured them they would receive more food and better living quarters. Many of the Jews in the ghetto agreed to go, but when rumors spread that the transports were going somewhere more sinister than work camps, the number of people willing to go diminished. The Judenrat had a quota that the Nazis demanded that they fill. They needed a certain number of people to board the transport, so they began offering a slice of bread with jam to anyone willing to go. And because people were starving and jam was almost impossible to get, the Judenrats were filling their quotas.

Ava's husband was convinced that things would be better if the Jews had jobs where they were useful to the Germans. He told Ava this and said he wanted to volunteer to go, but no matter what her husband said, Ava didn't trust the Judenrats. And she was glad that the transport had stopped. She had more friends than her husband, and she had heard from several reliable sources that the work camps were nothing more than lies. She'd heard that the Jews who went on these transports were on their way to death camps, where they would be systematically murdered. It was difficult to believe such a thing could be true, but somehow, she felt it was. So, she told her husband that she refused to go. He was angry, and it caused a rift between them. She couldn't take such a terrible risk. It was bad enough that she might put her husband and herself in danger, but most importantly, she refused to take this risk with her little girl.

Ava felt overwhelming sadness as she thought about all the arguments she'd had with her husband since they were arrested and forced to come to the ghetto. Before they came here, they had a good marriage. There had been occasional disagreements, but they had always come to terms that were acceptable to both of them. Most importantly, they never went to bed angry. But Louis, her husband, was a different man since they had arrived here in this ghetto. A side of him she had never seen before appeared. Louis had become an angry man who often took his anger out on those he loved.

Ava closed her eyes and remembered how she had first met her husband. It was a Yom Kippur dance that took place at the synagogue after the fasting ended on the highest holiday in the Jewish calendar year. Yom Kippur was the day of atonement when Jews fasted to ask God for forgiveness for their sins. Ava was young and very pretty at the time. She had always been a vivacious girl who loved music and loved to dance. As a teen, she had won a dancing competition. So, when the opportunity arose for her to attend the Yom Kippur dance with her girlfriend, whose family were members of the synagogue, she accepted.

As she sat on the bench watching Jakup and Chaya play, Ava remembered all the excitement she had felt when she was combing her chocolate brown curls before she left for the dance. She knew she would have a wonderful time, but never in her wildest dreams had she thought that she would meet her future husband that night.

When Louis Stalsky walked up and introduced himself, and she looked into his dark eyes, she knew that something significant had just happened in her life. She didn't know what to say, so she asked him to get her a glass of punch. He had gone willingly but had tripped and fallen, spilling the punch all over the floor. The other students laughed at him. It hurt her so much to see him humiliated that she got up and went to his side. "I'll get us both some punch," she said, and she saw the gratitude in his eyes.

They talked and danced together without missing a single dance, all the way until the band played its last song. Then Louis thanked her for the lovely evening and left. She was disappointed that he hadn't asked to see her again. As she and her girlfriend walked home, Ava told her friend what happened and how disappointed she was that Louis had not asked her out. The following day, Ava couldn't get Louis out of her thoughts.

It wasn't that he was terribly handsome. In fact, he was significantly overweight with an unremarkable face, but there was just something about him that made her feel warm and safe, like a fire in the fireplace on a cold winter night. Then, to her surprise, a few evenings later, Louis came to her home. She was in the kitchen chopping vegetables when she heard someone knock on the door. Her mother was in the living room, so she opened the door. That was when Ava heard Louis's voice. She felt a tingling in her heart as he said, "Hello, my name is Louis Stalsky. I was wondering if it would be possible to speak to Ava's father."

"Of course. He just got home from work, and he is currently washing up and getting ready for dinner. If you would like to wait in the living room, he'll be coming out soon."

"I would be happy to wait," Louis said.

Ava remembered how her heart hammered in her chest as she made her way through the back of the house to her bedroom. Then she hid behind her bedroom door, where she could hear everything that was taking place in the living room.

When Ava's father entered the room, Ava heard Louis introduce himself.

"It's a pleasure to meet you, young man. Now, why are you here? What can I do for you?"

For a few moments, there was silence. Then Ava almost fainted when she heard Louis ask for her father's permission to ask Ava to marry him. She was holding her breath as Louis was telling her father that he had a nice apartment and a very good job. *Please, Papa,* she had thought. *Give him your permission and your blessing.* It seemed like forever until her father answered, and when he did, he told Louis that he could propose. Then, he gave Louis his blessing.

The following day, Louis visited again. When he knocked on the door, Ava's mother answered excitedly. She already knew about the conversation Louis and her husband had the day before.

"I would like to speak to Ava, please," he said.

"Of course, she's out in the garden," Ava's mother chirped, gesturing toward the door.

"Thank you," Louis said, smiling as he made his way outside. "Hello, Ava."

"Hello," she replied, smiling back.

"Would you like to take a walk with me?" Louis asked.

"Yes, that's a good idea. Let's take a walk," Ava said. She could feel her knees grow weak because Louis did not say anything for a while. They continued to walk, and she decided he was as shy as she was. Louis began making small talk about the music and the weather at the Yom Kippur dance. In fact, it took him almost fifteen minutes to stop walking and stand beside her, looking into her eyes. Finally, he asked her to marry him. She paused for what felt like forever, but then she looked up at him and her eyes met his. Her face broke into a big smile and the word, "Yes," came out from her lips. *Up until that moment, the day Louis proposed was the most wonderful day of my life.* And there had been so many wonderful days since, especially the day her daughter was born.

CHAPTER FIFTY-TWO

Anshel left his flat and began his walk through the ghetto to start another long day of work at the Jewish Council. He was so hungry that his stomach ached. To make matters worse, he knew there would be nothing to eat for several more days. He and his wife had run out of their ration cards for the week and had not been able to buy any food for the last two days. He'd already sent the family who roomed with his family away on a transport because the husband had a tendency to steal food from the pantry. Sometimes, because he worked as a Judenrat, one of the Nazis might toss him a scrap—a half-eaten sandwich or a stale crust of bread. Though he knew he should save whatever he received and take it home to share with his wife, he had never been able to do so. His stomach was always so empty that even the tiniest morsel of food was like a dream, and he gobbled it as soon as he was able.

Just then, Horst walked by, hands jammed into his pockets as he made his way quickly through the ghetto. He was moving as fast as he could so he would be able to tell *Obersturmführer* Weaver that he'd followed his orders and he'd gone through the ghetto on his way home. This would not satisfy the *Obersturmführer*, who wanted Horst to go into Warsaw and find him a child, but for now, it was going to have to do. As he fiddled around in his pocket, he realized he still had a bar of chocolate that he'd purchased the day before. He pulled it out and opened it, throwing the paper on the ground. His first bite was heavenly. The sweet chocolate melted in his mouth, and for a single moment, he closed his eyes and savored the delicious flavor. When he opened his eyes, he saw a young, dark-haired man staring at him. *That's definitely a Jew. Look at him; he's watching me eat. He's like a pig, almost drooling over my chocolate bar. I've heard that Jews were swine, and this one has no manners.* Disgusted, Horst sneered, "What do you want?"

"Nothing," the young man said, turning to walk away quickly.

"Wait." Horst was annoyed, and he wanted to take out his frustration on someone. *Who better than a Jew?* "Who are you?"

The young Jew stopped, frozen in his tracks. Horst could see that the young man was shaking. "My name is Anshel Minsky. I am a member of the Jewish Council."

"Ahhh, yes, the Judenrat. I see, so you're a collaborator. A friend of the Nazis. Isn't that right?'

"Yes, sir. Yes, of course," Anshel was trembling.

"Would you like a piece of my chocolate bar, Anshel Minsky, traitor to your own people?" Horst laughed at his own joke. He thought he was being quite funny.

"No, no, thank you," Anshel said. He wished he could run away but was afraid the Nazi officer would pull a gun and shoot him.

"Oh, come on, Jew. Of course you'd like a piece of chocolate," Horst was toying with Anshel, and then a thought occurred to him. *Well, perhaps he can help me.*

"Do you have any Polish friends?" Horst asked. "I mean, perhaps you are friends with some of the Poles who come into the ghetto to deliver supplies? I would assume you must have plenty of contact with the Poles who come in and out of this hell hole if you are a Judenrat."

"Yes, sir, I know many Polish people, sir," Anshel stammered, growing more anxious. "But, never mind about the chocolate. I am going to go home. I'm sorry I bothered you."

"Not so fast." Horst's voice dropped to a dangerous edge. "Don't you dare walk away when I am talking to you. Now, I need a favor. Don't be afraid of me, Jew. Just help me, and I will give you the rest of this candy."

Anshel looked down at the ground. "I don't know what I can do for you. Please, can I just go home?"

Horst ignored Anshel's request and went on, "I need to find a Polish child under ten years old. Not just any child. It must be a beautiful child with blond hair and blue eyes. Can you direct me to the home of one of the Polish vendors who you know that has such a child?"

Anshel hesitated for a moment. Then he looked at the Nazi who was dangling the chocolate bar in his face and said, "I'm sorry, I wish I could help, but I don't know of anyone."

"Liar! You are a lying Jew. Do you know what I could do to you for lying?"

"Please, just let me go," Anshel begged.

"All right, well, since I think you do know of someone, how about this... how about I sweeten the deal?" Horst laughed again. "Not with more chocolate, but with thirty pieces of silver. I'm sure you know the story of Jesus and Judas. Don't you?"

Anshel shook his head. "I'm sorry. I don't know that story, and I really can't help you. I have to go home now."

"I said, not yet," Horst growled. "Think hard, little Jew. Your very life might just depend on it. Come now, you must know some Pole who has a blond, blue-eyed child."

And suddenly, the answer came to Anshel. "I can show you a child who I believe will fill your expectations. He is right over there playing with another child. Do you see him?" Anshel pointed his finger.

Horst turned and saw the most perfect, beautiful little boy with golden curls that shone in the afternoon sun. *That little boy is exactly what I need to appease the Obersturmführer. I know the child is a Jew, but no one will ever suspect.* Smirking, Horst tossed the candy bar into the mud, laughing as Anshel picked it up. Then he said, "And about those thirty pieces of silver? I was just fibbing."

CHAPTER FIFTY-THREE

Ava was so lost in thought that she didn't notice the Nazi officer approaching from behind. But when she saw him in his black uniform, she became instantly alert and was transported out of her thoughts and back into the present moment. Fear pierced her heart like an ice pick.

"Hello," he said, smiling. He was a tall man with blond hair and thick glasses.

"Hello," she replied cautiously, her mind racing. *What does he want?*

"Who is that little boy?" the Nazi asked, studying Jakup intently. "He is surely not a Jew."

Ava didn't know how to answer. She wished Mila was there because she didn't want to say the wrong thing and possibly put Jakup in danger. She remained silent, paralyzed. She didn't know what to say, so she didn't answer the Nazi's question. He glared at her, and his face turned red with anger. "I asked you a question, you ignorant Jew. Are you too daft to answer?" he snarled. Then he walked over to Jakup. "The child is so clean. He can't be a Jew. What is he doing here? There must be some mistake. Is he or is he not a Jew?"

"He's not Jewish," she said, thinking she was protecting Jakup.

But then the Nazi picked Jakup up and began to carry him away.

"Where are you taking him?" Ava's voice shook.

But the Nazi officer didn't answer.

Ava felt her heart beating hard in her chest. She didn't know what to do. *Should I take Chaya and follow him? Or should I stay here and protect Chaya? Where is Mila? I don't know what to do, but I have to do something. In a few seconds, that Nazi will turn the corner, and Jakup will be gone, maybe forever. I can't let this Nazi take Jakup.* She mustered all of her courage, and before the Nazi got far enough away that he wouldn't hear her, she yelled, "That little boy is a Jewish child. He's my friend's son. You can't take him!"

The young Nazi officer stopped in his tracks and spun around. He yelled loud enough for anyone in the area to hear him, "Are you trying to tell me what I can and can't do? Just who do you think you are speaking to in this manner?" Still holding Jakup, he walked back over to where Ava was standing with her fists clenched at her sides. Then he slapped her across her face. Blood burst from her nose, and she stumbled, reeling from the pain. "I'm sorry. I didn't mean to offend you," she gasped. "But please, you can't take that little boy. Please."

The Nazi officer ignored Ava. Jakup, wanting to get away from the stranger, began to run away. But the Nazi caught up with him in a second and scooped him back up into his arms. Then he carried Jakup away. It looked like he was headed for the entrance to the ghetto. Ava thought she should go after him before he and Jakup left the ghetto, but she was terrified. She reached up to touch her nose, and when she looked at her hand, it was covered with blood.

Just then, Mila walked out of the building and then made her way over to Ava. She was carrying two cookies, one for Jakup and one for Chaya. As she got closer, she saw Ava's bloody face, and then she looked down at the ground where Chaya was sitting amongst the colorful autumn leaves. Mila gasped. Chaya was playing alone. "Where is Jakup?" Mila asked nervously.

Ava could hardly speak. Her face was flushed, and her hands were shaking. Mila shook her and repeated her question in a panicked voice, "Ava, where is Jakup?"

Tears rolled down Ava's face as she tried to explain what had just happened. "A Nazi came up to us, and he took Jakup. I tried to stop him, but I couldn't. I tried Mila. I really tried."

"Which way did they go?" Mila demanded, fighting to keep her composure.

"Towards the entrance." Ava's hands shook as she pressed a cloth to her nose, blood and tears mixing on her cheeks. "Mila... I am so sorry. Please forgive me. I don't know what else I could have done. He hit me hard enough to make my nose bleed. I think it might be broken."

Mila didn't have time to talk or listen to Ava. The cookies she'd brought down for the children, a treat so difficult to come by, dropped from her hand and fell on the dirty ground. She didn't pay any attention to them. Mila's heart was pounding hard as she ran as fast as she could towards the entrance to the ghetto. She cried out to her son in a loud voice, "Jakup! Jakup, where are you?"

On her way to the gate, she ran past a group of old men sitting outside a tavern. They were drunk and ragged, and they looked like they had given up on life and were just waiting to die. If she hadn't been so concerned about her son, she would have pitied them. Instead, she stopped for a moment and asked them, "Did any of you see a Nazi with a little blond-haired boy?"

The men looked at each other. Some of them shrugged, others said no.

Mila persisted. "Are you sure you didn't see them? Please, you must try very hard to remember. They would have passed here only a few minutes ago," Mila begged, hoping one of the drunken men might remember something. She could feel her skin breaking out in hives from nerves.

One man shook his head. "Didn't see anyone. Sorry, lady."

Time was of the essence. Mila gave up on the drunks standing outside the tavern and began to run towards the entrance again. By the time she made it to the gate, she was out of breath. She looked around her for Jakup but did not see any trace of him. Then, looking up, she noticed the guards in the tower, their rifles trained on her. A shiver ran down her spine as she saw they were watching her. Mila got as close as she could to the gate and looked outside the wall. A pain shot through her chest when she saw a young man in an SS uniform holding Jakup's hand as they walked down the street. Mila began to run towards the gate. She had to save her son, even if it meant that the guards above would shoot her. Mila had lost sight of all logic and reason. All she cared about was her child, and she had to find a way to get him back.

Suddenly, she felt a strong hand on her shoulder, pulling her back and holding her tightly. "Mila, stop. They are watching you up there in the tower. If you try to leave here, they will shoot you. Then you will be dead and of no use to Jakup or anyone else." It was Ava. Her eyes were red with tears. Chaya was standing beside her mother, looking frightened and bewildered.

"That Nazi has my son. My only child," Mila choked out, her voice breaking. "Please, I have to go. Let go of me!"

Ava still held tight to Mila's shoulder even though Mila was struggling with all of her might to break free. "No, you can't go through that gate," Ava said. "Listen to me, please. The guards are watching us, and they will shoot you. You know that they don't think twice when it comes to killing one of us. We are less than human to them."

"I don't care, just let go of me," Mila pleaded desperately. "I have to get to Jakup."

"If I let you go, you will be dead. You will never get out of here, and you will never get to Jakup. If you are dead, then where will Jakup be? Come with me. We will go and tell Pitor what happened. He'll know what to do."

"I can't," Mila sobbed. "If I leave here without Jakup, I may never see him again."

"I know, but if you're killed, you will never see him again anyway," Ava said firmly.

"How could you let them take my son?" Mila cried, her voice filled with anguish.

"I didn't. Believe me, I didn't. I tried. But what could I do? What could I do, Mila?"

Mila didn't answer. All the fight left her body, and she began to let out loud, wrenching sobs. Then Mila allowed herself to be turned away from the entrance. Ava picked Chaya up and held her tightly in her right arm. With her left hand, she put her arm around Mila and led her towards the factory where Pitor was working.

When they arrived, the workers had not yet been released for the day. "We'll wait here," Ava said.

"How are we ever going to find my son?" Mila murmured. "He's gone. Oh, dear God, help me."

They waited for over an hour for Pitor to be released. Ava sat on the stoop outside the factory while Mila paced. "I am so sorry," she said again and again, but Mila no longer responded. She just kept pacing, a frantic, empty look in her eyes. Finally, a large group of men came out of the factory and began walking by. When Mila saw Pitor, she ran to him. "What's wrong?" he asked. "Why are you crying? Where is Jakup?"

Mila could barely speak as she fell into her husband's arms and began to weep even harder. Her cries were like the heart-wrenching sound of an animal dying.

Pitor held her tightly, trying to calm her. Then he saw Ava standing next to Chaya, who was still sitting on the stoop. With his arm still around Mila, he led her over to Ava. "Your nose is bleeding," he said to Ava. "What's going on? What's wrong with Mila? Where is Jakup?"

Ava, who was still trembling, told Pitor everything that happened. "I'm so sorry. I tried to stop him. I should have tried harder. But how? I don't know what I could have done. Even so, it's all my fault."

Pitor shook his head. "Blame will get us nowhere. We have to find a way to get to Jakup. Can you describe the Nazi?"

She nodded and did her best to give him a description. "He was about your height with blond hair and glasses. He wore a black uniform with an SS badge on his chest." When she finished, Pitor shook his head, frustration twisting his expression. He muttered questions she couldn't answer, more to himself than to her. "Why would an SS officer come into the ghetto and take Jakup? What would he want with my son?"

But Pitor had no answers. He knew the Judenrats were fakes. They were not on the side of the Jews. Yet, they were the only people who might know where that Nazi had taken Jakup, so he told Mila to go home and wait for him there. "I am going to speak to the Judenrat," he said. "The line is long, and it will take me a while to get to the front, so you go home, and I will be there as soon as I can."

Then he got in line and waited to speak to one of the Judenrat. Mila stood beside Ava for several moments and watched Pitor. The long line was not moving.

Without consulting her husband or her friend, Mila walked to the front of the line. An older man, heavy-set and visibly weary, turned to look at her. "Where do you think you're going, young lady?" he asked irritably. "Can't you see that there is a line here? We are all waiting for the same chance to speak to a council member. If you want your turn, I suggest you go to the end of the line and wait like the rest of us."

"Please, please, just let me pass. A Nazi took my four-year-old son. I have to get there and find out where he took him."

The old man softened. "All right, I will have *rachmones*, a little pity, for you," he said. "Go ahead."

Mila ran into the building. Then she saw Anshel, who was sitting at a table, looking exhausted. "Anshel!" she called out desperately.

Anshel looked up from his desk, and when he saw Mila, he

smiled. She knew by the look on his face that he had never stopped wanting her, but the smile disappeared as fast as it came. A hardened look of cold triumph replaced it, and she knew he was reveling in his power as he remembered she had chosen Pitor over him.

"What do you want?" Anshel stared at her coldly.

Mila did her best to remain calm as she explained what had happened to Jakup.

"And what would you like for me to do about this?" Anshel's voice dripped with indifference.

"Anything you can do would be so helpful. Please, Anshel, Jakup is my son, my only child. Help me please."

Anshel leaned back, his voice laced with mockery. "Now, after all this time, you come to me for help? Did you forget that we were just weeks away from being wed when you abandoned me? How do you expect me to feel about you now that you need something from me?"

"Please don't hold that against me," Mila whispered, desperate. "I never meant to hurt you. If you won't do anything for me, at least please consider the fate of my little boy. You have children, too. How would you feel if you were in my place right now?"

"I wouldn't be in your place," he said smugly. "I was smart enough and important enough in our community to be selected for this job. That's why my children are safe. If you were my wife, your child would be safe, too. But as things stand, there's nothing I can do for you. And to be quite honest, even if I could help you, I wouldn't."

She glared at him. "You should be ashamed of yourself. You call yourself a religious man, but you are vindictive and a terrible person. I always respected you because you are a scholar, but the truth is, Anshel, you are only a scholar on paper. You read books and argue about concepts with your fellow intellectuals, but your reaction to what has happened to my son tells me that you are a fake. In your heart, you are nothing but a no-good louse. I am glad I never married you. I feel sorry for your wife. She's stuck with you, but I'm not." With that, she turned and walked out, head held high.

On her way back, she saw Pitor was still waiting in line. She hurried to him and told him what happened with Anshel.

"When I get inside, I will try to speak with one of the other Judenrat. Maybe someone who doesn't know us will be kinder than Anshel. Please go home. Wait for me there," Pitor insisted.

"Did Ava leave?"

"Yes, she had to give her husband his dinner."

Mila's face darkened. "I don't know how she could have let this happen."

"Look at her face, Mila. The Nazi broke her nose. I'm sure she tried to help Jakup, and that's why he hit her. Don't be too hard on her. She feels so guilty."

Mila shrugged. Her face was still tear-stained. "I would rather be feeling guilty right now than feeling like I have lost my son forever." Then she turned away from Pitor, and without looking back, she walked slowly towards her apartment.

When Pitor finally made it to the front of the line, he was able to speak with someone other than Anshel. He explained everything that had happened as calmly as he could to the young Judenrat.

"I'm sorry. I haven't heard of anything like this before," the young Judenrat said when Pitor finished explaining. Then he added, "Go home and wait. Perhaps he needed Jakup for something like a propaganda photo, and when he's done, he will bring the child back. You know how the Nazis are always making fake photos to show the world how good they are to us."

"Yes, I know. But what if he never brings Jakup back? Is there anything you can do to help?"

"Give it a week or so, and if he doesn't bring Jakup back, I will ask about this incident the next time we meet with the Germans," the Judenrat said.

At that point, Pitor knew the Judenrat was only trying to appease him. There was nothing this young man could do to bring Jakup back. For some inexplicable reason, this Nazi had wanted his son. The very thought of this made Pitor feel sick to his stomach. He would never tell Mila what he was thinking, but Pitor was afraid that the Nazi who had taken Jakup was a pedophile and that he was going to hurt Jakup.

The Judenrat proved to be powerless. Pitor realized that this man's job was to calm his fellow Jews down and then send them home. Pitor looked at the young Jewish Nazi collaborator and wanted to punch him in the face, but it wasn't worth the effort. Pitor knew that if he did this, he would end up in jail or, worse, he might be shot dead. How could he help Mila find their little boy?

Pitor took a deep breath and forced himself to leave the building. When he got outside, he felt a sharp pain in his chest and forced himself to sit down. The discomfort and heaviness in his chest were so painful that he couldn't walk. He sat on the ground and tried to catch his breath. Pitor waited for nearly a half-hour before the pain subsided and became a dull ache. Then, he felt calm enough to go home to Mila.

That night, Pitor spoke to his network of young people with whom he had worked on the black market. He told them everything that had happened, then he showed them a photo of Jakup and made them promise to keep a lookout for Jakup when they were in Warsaw. "And, please do whatever you have to in order to get any information about why a Nazi might have kidnaped a Jewish child. If you need to pay someone for information, pay them, and I promise I will give you your money back."

Pitor went into the city of Warsaw that night and questioned all the Polish people he had met through the black market. At first, no one had any idea what had happened to Jakup or why a Nazi might have taken him. But then one of the Polish men who was in the Polish underground said, "I don't know if what I am about to say is relevant to your situation, but I know for a fact that the Nazis have been stealing Polish children who are blond with blue eyes. Since you have blond hair and blue eyes," he gestured toward Pitor's hair, "I figured your son might have the same coloring. This could be why the Nazis took him."

"Jakup looks like me. He is blond with blue eyes," Pitor said, hope and dread mixing in his chest. He was listening closely now.

"Well, maybe the Nazi thought your boy was a Pole and not a Jew. It's possible."

"But why would a Polish child be in the ghetto? Besides, why would an SS officer want a child who was Polish or Jewish?" Pitor shook his head. "It doesn't make any sense."

"I have heard that they are Germanizing these children."

"What does that mean?"

"It means that they are taking young children and raising them to be Nazis. From what I understand, they take these youngsters and place them in homes with SS officers and their wives where they learn how to be good little Nazis."

"But you and I know that all Nazis hate Jews. They would never want a Jewish child to live with one of their SS officers."

"Perhaps the Nazi thought Jakup was someone else. He must have thought Jakup was Polish. This is the only conclusion that makes sense," the man said.

For Pitor, nothing made sense right now. He had played by their rules, and still, the Nazis had taken one of the most important things in his life. Pitor showed every one of the people he met with that night the only picture he had of Jakup. It was a few years old, he explained, and Jakup had changed so much, but Pitor begged them all to use their imaginations when they kept an eye out for his son. "I have a gold ring. It is my wedding band, and it is worth a lot of money. I will give it to anyone who can give me relevant information about the whereabouts of my son."

Pitor had done everything he could do. Weeks turned into months, and no one was able to find out anything about Pitor and Mila's son. Jakup had disappeared into thin air. Ava was burdened with guilt, so she and her husband brought Chaya with them when they came to visit Pitor and Mila at least three times every week. Ava constantly told Mila how terrible she felt. She blamed herself. "I should have done something. I should have chased that Nazi down and pulled Jakup away from him," she said as the tears ran down her cheeks. But Pitor knew that there was nothing Ava could have done. If she had tried to stop a Nazi officer from taking Jakup, he would have killed her on the spot, and probably Chaya, too.

On the nights when Pitor did not leave the ghetto to buy food on the black market, he found he had trouble sleeping. He was exhausted from his job at the factory, and yet, when he closed his eyes, all he could think of was his son. Lying in bed did no good, so Pitor would get up quietly and go into the living room. He would sit on a chair and look out the window. For the first time in a long time, he prayed silently. *Dear God, I know I have done some pretty bad things, like breaking your commandments. But I am begging you to please let Jakup be alive and well. Show me where he is and how I can bring him home.*

Mila had trouble sleeping, too. Whenever Pitor left the ghetto to go into Warsaw, she worried constantly until he returned. On the nights when he did not leave to deal with the black market, he would stay at home. They would go to bed early because they were both exhausted. But even when Mila managed to sleep, she would feel the emptiness in her bed and know that Pitor needed her beside him. So, she would get up, and without saying a word, she would walk into the kitchen, hoping she would find her husband. As she walked from her cot through the small apartment, she was terrified that Pitor would not be there. She was afraid he had done something stupid and even more dangerous than working with the black market.

But each time when she saw him sitting on a chair and looking out the window, Mila would sigh and then take a deep breath. She was relieved to see him. For now, at least, he was safe. He was at home, not roaming Warsaw. Pitor would smile a sad, tired smile when he saw her, and she would pull a chair beside him, taking his hand in silence. Pitor was always lost in thought, unable to bring himself to tell his wife what he was thinking. However, he felt that she probably had the same worries about Jakup that he did.

CHAPTER FIFTY-FOUR

January 1943

At six o'clock in the morning of January 18, 1943, the transports resumed. But now, many more of the Jews living in the Warsaw Ghetto had heard the rumors about the death camps, and they were refusing to board the trains. In response, the resistance groups in the ghetto grew stronger. Many Jewish families tried to hide, and some of the Jewish men began to fight back with the guns and arms they'd either stolen or purchased on the black market. When the Judenrat went to their homes to convince them to take the transports, they pulled out their guns and refused to board the trains. This went on for several days.

One day, while looking out the window, Mila saw Anshel walking through the street. His head was bent, but when he looked up, she saw that both of his eyes were black and blue, and there was dried blood on his face and shirt. Mila felt sorry for him despite how mean he'd been to her. Their eyes met for a moment, but Mila turned away.

After Anna's death, Miriam and Hymie were barely alive. They went through the motions of everyday living, but they never smiled or laughed. Then one morning, Miriam and Hymie told Pitor and Mila that they were going to board the next transport and they were planning to take Lena with them.

Pitor tried to discourage them. "I have heard a lot of things about these transports. I'm sure you must have heard them, too. Everyone in the ghetto has heard rumors going around that say that the Nazis are not sending the people on these transports to work camps. I've heard from very reliable sources that they are sending them to a camp somewhere in Poland and then murdering them there."

"But the men in the Jewish Council promised us we would be safe if we boarded the next transport," Hymie argued. "We are so tired of not having enough to eat."

Pitor looked at Hymie and saw how thin he and Miriam had become. The apartment would be less crowded without them, but Pitor could not let them go to their deaths. "You can't trust the Judenrat. They are only out to save themselves, so they conspire against the rest of us with the Nazis. They are worse than the Nazis because so many of the Jews trust and believe everything they tell them. Mark my words, Hymie, one day, the Nazis will turn on their Jewish collaborators, and the entire Jewish Council will be sent away to death camps."

"I have also heard this about the transports. People are saying that the trains are going to death camps and the Nazis are systematically slaughtering us. Still, I just can't believe it is true. It's just not logical. If we provide them with free labor, why would they want to kill us? For a little extra food, we are all willing to work. This saves them a lot of money. Now, don't get me wrong, I understand your point of view, and I appreciate that you care about us when you are telling us not to go. But I am sorry, I just don't believe that the transports are on the way to death camps. So, Miriam and I are taking Lena and getting on the next transport."

"Leave Lena with us. We'll take care of her," Pitor pleaded.

"Miriam and I could never leave our daughter behind. Besides, she is a growing girl. She needs more food, and if we go to a work camp, she will get more food."

Pitor shook his head. He wished he could shake some sense into Hymie, but Hymie's mind was made up. He was never going to change Hymie's mind.

"I have often wondered if Anna would still be alive if she had been given more food. Who knows, right? Miriam and I have already lost one daughter. We don't want to lose two."

A week later, Pitor and Mila stood at their apartment window and watched as hundreds of Jews stood in line to board the transport. Mila felt the hot tears prick her eyes as she watched Miriam, Lena, and Hymie climb on board. "I hope we are wrong," Mila said. "I hope they are right, and this transport is going to a work camp somewhere. It's hard to imagine that they will be murdered."

Pitor nodded. "I hope we're wrong, but I really don't think so."

Then Mila saw Anshel. He looked frightened and defeated as he and his wife, Esther, and their two young boys stepped up on the platform and boarded the train with the rest of the Judenrat.

"Look, Pitor, there is Anshel. He and his family are in line with the rest of the Judenrat to board the train. I know he never forgave me, but even so, I feel sorry for him and his family."

"He should have tried to help us find Jakup," Pitor replied.

"Yes, he should have," she agreed quietly. Then, in a voice barely above a whisper, she asked, "Do you think we will ever find Jakup?"

"I don't know, love, but I will never stop trying," Pitor said. Then he put his arm around Mila's waist and led her away from the window.

The fighting between the Nazis and the Jewish resistance continued, and by January 21, about 6000 Jews had been sent to death camps.

Once again, the deportations stopped.

CHAPTER FIFTY-FIVE

The child is perfect, Horst thought, holding Jakup's hand tightly in his own hand as he entered the Lebensborn home. He'd driven for two days with the child crying in the back seat of the automobile, making his way to Heim Hochland, which was in Steinhoring, just outside of Munich. *No one will ever suspect that this Aryan-looking boy is really a Jew. The way he looks, I am sure that the nurses here at the Lebensborn home will love him. I will receive a lot of credit for delivering him to them. He is so young and will quickly forget his family. Once Reichsführer Himmler renames him, he will be adopted by a German family. I have inadvertently given this little boy a second chance at life. He is a lucky child. He will leave all knowledge of his Jewish ancestry behind. Because his looks are so perfect, it won't be difficult for the little brown sisters to "Germanize" him; after all, that is their job.*

After Horst filled out a pile of the paperwork, he was directed to a room where two women with brown hair and brown eyes sat on a large blanket on the floor, playing a game with two blond-haired, blue-eyed boys. Horst knew that these two girls were little brown sisters. He knew that both of them had been carefully screened to be sure that they were of pure Aryan blood. Since they were not blessed with the desirable Aryan traits of blonde hair and blue eyes, they were demoted to the job of being little brown sisters. Little brown sisters could live at the Lebensborn home, but because they had the wrong genetics, they were not permitted to mate with the SS officers in order to produce children. One of the sisters saw Horst and Jakup, and she stood up to greet them.

"Heil Hitler," she said sweetly.

"Heil Hitler, *Fräulein*," Horst answered, smiling. "I've brought someone you might like to meet." Horst gestured to Jakup.

"Well, well, aren't you a handsome little fellow," the sister cooed at Jakup, who stared back at her wide-eyed.

"I filled out quite a bit of paperwork, though I am not sure if I filled out everything you will need for this child," he said.

"Oh, that's all right. I'd be glad to help you," she said. "By the way, I am Heidi, and my coworker over there sitting on the blanket is Gretchen."

"It's very nice to meet you," he said with a nod.

Heidi smiled. "Likewise, I'm sure," she said, then she took Jakup's hand and led him to the blanket, where Gretchen began showing him toys to distract him. Then Heidi said, "Come into the office with me, and we'll finish the paperwork."

A half-hour later, Horst completed the remaining forms and prepared to leave.

Horst walked out of the office, and as he did, he saw a group of pretty, athletic, blonde-haired women walking in a group. They all wore white sports clothing that showed off their toned bodies. He felt aroused as he watched them saunter by him. He thought he saw one of the girls glance at him. He was not an attractive man, but he was of pure blood. *I'm a perfect Aryan,* he thought as he winked at her. When she winked back, he decided he could spare a night away from work. He smiled to himself. This was one of the benefits of being an SS officer. He would stay here at Heim Hochland and see if he could find the girl who had winked at him. If not, he could always pick one or two of the other attractive women who were doing their patriotic duty to the Führer by producing more pure Aryan. Then, he would do his duty to his country by impregnating them with his unquestionably pure German sperm. Horst licked his lips in anticipation.

CHAPTER FIFTY-SIX

JANUARY 1943

Perhaps because Louis was an only child who'd always been overweight and clumsy, his parents had a tendency to coddle him. His mother was afraid he would get hurt if he tried to join in a game of *futbol* with the other boys on the street where he had once lived. So, she would find things for him to do rather than allow him to play with the other boys his age. Louis didn't mind. In fact, he preferred to stay inside and read rather than to go out and risk skinning his knee or elbow. In school, he was an above-average student whose teachers said he was a joy to have in class, especially in math classes, because he had a talent for numbers. His favorite uncle, Mikey, his mother's older brother, who was an accountant, told Louis he would be perfect for the profession. Since Uncle Mikey had his own firm, he promised to hire Louis someday.

Despite his doting parents and an uncle who adored him, he was very lonely. His father tried to ease that loneliness by bringing home a scrappy mutt, whom Louis affectionately named Buddy. Buddy was a good friend, and Louis loved him like a brother.

As he entered his teen years, Louis watched his fellow students start to date and then couple up and get married. He'd had no friends his own age, and although he got secret crushes on the pretty girls at school, he never had the confidence to speak to any of them. So, he was certain that he would never marry.

When he met Ava, he was instantly smitten. Even now, so many years later, as he walked towards his makeshift home in the Warsaw Ghetto, which was little more than a cramped apartment that he, along with his wife and child shared with two single men, he marveled at his good fortune to have found a woman like Ava.

He'd met Ava at a dance. It was the first and only dance he had ever attended. And he would not have gone had his uncle not insisted. When he walked in, he was intimidated by the small groups of young people who all seemed to be friends. Louis felt like an outcast and was about to leave when the prettiest girl he had ever seen was sitting on the sidelines of the dance floor. It took all of his courage to speak to her, but he knew he had to meet her. So, he walked over and introduced himself. She smiled and asked him if he would get her a glass of punch. He looked at her dumbfounded, knowing full well that she could easily have gotten her own punch. Louis was stunned that this girl was speaking to him, and he immediately agreed to get her the refreshment. He was so nervous that on his way back, he tripped and fell, spilling the punch on the floor. Several of the other young people at the dance saw him fall and started laughing. He was not hurt, but he was humiliated and wanted to leave the dance, run out the door, and keep running until he was far away.

But Ava rushed to his side and knelt down. "Are you all right?" she asked.

"Yes, I'm fine. Just clumsy, I guess," Louis replied, embarrassed.

She smiled, looking into his eyes and holding out her hand to help him up. "Let me get us both some punch," she said, pointing to a nearby table. "Why don't you sit down here and wait for me. I'll be right back."

She returned with two cups of punch and sat down beside him, where she stayed the entire evening. They talked and laughed and danced all night, and by the end of the evening, Louis was feeling far more comfortable.

Louis could not sleep that night. He was so excited that he could hardly believe what had happened. He went over it in his mind a thousand times and even told Buddy all about Ava. The following morning, when he got up, his mother was preparing breakfast for him and his father. "You look cheerful," she said. "Did you have a good time last night?"

"I did," he said, unable to contain his excitement as he told her all about Ava.

His mother listened quietly, and when he was finished, she insisted he find out where Ava lived and then speak with her father. "Ask her father for his permission to court his daughter."

"What if he says no?"

"Let's not get ahead of ourselves," his mother said. "Go and ask him."

Louis nodded. After school, on his way home, he stopped at the bakery, as he did almost every day, and bought a pastry. He'd become friendly with the owners, who were a young couple living in an apartment above the bakery. In a quiet voice, he asked the owner's wife if she knew Ava Goldstein.

"Of course, I know her," she replied. "Her mother comes in here once a week. She lives around the corner."

It was no surprise that it had been that easy to find out Ava's address. They lived in the same Jewish sector of Warsaw, where everyone knew each other. Although he had not met Ava before the dance, he lived only a few streets away from her.

All day, he had been nervous and anxious because he had decided to make a bolder move. Instead of just courting Ava, Louis was going to ask her father for his permission to propose to Ava. Her father liked Louis right away. He agreed to give him his permission and blessing. Louis was thrilled. However, he was even more nervous now because he had to ask Ava. He was afraid that he might have misread her signals and was terrified that she had spent the evening talking to him because she pitied him.

Louis told his mother about the plan prior to speaking with Ava's father. "You will need a ring if you are going to propose," his mother said. Then she went into her *knipple*, took out several bills, and handed them to Louis. "Take this money and go to the jewelry store and pick out a ring." The money was enough to buy a small engagement ring.

"I can't take your money," he said. "I'll get a job and save."

"You can get a job and pay me back if you'd like, but take the money and buy the ring now," she insisted, placing the money firmly in his hand.

He nodded and put the money in his pocket.

On his way home, after school, he stopped at the local diamond cutter, where he spent two hours looking at rings. Finally, he chose one. The diamond in the center was small, but it sparkled, and it gave him courage, even though deep inside, he was afraid she was going to refuse him. She was as sweet as she was beautiful, and he was certain that she would find a way to let him down gently.

When Louis arrived, Ava's mother answered the door. He smiled when he saw Louis and told him that Ava was out in the backyard. She was busy with her garden, but if he wanted to speak to her now, he could go into the back of the house. Louis practically stumbled over his own feet as he walked through the gate into the backyard of Ava's home. She was on her knees planting something, and as he looked at her with the sun illuminating her dark hair, he was overwhelmed by her beauty and his own anxiety. He was about to leave when she looked up and saw him.

"Hello, Ava," Louis said, hardly containing his excitement about seeing her.

"Louis?" she said warmly, "Hello, come in. Please excuse my hands. I know they are dirty." She wiped them on the apron she wore over her pink house dress.

"Would you like to take a walk with me?" He asked.

"I would love to."

After several minutes of walking and much small talk, Louis couldn't contain himself any longer. All the anticipation was making him nervous, so he quickly forced himself to blurt out the question that was burning in his mind.

"Will you marry me?" he asked, his hand trembling in his pocket where he held the box with the ring inside. He couldn't look at her. His stomach felt queasy, and his heart was beating so hard that he could hardly breathe. *Who am I to think someone as pretty and smart as Ava would want to marry me?* "I'm sorry," he stammered. "I don't know what I was thinking. I should never have put you in such an uncomfortable position. I'll go now." He turned to walk away.

"No, don't go. Please," she said softly. Then she smiled, and his world lit up. "My answer to your question is yes. Yes, Louis, I will marry you."

"What? Really? Do you mean it?" he asked, trembling.

"I mean it," she replied with a gentle laugh.

Louis's hand shook so badly that he dropped the ring when he took it out of his pocket. She giggled, picked up the box, and handed it to him. "Sorry, I'm clumsy when I am nervous," he said.

"It's all right," she smiled. "No harm done."

Her smile warmed his heart, and he took the ring out and carefully slipped it onto her finger. "I'm sorry the stone isn't bigger," Louis said. "But someday, I promise you that I will buy you a ring with a large diamond worthy of a woman who is as wonderful as you."

"It's beautiful. I love it," Ava said, then stood on her toes so she could reach his face, and then she planted a kiss on his lips.

From that day forward, and even now, Louis adored Ava. He did anything and everything he could to ensure that she was happy.

But Louis didn't have to try so hard. Years later, after their daughter was born, she told him she had loved him from the first night she'd met him. She turned out to be a good wife. She'd been at his side when his mother passed away, followed by his father's passing a few months later.

True to his word, Uncle Mikey hired Louis as soon as Louis finished school. He was brilliant and proved to be an excellent accountant and a hard worker. Not only that, but he was a kind husband, and within a short time, Ava became pregnant. That was when Louis purchased a home for his wife and coming child. When Chaya was born, Louis was so happy that he often wondered if he was dreaming. The joy of those early years felt like a dream he never wanted to wake from. But then Germany invaded Poland, and the young couple's happiness was torn, casting a dark shadow over their small Jewish neighborhood. The Nazis came without warning and arrested all the Jews. Louis had protected his wife and daughter the best he could. But in the end, he and his family were ushered into the Warsaw Ghetto along with all of their neighbors.

Uncle Mickey was murdered when he refused to cooperate with the Germans who came to his house to arrest him. Later, when Louis saw his uncle's wife, she wept as she told Louis that Uncle Mikey was shot immediately. Then, the rest of his family, like Louis and his family, were forced to go to the Warsaw Ghetto.

Louis missed his uncle terribly. They had worked together every day, and he longed to speak to him again. Louis tried, but he could not find a job as an accountant in the ghetto, so he took a job working in a factory. With Ava's support, he did what he could to help Mikey's widow.

Every day, Louis wished he could find a way to get his family out of this ghetto. When he got to the building where he was living, he was already exhausted from his mile-long walk home. He was out of breath by the time he climbed up the two flights of stairs to his apartment. When he entered the apartment, he plopped down into a chair to catch his breath, and that was when he noticed that Ava and Chaya were both dressed to go out.

"Where are you two lovely ladies going?" he said as cheerfully as he could between labored breaths.

"We are going out, and you're coming with us," Ava said to her husband.

"All right. So you want me to come with you. May I ask again, where are we going?" Louis said as he tightened the belt, which barely held up his loose pants. All of his life, Louis had been considerably overweight. In school, the other students had nicknamed him Fat Boy. Though he was still overweight, he had lost weight since he and his family were put into this ghetto, and now none of his clothes fit him. There was a time before the Germans came and before the rationing when Louis tried to lose weight and couldn't.

"We must go to Mila and Pitor's apartment," she whispered. "Mila asked us to come. She said that Pitor wants to talk to us."

Louis heaved a sigh. He would have preferred to stay at home. He longed to sit down at his own table and have a quiet dinner, followed by a few hours of playing with Chaya before she went to bed. But he had become used to Ava's attempts to assuage her guilt about what had happened when she was watching Jakup. Because she felt guilty, she and Louis always did things to help Pitor and Mila. "Do you know what it's about?" Louis asked Ava.

She shook her head. "I asked Mila, and she said she didn't know. All she said was that Pitor would explain everything."

"My guess is that he has come up with another one of his schemes to find Jakup," Louis murmured.

"You can't blame him," Ava replied, her voice catching. "I know I can't. I don't know what I would do if someone kidnapped Chaya. It is my fault that the Nazi officer took Jakup. I should have done something, Louis. I should have tried to protect that little boy, but I was so afraid. I was terrified, not only for myself but mostly for Chaya. I was paralyzed by fear."

Louis put a gentle hand on her shoulder. "What happened to Jakup was not your fault. And Pitor knows that too."

But he knew she didn't believe him and probably never would forgive herself. "All right," he said, stroking her cheek. "We'll go and see what Pitor has to say. But if it's alright, I'd like to change clothes quickly before we leave."

"Of course," she smiled. "Would you like a bowl of soup before we go?"

"Yes. I would. Did you and Chaya already eat?"

"We did. Now go and change while I pour you a bowl of soup."

He nodded. He loved her so much that he would sacrifice a peaceful night at home in order to help her lift her guilt.

CHAPTER FIFTY-SEVEN

When Ava and Louis arrived with Chaya, Mila answered the door. "Pitor is not home from work yet, but I expect him to be home in a few minutes. For now, would you both please sit down? I have some cookies," she said.

Louis saw Mila had put a small plate with a few cookies on the table. He and Ava knew Pitor worked with the underground, and that was how he got his hands on these cookies, which looked like they came from an authentic Polish bakery. But Louis didn't care how Pitor got them. He was just glad to be offered this delicious indulgence. It had been at least a year since he'd enjoyed a cookie. Louis reached over and took one of the cookies off the plate. He split it in half, offering half to Ava, who refused, and then giving the other half to Chaya.

A few minutes later, Pitor arrived. He slipped off his coat and hung it on a hook by the door. Each time Louis and Ava saw him, Pitor looked more and more weathered. Lines had formed around his eyes, and his blond hair had streaks of gray. "I'm glad you both could come by," Pitor said to Louis and Ava. Then he sat down at the table. "I know you're both probably very tired. So, I won't sit here and make small talk. I'll get right to the point." He cleared his throat.

"Yes, I must admit, I am tired. I had just arrived home from work when Ava said you needed to meet with her and me to talk about something."

"That's right," Pitor said, "As you know, the Judenrat is encouraging us to board these transports. Now, I don't know if you've heard this or not, but there are a lot of rumors going around that say that these transports do not go to special work camps. This information about the transport is being spread by reliable sources. They are being spread by Jews who, until they were captured and brought here to the ghetto a few weeks ago, were free. Many of them were in the forests, living with partisans. They said that they followed the trains to see where they were going, and what they saw was very disturbing. They told us that they saw that the people who took the transports were not going to a work camp. They were going to death camps where they're being murdered."

Louis had heard this before, but he found it hard to believe. "Why would they kill us? We are free labor for them," he said, taking another cookie, splitting it, and giving half to Chaya. "I think all of these rumors are lies."

"I don't. I believe these people, and so do several of my friends. We have formed a resistance group here in the ghetto, just in case they try to force us to go on the trains."

"A resistance group? Here in the ghetto?" Louis repeated what Pitor had said, suddenly feeling sick to his stomach. "Do you really think this is necessary?"

"Oh yes," Pitor replied firmly. "I think it is the key to our survival. And if we don't survive... at least it will give us an opportunity to fight back instead of going like lambs to the slaughter."

Louis looked at Pitor in disbelief.

"And the reason Mila and I asked you to come here is because we want you to join us."

"Me?" Louis's voice wavered. "I'm not much of a fighter."

"It's all right," Pitor assured him. "Just join us and do what you can to help."

Louis glanced over at Ava, who looked tense. "What do you think?" he asked her.

She hesitated, then nodded. "I am afraid that Pitor is right."

"So you asked us to come here tonight because you want us to join this resistance group?" Louis repeated nervously.

"I know it's scary and uncomfortable, but we have no choice. So, I think you should join. Look at the Judenrat," Pitor said, his tone urgent. "Watch them. Can't you see that they are nervous? They have a quota to fill. Do you understand what I am telling you?"

"Not exactly," Louis admitted.

"The Nazis are forcing the Judenrat to do their dirty work. They are required to send a certain number of Jews on each transport. From what I've heard, if they don't meet their quota, the Nazis will send the Judenrats and their families. If you have noticed, the Judenrat don't want to go and will do anything possible to avoid getting on those trains. That tells me that our Jewish Council knows more about where those trains are going than they are willing to tell us."

Louis nodded slowly, dread settling in.

"Think about it," Pitor continued. "If this crap the Jewish Council is telling us about being relocated to a better place with more food and less crowding were true, wouldn't they want to be the first ones on the transports? Wouldn't they want to get their families out of this disease-ridden ghetto? Think about that for a minute."

Louis' hands were shaking. He knew in his heart that what Pitor was telling them had to be true. But he wished it were not, and so he hesitated for a few moments. He took a long, deep breath, feeling as though he had been defeated. Then he looked at Ava and nodded. She nodded back at him. Her face was scrunched and lined with wrinkles like a map.

"All right, we'll join you. What do you want us to do?" Louis asked.

"We need money or valuables to trade for guns."

"Trade with who?"

"With the Polish underground. For the right price, they will get us guns. I have a feeling we are going to need them."

"Do you really believe it will come to that?" Louis asked.

"I am certain it will. Once the Judenrats have filled the transports with everyone willing to go, the Nazis will start forcing the rest of us to get on the trains. Have you ever heard of Treblinka?"

"I don't think so, why? What is Treblinka?"

"It's a village where they built a death camp where Jews are being murdered. Treblinka is the name of the camp where these transports are going."

"You're sure of this?"

"I'm not positive because I haven't seen it with my own eyes," Pitor admitted, "but like I said before, I received this information from very reliable sources."

"So, you want me to go to see everyone I know and ask them to contribute to this cause?" Louis said.

"Exactly."

"Who is buying these guns?" Louis asked.

"I am, and there are also others who are involved. I am sorry, but right now, I am not at liberty to tell you their names."

Louis's head spun. "This all sounds... so serious and really frightening. Things are bad enough here. I can't believe that the Nazis don't realize that with the overcrowding, disease, and starvation, we're already dying at an alarming rate."

"They know, but it's not fast enough for them. They want to kill us all as quickly as possible," Pitor said grimly. "So, now that you know our plans, are you still willing to help?"

Louis swallowed hard, then nodded. "I'll do what I can. I'll ask everyone who I feel I can trust."

"Good."

CHAPTER FIFTY-EIGHT

When two young men from the resistance approached Pitor nearly a year before he met with Louis and Ava, asking him to join their cause, Pitor did not hesitate for a second. The two men who had come to him knew about Jakup having been kidnapped. They expressed their sympathy right away and said that they hoped Pitor would find his son again. But Pitor could tell by the way they spoke they were both certain that he would never see his little boy again. Deep in his heart, Pitor was afraid that they were right, yet a little light inside of him told him not to quit trying. Fueled by his love for Jakup and Mila, he listened to the light and continued to believe that his child was still alive by some miracle.

For months now, Pitor had been taking dangerous risks to buy guns. He had never wanted to bring Ava and Louis into this. That was because he thought of Louis as weak, and he didn't think Louis could find the strength to be a part of a resistance group. Pitor was sure that if Louis were questioned by the Nazis, he would not be able to withstand the torture, and he would tell them everything he knew. That was why Pitor decided that the only responsibility he would give Louis was fundraising. Louis would not know the details or anything else about the plan for the uprising until it was almost upon them.

Each night, Pitor slipped out of the ghetto and into Warsaw, where he paid exorbitant prices for guns and ammunition. Then, each morning, he brought the firearms back to the ghetto and gave them to other resistance members who stored them in one of their apartments.

At first, Pitor couldn't bring himself to tell Mila about the plans for the uprising. He knew it would scare and upset her, but after many agonizing nights of sitting up and wondering what to do, he finally told her. At first, she seemed unable to grasp what he was saying, and he knew it was because she was terrified. He was frightened, too, but he knew the Nazis had given the Jews in the ghetto no choice but to fight back. He truly believed that the Nazis meant to kill them all, and if he and those he loved were going to die, he was going to take as many Nazis with him as possible. Mila began to cry when he told her what the plans were for the uprising.

"I just want my son back," she sobbed, clinging to him. "I don't want you to fight. I can't lose you too. Oh, Pitor, I just want Jakup to come home."

He took her in his arms and held her close to his chest. He wished more than anything that he could find Jakup and take his family far away from this place and from these people who wanted to murder them.

"Maybe... maybe we should get pregnant again," Mila whispered. Pitor knew it was her sorrow speaking.

"No love, not now," he said gently. "Not now."

"I don't want to go to war against the Nazis. I just want to go home," she wept. "I want my son back."

"I know. I know," Pitor murmured, stroking her hair softly. They missed Jakup terribly.

"I miss him every day."

"I know. Me too," Pitor said, and he knew how hard this was on her. Many times, he had come home to find her holding Jakup's blanket to her face and crying. Once, he walked in on her accidentally, and she told him that in the beginning, when Jakup was first taken, she could smell Jakup's freshly powdered fragrance easily. However, as time passed, his essence faded away. Sometimes, he would find her crying for no reason, and he knew it was because she missed their son. Several times, she asked him, "Do you think he is still alive? God forbid, what if that Nazi is a pervert who takes advantage of young boys?" He always tried to comfort her by saying he didn't believe that Jakup was taken by a pervert. He said he thought Jakup might have been taken by someone who wanted a child and couldn't have one of their own. This seemed to quiet her mind, at least for a while.

"Promise me, Pitor, that if we get out of here alive, you will try to find Jakup. Promise me," she said as she tore at the hair on his chest.

"Of course, I will," Pitor vowed.

"Do you think we'll survive?" she asked.

He shrugged. "I am going to do everything I can to make sure that we do," he replied, gently brushing a hand over her hair.

She nodded, but he could see the despair lingering in her eyes. "But you will never give up searching for Jakup, will you?"

"Never," he promised. She was quiet in his arms, but he knew her mind was heavy with fear and sadness.

Pitor turned off the light. "Let's try to get some sleep," he said. But he couldn't sleep. He lay there staring at the ceiling and thinking. He didn't want to be a coward. Pitor didn't want to run away and leave the others to fight without him. He would gladly have given his life to help this cause that he believed in so deeply. However, he would do anything in his power to protect Mila. So, in the morning, when she awakened, he turned to her, and in a soft voice, he begged Mila to leave the ghetto with him.

"We can get out. I know how. You and I will leave here after dark. I go into Warsaw all the time through a crack in the fencing. Almost no one knows it's there. But I know exactly where it is, and we can get out. Once we escape, we'll make our way into the forest, where there are partisans who might be able to help us find Jakup," he said. He was sure that they would find the partisans, but he doubted that the partisans or any other human being could help him and Mila find their son. He was afraid that Jakup was dead, but he held on to a tiny shred of hope. *Only God, if he really exists, can help Mila and me find our little boy.*

She shook her head, her hands trembling. "I am afraid to try to escape. I still hate it every time you leave the ghetto. I am always terrified that you will get caught. I am not as graceful or athletic as you are, and I can be clumsy when I am frightened or nervous. If I tried to leave, I think I would be paralyzed with fear, and because of that, I wouldn't move quick enough to get out. Then the guards in the tower would spot us."

"I will help you. I won't let you get caught. You must at least try to get out of here with me. This uprising is going to be bloody. People will be killed. It's dangerous for you to be here, and more than anything, I would like to get you out of here before it starts."

"Oh, Pitor, is that fair to the others? Is it fair to those who can't get out?"

"I don't care what's fair. All I care about is you. Don't you realize that?"

"Yes, I know how much you love me, and I love you too," she whispered, "but I don't know exactly what you have planned."

"You don't need to know. Just do what I ask, please, Mila."

"Pitor, I want to know exactly what is going to happen here. You tell me there will be an uprising, but I don't know what that means exactly. I want to know when it's going to happen and who is involved."

"Will you try to escape with me if I tell you everything I know?"

She looked away, struggling with her fear. Finally, she sighed, shaking her head. "I... I can't," she admitted. "I am too afraid."

He nodded, defeated. "I know you are, but I wish you would just trust me and, for once, just do what I tell you to do."

"You are a big part of this uprising, aren't you? I know you have been attending meetings from the resistance, but you won't tell me the details."

He nodded again. "Only because I wanted to protect you."

"I thought so."

Pitor trusted Mila. He was sure that he could tell her everything, and she would never tell the Nazis or the Judenrat. He took both of her hands in his and said, "You really want me to tell you everything?"

"Yes, Pitor. If you want me to try to escape with you, then I want to know everything."

"Very well. I'll tell you," he said. "There are several groups of people involved in the planning of this uprising. We are sure that the trains that the Judenrat are loading Jews on are being sent to death camps. So, we have set up places to hide throughout the ghetto where there will be guns and ammunition waiting."

She nodded and said, "Go on. I know there is more. When is this uprising going to happen?"

"Yes, there is more," he said, clearing his throat, "On the eve of April 19, a day before Passover and also a day before Hitler's birthday, we are going to wait until the Nazis come into the ghetto. Then we plan to shoot down the Nazis from the windows of several different apartments. We will be in constant motion. No one will stay in one bunker for very long. After we each fire a few shots, we will leave that apartment and move to another bunker where we will do the same thing again. This way, when they come running up to the apartment where the shots were fired from, there will be no one there. We will already be shooting from another bunker."

"I think I understand, but why are you constantly moving?"

"Because we don't have as many guns or fighters as we would like to have. If the shots are coming at them from different directions, the Nazis will think we have far more firearms and fighters than we actually do."

"Why didn't you get more members? I'm sure there were a lot of people who would have joined."

"Yes, I believe there are a lot of people who would have been honored to work with us. However, we had to be careful of who we took on to join us because once they were members, they would have access to all of the information about the resistance and the uprising we were planning. As you know, this information could get us all killed."

"The uprising could get us all killed, too."

"Exactly. That's why I want you to escape with me," Pitor said firmly.

She sucked in a ragged breath. "All right. I'll try to escape with you."

"You mean it?" He was elated.

"I mean it. Do you want to go tonight?"

"Yes. The sooner, the better. I have to let everyone else in the resistance know that we're leaving before we go. I think it's only fair to them."

"So why don't you go over there now and let them know quickly. Meanwhile, I will pack a few things for us."

"Mila, don't pack too much. Once we get out of here, we are going to be on the run, so we can't carry a lot of things. In fact, the less you pack, the better. I would prefer you to only take the clothes you can wear. Layer them."

She didn't answer him, but he knew she would probably insist on taking a small bag at least.

Pitor grabbed his coat and turned to Mila. "Do what you need to do to get ready," he said as he walked out of the apartment. Pitor walked as quickly as he could to the apartment where the man from the resistance to who he brought his guns lived. When he arrived, he knocked on the door and waited. A pretty young girl of about ten years old, with red hair and freckles, opened the door. She knew Pitor from the meetings and so she invited him inside. Then she pointed at a worn sofa and said, "Wait here. I'll get my papa."

"Thank you, Sadie," Pitor said. A moment later, a tall, well-built man walked into the room. "Pitor," he said, and he looked genuinely happy to see him.

"Levi," Pitor acknowledged the other man. "I have to speak to you."

"Yes, go on."

Then Pitor told Levi, the man who was his contact in the Jewish Combat Organization—the *Żydowska Organizacja Bojowa* (ZOB), that he and Mila were going to get out of the ghetto before the uprising. Levi's expression shifted from surprise to anger.

"How can you just leave? Don't you think we would all like to run away? I have a child who I love, and I would like to get her out of here. But we must stay and fight. You can't do this. We need you. Besides, we still need more guns. You are our best contact with the Polish underground. They will sell firearms to you because they trust you. Pitor, think of the greater good. You just can't go and leave us like this."

Pitor did not answer.

"Listen to me," Levi went on, "I am working with the Jewish Military Union to place the guns so that we have arms in several apartments. But we still need more. I have money to give you to buy the guns."

Pitor knew he was right, but he wanted to save Mila, so he just shook his head and said, "I'm sorry. I know that you have other people helping you. They can buy the guns."

"Of course, we have others, but we need all the help we can get."

"I have done what I can. Now, I need to take care of my wife. We have lost our only son, and I want to get out of here so I can search for him."

Levi's face hardened. "Don't be a fool, Pitor. I hate to break this to you, but the child is probably dead."

Pitor had been dealing with that frightening thought every day since Jakup disappeared, but he was still stunned to hear someone say it aloud. He grabbed Levi by the collar, backing him against the wall. "Never say that again. Do you understand me?" he hissed.

Levi nodded, and Pitor let go of his shirt.

"Will you at least tell us where the break in the fencing is located so we can get someone else to go out and buy guns?"

Until now, Pitor had kept the place where the wall was broken a secret. Many times, he considered telling the rest of the resistance how he was able to come and go from the Warsaw Ghetto. But he was afraid that if he gave away the location of the small break in the fence, too many people would escape, and this would make the Nazis take notice. If they started to take notice, he was sure they could easily find his escape route, and all they would have to do was fix the barbed wire, and Pitor would not be able to get out that way again. Now that he and Mila were leaving the ghetto that night, Pitor decided he would share the location of the break in the fence. "I will tell you how I get in and out of the ghetto, but you must promise me that you will not tell anyone else until tomorrow because Mila and I are leaving tonight."

"I promise," Levi said.

Pitor nodded, and then he told Levi the location of the break in the fence.

CHAPTER FIFTY-NINE

That night, when the sun went down and darkness fell like a soft blanket over the ghetto, Pitor took Mila's hand, and they made their way to the break in the fence. Pitor was nervous, but he was glad that Mila would not be in the ghetto when the uprising took place. A wave of guilt came over him. He would have gladly fought beside the rest of the resistance fighters had it not been for Mila. But she came first, and he was always protective of her as he had been protective of Jakup. Now that Jakup was missing and he might never see him again, Pitor grew even more careful with Mila's safety.

As the Nazis in the tower shined their light over the ghetto, Pitor quickly pulled Mila into the doorway of an apartment building. She was trembling. Knowing how terrified Mila was, Pitor took her into his arms and held her close to him while the guards in the tower looked over the dark, empty streets of the ghetto. They shined this light several times each night because they were searching for the children who went out and purchased things to sell in the black market. The guards had discovered some of their escape routes and had shot the children on sight. However, they had not yet discovered this one. Since Pitor began working with the black market, he'd learned how to hide in the shadows. He knew which apartment buildings had locks and which were open. When he saw the guards shining their light, he knew where to hide.

A few minutes later, the light went off, and the ghetto was once again wrapped in the cover of darkness. Pitor could feel Mila's heart racing against his chest, and she was still trembling. "It's all right, my love. The guards in the tower shine the light over the ghetto every so often. I know how to hide us if it happens again, so please don't worry or be afraid. You trust me, don't you?" he asked.

"Of course, I trust you," she said, her voice a quiet tremor.

"Then give me your hand, and we'll keep moving."

Mila had packed a suitcase with things she thought they would need, but at the last minute, with Pitor's coaxing, she decided it was best to leave it behind. Carrying something like that could be very dangerous. Now, she was glad that she had no baggage. Instead, as Pitor suggested, she layered her clothing and wore her winter coat. She stuffed the only jewelry she owned into her bra. So, there was nothing to carry. Pitor did the same.

When Mila and Pitor arrived at the break in the barbed wire, Pitor was stunned. Someone had come and fixed it. It had to have been repaired earlier that same day. He wondered what happened. He didn't want to believe that Levi would have turned this information over to the Judenrat. *But who else knew about this place?* A few of the children who went in and out of the ghetto knew. However, Pitor was sure that they wouldn't tell. So, there was only one person who could have done this. He hung his head. He had trusted Levi, but he shouldn't have, and he knew it now. Levi needed him in the ghetto not only to buy firearms but also to fight. Pitor clenched his fists, murmuring to himself, "I made a terrible mistake."

Mila looked at Pitor. Her eyes were as large as the moon. "What are we going to do now?"

Pitor shook his head, struggling to keep his voice steady. "I don't know. I guess we are going to be stuck here in the ghetto during the uprising."

"I'm scared," Mila said.

"I know," he said, pulling her close, "but don't be afraid. I'll protect you. I promise"

CHAPTER SIXTY

Since July 22, 1942, when the Judenrat published a notice that deportations were to begin, over 300,000 innocent people, men, women, and children had been deported to Treblinka, an extermination camp. Most of them had already been slaughtered. Now, only 50,000 people remained in the ghetto.

CHAPTER SIXTY-ONE

APRIL 19, 1943

At sundown, it would be the Jewish holiday known as Passover or *Pesach*. The following day, April 20, was Adolf Hitler's birthday. But this was also a very important day for the Jewish resistance. It was to be the beginning of the Uprising in the Warsaw Ghetto. History would record this as the strongest and longest resistance fight put up by the Jews against the Nazis. Approximately 700 brave Jewish resistance fighters, armed with limited guns, ammunition, and homemade weapons, went to battle against the German army.

The night before it was all about to begin, the imprisoned Jewish people shivered with fear. They glanced at their beloved children and family as they said their prayers. They needed God's help, and they silently asked for it as they shared a meager Passover dinner. Most of them, even those not affiliated with the resistance, knew what was coming. This time, they would not board the transports without a fight. The Jews of the Warsaw Ghetto were ready to rise.

CHAPTER SIXTY-TWO

On April 19, a troop of Nazi soldiers led by SS General Jurgen Stroop marched into the Warsaw Ghetto. Stroop had recently replaced Ferdinand Sammern-Frankenegg, who the Nazis felt was incapable of liquidating the ghetto. The Nazi soldiers planned to clear out all the remaining Jews. But when they entered the ghetto walls and called out for all the Jews to get in line to board a train, they were met with fierce resistance, a force they had not expected. Surprised and horrified, the Nazis encountered a powerful uprising that defied their grim intentions.

CHAPTER SIXTY-THREE

Pᴵᵀᴼᴿ ᴀɴᴅ Mɪʟᴀ'ꜱ ᴀᴘᴀʀᴛᴍᴇɴᴛ ɪɴ ᴛʜᴇ Wᴀʀꜱᴀᴡ Gʜᴇᴛᴛᴏ
Aᴘʀɪʟ 19, 1943

Pitor held Mila's hand tightly as they knelt by the window of their apartment, watching the streets below. She was cold and scared, and he could feel her shivering. "We'll be alright," he said, trying to sound confident. "I have a plan."

Most of the resistance fighters were resigned to the fact that it was highly likely they would not survive this uprising. But they were also certain that if they cooperated with the Nazis, they would be murdered. So, they formed strong resistance groups anyway, one of which was the ZOB, of which Pitor was a member. This group, as well as the other resistance groups like the Jewish Military Union, were headed by a twenty-four-year-old Jewish man by the name of Mordechai Anielewicz. There were differences between the two groups, and in the beginning, they bickered. That was until they realized that the only way to fight the Nazis was to band together. The Jews in the resistance decided that they would rather die fighting than die passively. Pitor agreed with them. They were sure now that

"

those who boarded the transports in the past were murdered. So, these brave resistance fighters all decided that if they must give their lives, then they would die fighting. Then, they set up secret meetings where they informed everyone in the ghetto who would listen that they must not board the transport. "Hide if you can, but don't ever board one of their trains willingly. It is a death sentence," Mordechai warned.

If it weren't for his family, Pitor would have been ready to die for this cause. However, he couldn't bear to leave Mila alone while he went to fight the army that the Nazis would send. And even worse, the thought of Mila being shot and killed was unthinkable for him. Pitor knew he must survive in order to protect his wife. He still held on to the hope that if he could get himself and Mila out of the ghetto, it might be possible to find Jakup and become a family again. Somehow, somewhere, there had to be a place where Jews could live safely. So, while the others were planning the attack, Pitor was planning a way to escape with Mila during the chaos. He knew there was a strong possibility that they would be unable to get out, but he knew he must try.

Then, as was expected, a troop of German soldiers headed by a strong leader whose name Pitor did not know entered the ghetto. The Nazis entered the ghetto walls. Pitor and Mila could see them from their living room window. The Germans were fearless as they walked through the streets of the ghetto, laughing and chatting amongst themselves. From their casual, relaxed demeanor, Pitor knew they did not know what the Jews had in store for them.

When they reached the center of town, the Nazi soldiers congregated. "Come out now, you Jewish swine!" General Stroop's voice echoed through the streets, met only by silence. No one came. "Come on now," Stroop said in a condescending voice as if he were speaking to children who were playing hide and seek. "You Jews are a filthy lot. So now, this place has become uninhabitable. It's full of diseases. Come out now and get in line. If you listen to me and don't cause any trouble, you will be sent to a work camp in the east. There, you will be given more food, and there will be less crowding and more room to live."

Pitor watched the apartment across the street, waiting for the man who was kneeling at the window there to give him a signal. "Stay down. Don't look out the window," he whispered a warning to Mila. "Don't move until I say."

She lay beside him on the floor, and seeing her so vulnerable gave him courage. *I must protect her, no matter what it takes.* The love he felt for his wife was even stronger than ever. *I will not let them take her or hurt her.*

Pitor's gaze locked onto the man across the street. His finger twitched on the trigger as he waited. Then he saw the signal. Fixing his aim on the cluster of unsuspecting Nazis, he steadied himself. The second signal came, and suddenly, the sound of gunfire was deafening. Pitor shot at the group of German soldiers, too. The Nazis were falling to the ground. Pitor was sure that many of them were dead. He'd never been a violent man, but it felt good to get back at them for all they had done to the Jews. Pitor was still firing, but it was impossible to determine if he hit his target or not because gunfire was coming from all directions. The Nazis did not move at first. They stood there frozen, looking stunned and terrified. Stroop's bellowed order cut through the chaos, and the soldiers frantically raised their guns, trying to aim. The bullets were coming from all directions, and they could not decide where to aim. Fifteen minutes later, the Nazis fled the ghetto.

"Are they gone?" Mila asked.

"For now, yes," Pitor replied, glancing toward the watchtower. "But the guards up there are still watching, and the Judenrat that are left here are still patrolling the ghetto like the damn fools they are."

"So, what do we do now?"

"We wait until this uprising becomes so chaotic that the guards are distracted, and we can escape from this place."

The next day, the Nazis returned with new tactics. They began their attack by setting apartment buildings ablaze, demanding the

Jews come out immediately, or they would be destroyed by the fire. The Jews did not yield. They had created underground tunnels that led to other bunkers. The shooting continued, but the Nazis still could not figure out where to shoot. Mila and Pitor watched in horror as entire buildings were engulfed in flames.

"There were people inside that building," Mila said, her voice shaking.

"I know," Pitor replied, unable to tear his eyes away. "Don't look. We can't help them."

For several days, Pitor and Mila barely slept. They watched the battle from their window. Pitor knew how limited they were on ammunition. So, he only shot at the Germans when he thought he could hit one.

Ten days later, the battle still continued. Then, the building across the street from Mila and Pitor burst into flames. Mila gasped. Her hand covered her mouth. "Look, Pitor, that is where Ava, Chaya, and Louis live. Do you think they are all right?"

"I don't know," he said, pained. "I hope so."

Tears welled in Mila's eyes. But there was nothing she or Pitor could do to help their friends. When she thought of sweet little Chaya lying dead in a burned building, she gagged and vomited.

Pitor placed a hand on her shoulder, wanting to console her, but there was no time. There was a loud explosion, and then the synagogue, which was a few streets away, was consumed in flames.

"We have to go right now. We have to leave this apartment," Pitor told Mila.

"Go where?"

"There's a tunnel that will lead us to another location."

"But why can't we just stay here?"

"Because it's not safe. They are burning down buildings all around us, and this one is probably next. Besides, to keep fighting, everyone in the resistance must keep shooting from different locations. Remember, love? I told you that." He rubbed her upper arm. "Now, listen to me," he said gently. "Stay down so they don't see you through the window. And we will crawl to the exit door. As soon as we leave this apartment, we must leave this building as quickly as possible. I am pretty sure they are about to burn it down."

Mila nodded. "All right. Let's go."

They crawled to the door. Pitor reached up to open it, then he pulled Mila to her feet and took her hand. "Run with me."

"Which way are we going?" She was nervous.

He could tell. "It's not far. Just follow me."

"Are we going to an underground tunnel that will lead us to another location?"

"Yes."

Mila did as Pitor requested, her trust outweighing her fear. The Jews who were living in the same building as Pitor and Mila were frightened by the fires. They stood paralyzed with fear in the building's hallway. One of them turned to Pitor. "What should we do?" he asked. Pitor felt sorry for the man, but at this moment in time, even seconds counted, and he did not have time to stop and talk, so as he was running by, he called back, "Get out of this building!"

As Pitor and Mila were making their way to the tunnel, Pitor heard gunshots, and he knew that one of the other resistance fighters who lived in their building was still there and still shooting. He knew he should have stopped and told him to get out, but he was afraid to take the time. He had to get Mila to safety.

Pitor had never been as jittery as he was when he and Mila left the apartment building through the back door. He held a gun in one hand and Mila's hand in the other. He was leading her to an underground tunnel in the sewers, which led out of the ghetto. They were behind the apartment building where they lived and only a few feet away from the tunnel. Pitor looked around. His heart was beating so hard that he felt as if it might explode in his chest. When he was sure that he did not see anyone. He took Mila's hand and pulled her towards the sewer. He removed the heavy sewer cover. But she was reluctant to enter for a moment.

"The sewer?" she said.

He nodded, "Yes, now hurry."

She was about to enter the sewer when everything in Pitor's world came to a standstill. It was the unmistakable sound of a gunshot that stopped his heart. His beloved Mila collapsed onto the ground. Pitor's lip was trembling when he looked up and saw a young Nazi soldier holding a gun and pointing it at Mila. Pitor was a skilled marksman, so he was quick to find his target, and his shot was right on point. Pitor saw the bullet hit the young Nazi in the face. His facial features were obliterated as he fell back.

Pitor dropped to his knees beside Mila. He could see that she was bleeding from her shoulder, but he couldn't tell exactly where she was hit. If it was her heart, she would die. Pitor took a moment and tried to find her injury, but he stopped when he saw that there was a raging fire inside the building. The fire was too close for comfort. He had to get Mila out of there and into the safety of the underground sewer. Then, once they were away from this danger, he would look to see where the bullet had entered her body.

He scooped her up, feeling the heat of her blood seeping into his hands as he carried her down into the sewer. As they descended, he whispered, "Don't you dare die on me, Mila."

But she didn't answer, her face pale and eyes half-closed.

Pitor trembled with fear, thinking of how meaningless his life would be without her.

"I promise you that if you live, I will do everything in my power to find our son. Please don't die, Mila. I can't go on without you." His voice turned to a desperate prayer. "Dear God, please, I'm begging you. I know I haven't always been the man you wanted me to be. I haven't followed your laws. I was arrogant. Forgive me, please. Please, God, take me instead of her. I am begging you, please don't let her die."

Mila was heavy in his arms in the hot, stifling sewer, but he would not put her down for a second. Not even when the fetid odor of feces and urine in the tunnel made him gag.

The darkness of the tunnel seemed to close in on him, and as her blood warmed his trembling hands, Pitor felt the depth of his grief and helplessness. "You can't die, Mila. You can't leave me here on earth without you. There is no reason for me to go on if you are not by my side," he murmured, voice breaking. Then, he broke the promise he made to himself many years ago. For the first time since his mother's death, Pitor Barr wept.

EPILOGUE

Heim Hochland, the Lebensborn home
Steinhoring, Germany
Less than a year later

Little brown sister Gretchen Auerbach reached down into the crib and wiped the infant's face with a clean white rag. Then she turned to her coworker, Heidi Nessler. "I have given all of the children baths and dressed them, so they are ready to go."

"Yes, I saw them. They look very nice," Heidi agreed. "Is Horst still meeting you at the party?"

"Yes, he is. I got permission to bring him with us."

"So, you are dating him?" Heidi raised an eyebrow. "He really doesn't have much to offer."

"That is not true! He is handsome and ambitious."

"He is hardly handsome," Heidi scoffed. "And with those looks, his ambition won't do him much good."

"You don't even have a boyfriend at all. So, you really have nothing to say about Horst," Gretchen said arrogantly. She knew Heidi was jealous; among the two of them, Gretchen was the better-looking one. Although Heidi had been working at Heim Hochland longer, Gretchen was from an old, respectable German family, and Heidi came from a lower-class background. Gretchen was tired of Heidi's constant criticism of everything she did. She was proud of the fact that she had a boyfriend, even if he wasn'pit one of the high-ranking officers in the SS or the most handsome. In fact, Gretchen knew most women would consider Horst ugly. His hair was so thin that his shiny bald scalp shone through like a giant lightbulb, and he had red and angry-looking pockmarked skin. But neither she nor Heidi, both being "little brown sisters" without the Aryan ideal of blonde hair and blue eyes, had many prospects among higher-ranking officials.

"You say you had to get permission to bring him? If he had been anyone of importance, he would have been invited. But he wasn't, now was he?" Heidi asked innocently.

Gretchen gave Heidi a frown. She knew Heidi was just being catty. She already knew the answer. "Stop it. You are just being mean."

"I just hate to see you sell yourself short. That's all. I think you could do better."

"It's not as if I see you dating someone better. Horst is a nice man, and he treats me well. Besides, he has offered to help us with the children if we need him."

"I don't need anyone's help. I can manage a handful of children, and I would think you would be capable of the same."

"Of course I am. I know you are, too. But he'll be there, just in case."

"What we really need is blonde hair and blue eyes," Heidi remarked, her tone dry. "Then we could find some men who would be worthy of our attention. But right now, this one is nothing to brag about."

"Just stop it already. You are jealous. That's what this is all about," Gretchen shot back.

"Oh please, don't make me laugh. I could never be jealous of anyone dating a man like Horst."

"Well, he's my boyfriend. So, I would appreciate it if you would just shut your mouth for a while," Gretchen hissed. She hated it when Heidi said things that reminded her that, being little brown sisters, they would always be inferior to the Aryan beauties who lived at the Lebensborn home and were chosen for their beauty to breed blond-haired blue-eyed children. *Horst is a good man. He cares for me, and I like him. He is the only man who has shown me any interest, and I know he is ambitious. If we get married, he will do his best to make a name for himself. He will try his best to rise in the world. As usual, Heidi is jealous.*

Heidi looked angry. Her face was turning red, and her fists were clenched. Gretchen knew her coworker could be mean, and since they were going to be together at the party at the Eagle's Nest that night, she changed the subject and tried to soften Heidi's mood. "Anyway, I'm sorry if I offended you. Let's change the subject. What do you say?"

"Of course. No harm done," Heidi replied, softening.

"I'm glad," Gretchen said. "Now, *Reichsführer* Himmler has honored you and me by choosing the two of us to bring these beautiful children to the party. I am very excited to be a part of all of this, aren't you?"

"Of course I am. Unfortunately, we can only get so far because we are little brown sisters, but yes, it's nice to be going to the Eagle's Nest."

"It's very exciting. As you know, he is very proud of his Lebensborn project, and he wants everyone to see what a good job we are doing here at Heim Hochland. Horst told me that he had heard that the Führer would be at this party. So, this is really a great honor. We just might get to meet him. Can you imagine? We might get to speak to the Führer. Now, that's quite an accomplishment for two little brown sisters. Isn't it?" Gretchen smiled and patted Heidi's hand.

"Oh yes, it certainly is. Not very many little brown sisters will ever see the Eagle's Nest or meet the Führer. I've heard the view is magnificent," Heidi said.

"Yes, I have heard that only top officials own homes up there, and I heard the ballroom is spectacular, too."

Just then, a little blond-haired boy and girl came running into the room. The little girl fell and began to crawl on the ground. "No, no, you must not crawl on the ground, little one. Come on now. Get up. You're going to get dirty," Gretchen said. Then she turned to Heidi as she lifted the little girl and dusted her off. "They really are beautiful children."

"Yes, they are," Heidi replied. "That little girl was born right here in the birthing room. In fact, I was here on the day she was born to one of the Aryan mothers. Poor thing labored for hours," Heidi said. "Then, I suppose because it was such a difficult birth, she didn't want to let the child go. She put up quite a fuss. She begged Himmler to let her have her daughter, but of course, she was refused."

"I have seen that happen with several of the children. It's very sad."

"Not really. The mothers know that they can't take their children with them. That little girl is to be adopted by an *Obersturmführer* and his wife as soon as Himmler does her naming ceremony. That child will have a wonderful life. Now, that little boy is another story altogether."

"Oh, did you witness his birth, too?" Gretchen asked casually. "Wasn't he recently named at Himmler's most recent naming ceremony?"

"I didn't witness his birth, but I was at his naming ceremony; Himmler has decided to call him Seigbert."

"Seigbert. What a wonderful name. It means 'bright victory.'"

"He is far from a bright victory. Wait until you hear this. I have a secret to tell you about him."

"About this little boy?" Gretchen said, pointing at the little boy with blond curly hair. "I was with you when Horst brought him in. What did he tell you about him?"

"You have to promise to keep everything I tell you secret. Can you do that?" Heidi asked.

"You know I can. Tell me what you know."

Heidi smiled, and her eyes narrowed. Then, in a whisper, she said, "He was stolen."

"Oh, from a Polish family?" Gretchen said in a conspiratorial whisper. "I heard something about that sort of thing taking place."

"No, not that little boy. He was not taken from a Polish family," Heidi giggled a little, then she added, "Not that one." Heidi was smiling a wicked smile that pulled Gretchen in. Gretchen felt the hair on her arms stand up straight. She was excited to hear the secret that Heidi was about to share. Even though she knew Heidi could be cruel and she should refuse to listen, she also knew that Heidi always had the privilege of knowing the deepest, darkest secrets.

"Well..." Heidi said, pausing for dramatic effect. When she saw Gretchen was listening intently, she put her arm around Gretchen's shoulder and whispered softly in her ear. "Someone told me in the strictest confidence that he saw a German officer walking out of the Warsaw Ghetto with that child. That little boy right there."

"Really?"

"Yes, don't tell anyone, but I heard that little boy has Jewish blood."

"Really?" Gretchen loved being a part of the inner circle, those who were privy to secrets and gossip. "Who told you that?"

"I can't tell you," Heidi smiled. Then she said, "But... here is something I think that you really should know."

"Oh?" Gretchen leaned in to listen.

"Do you know who it was that brought that child into Heim Hochland?"

"No, I wasn't here the day he arrived," Gretchen admitted.

"I know you weren't. But just so you know, it was none other than Horst Ackermann. Your boyfriend. He was seen leaving the Warsaw Ghetto with that child. Now... If this information ever gets out,

Ackermann's head will be on the chopping block. Aryan coloring or not, that child is a Jew."

"Never!" Gretchen said, horrified. "Horst would never do such a thing. This is unkind gossip. Some horrible person is trying to ruin Horst. It's simply not true."

Heidi smiled. "Oh, but it is..."

To be continued

A NOTE FROM THE AUTHOR

Dear All,

I always enjoy hearing from my readers, and your thoughts about my work are very important to me. If you enjoyed my novel, please consider telling your friends and posting a short review on Amazon. Word of mouth is an author's best friend.

Also, it would be my honor to have you join my mailing list. As my gift to you for joining, you will receive 3 **free** short stories and my USA Today award-winning novella! To sign up, just go to my website at... www.RobertaKagan.com

I send blessings to each and every one of you,
Roberta

Email: roberta@robertakagan.com

ABOUT THE AUTHOR

I wanted to take a moment to introduce myself. My name is Roberta, and I am an author of Historical Fiction, mainly based on World War 2 and the Holocaust. While I never discount the horrors of the Holocaust and the Nazis, my novels are constantly inspired by love, kindness, and the small special moments that make life worth living.

I always knew I wanted to reach people through art when I was younger. I just always thought I would be an actress. That dream died in my late 20's, after many attempts and failures. For the next several years, I tried so many different professions. I worked as a hairstylist and a wedding coordinator, amongst many other jobs. But I was never satisfied. Finally, in my 50's, I worked for a hospital on the PBX board. Every day I would drive to work, I would dread clocking in. I would count the hours until I clocked out. And, the next day, I would do it all over again. I couldn't see a way out, but I prayed, and I prayed, and then I prayed some more. Until one morning at 4 am, I woke up with a voice in my head, and you might know that voice as Detrick. He told me to write his story, and together we sat at the computer; we wrote the novel that is now known as All My Love, Detrick. I now have over 30 books published, and I have had the honor of being a USA Today Best-Selling Author. I have met such incredible people in this industry, and I am so blessed to be meeting you.

I tell this story a lot. And a lot of people think I am crazy, but it is true. I always found solace in books growing up but didn't start writing until I was in my late 50s. I try to tell this story to as many people as possible to inspire them. No matter where you are in your life, remember there is always a flicker of light no matter how dark it seems.

I send you many blessings, and I hope you enjoy my novels. They are all written with love.

Roberta

MORE BOOKS BY ROBERTA KAGAN
AVAILABLE ON AMAZON

A Million Miracles Series

I'll Never Cry Again

Searching for Jakup

A Million Miracles

Margot's Secret Series

The Secret They Hid

An Innocent Child

Margot's Secret

The Lies We Told

The Blood Sisters Series

The Pact

My Sister's Betrayal

When Forever Ends

The Auschwitz Twins Series

The Children's Dream

Mengele's Apprentice

The Auschwitz Twins

Jews, The Third Reich, and a Web of Secrets

My Son's Secret

The Stolen Child

A Web of Secrets

A Jewish Family Saga

Not In America

They Never Saw It Coming

When The Dust Settled

The Syndrome That Saved Us

A Holocaust Story Series

The Smallest Crack

The Darkest Canyon

Millions Of Pebbles

Sarah and Solomon

All My Love, Detrick Series

All My Love, Detrick

You Are My Sunshine

The Promised Land

To Be An Israeli

Forever My Homeland

Michal's Destiny Series

Michal's Destiny

A Family Shattered

Watch Over My Child

Another Breath, Another Sunrise

Eidel's Story Series

And . . . Who Is The Real Mother?

Secrets Revealed

New Life, New Land

Another Generation

The Wrath of Eden Series

The Wrath Of Eden

The Angels Song

Stand Alone Novels

One Last Hope

A Flicker Of Light

The Heart Of A Gypsy

www.ingramcontent.com/pod-product-compliance
Lightning Source LLC
Chambersburg PA
CBHW061651190726

48289CB00006B/1827